KIWI WARS

A Captain Jack Crossman Adventure

Captain 'Fancy Jack' Crossman has been sent to New Zealand, where the Maori Wars are in progress. His remit is to map the bush country and to set up a network of spies. During conflict he finds that the Maori are an honourable people. However, nefarious Europeans are at work, enriching themselves as land agents. Jack realizes just how heinous these crimes are, and he must hunt down and destroy these monstrous elements...

Garry Douglas Kilworth titles available from
Severn House Large Print

Rogue Officer

KIWI WARS

Garry Douglas Kilworth

Severn House Large Print
London & New York

This first large print edition published 2010
in Great Britain and the USA by
SEVERN HOUSE PUBLISHERS LTD of
9-15 High Street, Sutton, Surrey, SM1 1DF.
First world regular print edition published 2008 by
Severn House Publishers Ltd., London and New York.

British Library Cataloguing in Publication Data

Kilworth, Garry.
  Kiwi wars.
  1. Crossman, Jack (Fictitious character)--Fiction. 2. New
  Zealand--History--New Zealand Wars, 1860-1872--Fiction.
  3. Historical fiction. 4. Large type books.
  I. Title
  823.9'14-dc22

  ISBN-13: 978-0-7278-7894-6

Severn House Publishers support The Forest Stewardship Council
[FSC], the leading international forest certification organisation. All
our titles that are printed on Greenpeace-approved FSC-certified paper
carry the FSC logo.

MIX
Paper from
responsible sources
FSC® C018575

Printed and bound in Great Britain by the
MPG Books Group, Bodmin, Cornwall.

ACKNOWLEDGEMENTS

This novel is for my good friend Major John Spiers, who was at the time of the work's conception the curator of the Light Infantry Museum in Winchester. (He is now Rifles' Secretary, Property and Heritage.) His name has often appeared in my acknowledgements for the research material he has provided. He also suggested that the Maori Wars might make for a different, and interesting, Crossman novel.

John also supplied much of the historical material, but is in no way responsible for any errors in this work. I like to think I can get things wrong without any expert assistance.

One

Three sailors slipped over the side of the moored British man-o'-war into a stolen skiff to sail across the bay to the harbour of the small Australian port of Melbourne. They had contrived to serve watch together in the early hours, to provide themselves with this opportunity of jumping ship. The officer of the watch, a Lieutenant Urquart, was standing fast asleep with his head on the rail of the quarterdeck. Urquart was famous for his catnapping. By the time he lifted that sorry head of his, he would be in the deepest trouble of his so-far short life.

'Watch the prow,' whispered Danny, urgently.

He was too late, the stolen skiff's front end bumped against the ship's hull, not loudly, but with a definite thump.

'What?' called the officer above, obviously waking from his doze. 'Who's there?'

The three men in the skiff swiftly manoeuvred the boat around and under the stern of the man-o'-war. There they waited with hearts beating fast, knowing that directly above them was the captain's cabin. They could hear that very

7

man snoring like a pig with a blocked snout. Urquart's footsteps sounded on the deck. The three sailors followed them with their ears, knowing he had walked to the port side. There he would be searching the surface of the sea, looking for a log or whatever he imagined had made the noise. If they were caught the least they could expect was a term in the brig. Most likely it would be a flogging.

For the next few minutes all that could be heard was the lapping of wavelets against the hull of the great ship. Then the footsteps travelled again, probably to the quarterdeck, where the lieutenant would again rest his head on the rail. Urquart was nothing if not consistent in his habits.

'What now?' hissed Striker.

Abe said, 'Wait.'

They stayed where they were, holding on to the anchor chain for the next quarter of an hour.

'All right,' Abe murmured. 'He'll be off again now.'

They pushed off, out into the bay. All three looked anxiously at the man-o'-war for the next few minutes, as they slid across the quiet waters, but it seemed Urquart had indeed returned to his slumber. There was another seaman with him, a sailor by the name of Longfield, but he too had no doubt succumbed to the invitation of the sandman.

The dawn came up over the waters of the huge natural harbour which curved like a giant fish hook around the small skiff. To the east were

8

green hills, to the further west a flatter drier landscape. Ahead though, was the welcoming mouth of the Yarrow River. It was towards this stretch of fresh water the three sailors were heading. They did not intend to touch land, but, tacking through the other quiet ships which littered the harbour, they were desirous of sailing upriver towards gold country. It was a source of bitter disappointment to them that they could not go directly to the goldfields, where daily fortunes were being made, since they had no money. They did have a stolen ship's mainsail, which would stake them once they were there, but they had no provisions for the journey. They needed a horse or donkey to carry the canvas, since they could not sail all the way to Ballarat, their eventual goal.

They passed rather too close to a frigate where the officer of the watch was far more alert than Lieutenant Urquart. Striker gave the officer a friendly wave, relieved to see that it was a visiting American vessel and not a British ship. The officer, hands locked behind his back, merely returned Abe a hard stare.

'Bloody gentry,' muttered Striker, 'same everywhere.'

'They don't have no gentry in the United States,' stated Danny in his thick Irish brogue. 'They're a republic.'

'Oh, they have gentry all right,' Abe said, getting in on the conversation. 'They just don't call 'em lords and ladies. It's a fact of human nature to have your high brows and your low.

That one there, he comes from a family that don't speak civil to Chinamen, you can be sure of that. He'll have servants in the kitchen, same as our lot.'

'Was you in service, when you was a land-lubber?' asked Danny of the leader of the group.

'Me?' cried Abe in a shocked voice. 'I never served no one nothin'. I've got my pride. I was a lengthsman, me. Since I was fourteen.'

Danny, being Irish, did not know what a lengthsman was and requested more information.

'Why,' said Abe, loosening the sheet and letting out more sail as the wind dropped, 'it's a workman for the council who looks after a length of greensward and ditching. I had five miles on it, 'tween Rochford and Hockley, in the county of Essex. Scythe and spade was the tools of my trade. I cut the verges with one and kept the ditches clear with the other. That and help the sexton dig his graves. I've shovelled earth on many a gentry's corpse, I can tell you. I s'pose that's servin' 'em in a manner of speak-in', but all I've done for 'em direct is throw the dirt of county on their dead faces. All I ever intend doin' for 'em, what's more.'

Abe was tall and lean, with a huge scar that ran from the corner of his right eye down to the tip of his chin. The scar came from a knife fight with a Lascar seaman in a Liverpool tavern. He wore it proudly, as if it proclaimed him to be a man to be reckoned with. Privately his ship-mates said they would be more afraid of the man

10

who gave it to him. Still, it looked gruesome and worried them enough that they gave him a wide berth when he was in a temper.

The three made it upriver for five miles before they abandoned the skiff. Striker wanted to sell it to get money for provisions, but such a sale would have attracted too much attention, and they could not afford to be detained while their non-existent credentials were checked by the purchaser. Instead they lugged the mainsail, and the sail from the skiff, a further mile along the bank and hid them in some bushes. Then Danny led them to a tree-fellers' camp he had been told about by some Victorian sailors. Here they joined a self-employed gang of men who cut and sold eucalyptus wood for the boilers of the paddle steamers that plied their trade up and down the Yarrow.

'See them gum trees down by the water's edge, them's river reds,' explained one of the gang to the three sailors. 'Them others, further back on the drier parts, them's black box. River reds burn to charcoal, but black box goes down to dust. They wants both types of wood, see – they needs a mix. And a warnin' on the river reds—'

At that moment an explosion occurred on a paddle steamer that was about quarter of a mile downriver. A look of satisfaction spread over the faces of the cutting gang. They nodded to each other in grim fashion as they saw that the steamer's paddles had come to a halt and the boat was drifting on the current.

'What's that?' asked Abe. 'What's happened there?'

'Captain of that there vessel,' said the same man who had been explaining about the types of wood, 'went off without payin' us our dues.'

'And?'

'And so we packed some gunpowder in a hollow log.'

Abe laughed. 'I like that. They threw it in the furnace without knowin' its content?'

The rest of the gang smiled. 'Just so,' said the second man. 'It'll remind the captain of his debt. They won't not pay us again. That engine'll cost a tidy penny to get put right. Now, as I was sayin', don't stand at rest under the river reds. They call 'em widow-makers here. Boughs break and drop without a warnin'. Here watch.'

The sawyer hefted a log into the water and it sank quickly to the bottom of the Yarrow.

'Heavy enough to defy nature,' said the man. 'Imagine that coming down on your back.'

The three sailors only stayed with the cutting gang long enough to earn money for provisions. Then they struck inland for a short way to hire a beast of burden. They found a man willing to let go of an old camel called Bessie. Bessie was brought, not without protest for dromedaries are belligerent beasts at the best of times, to the spot where they had hidden the sails. They loaded her up and then set out for Ballarat, the town that served the goldfields.

It was about six o'clock in the evening as three sailors and a camel entered the Victorian town.

The camel was thirsty and so were the men. They tied the beast to a tree by a long piece of ship's rope and left it to drink from the town's lake. They themselves entered an eating house and ordered steaks and beer. The fare was eye-wateringly expensive. The cutting gang had warned them of the prices on the goldfields, most of them having tried their luck themselves before deciding that a steady job was more lucrative.

'I could buy the whole damn cow for that money,' grumbled Abe, 'let alone this bit of gristle and bone.'

But there was nothing they could do about it. Demand exceeded supply. While they were eating, a man shambled in and asked if anyone wanted to buy a cheap digging licence. Abe signalled to the fellow, who was in rags and said he had not eaten for three days.

'No luck, eh?' said Danny, who was beginning to realize that you could not pick up gold nuggets from the ground like pebbles as they had been told by a visitor to their ship. 'Giving up.'

'Giving up and going home,' said the man, who was a well-spoken and clearly educated gentleman. 'You can dig in a thousand holes and find nothing. That's what I've found, absolutely nothing. Look at these hands.' He showed them his palms. They were raw and bleeding with split skin. 'I've had it up to here.' He drew a line across his throat.

'Need some grub in your belly first, eh?' Abe said. 'Well, we could come to an arrangement...'

And so the licence to mine on the goldfields was purchased.

Striker kept a keen eye out through the open doorway. The load carried by the camel was very precious and the sailors did not want it stolen. They were aware that marines from their vessel *Comet* were searching for them in the brothels of Melbourne, but it was doubtful they would reach as far as Ballarat since the ship was due to sail. By the morning the *Comet* would be on its way to Sydney and the three deserters would be relatively safe. They believed themselves safe now and drank to that fact, laughing and joking, and cursing their old captain and his officers for pigs and pi-dogs, saying they were well out of it.

All three had spent time in the brig and one of them, Abe, had felt the lash on a number of occasions. Punishment did not greatly bother Abe for very long. Oh, he got mad all right, spitting mad, and cussed and swore at the man wielding the cat, but his body seemed to absorb the hurt and pain. Abe had eyes like chips of flint. There were few who liked him as a person, but they respected his eyes.

Danny and Striker were typical seamen of low birth. As young men they had been press-ganged into the Royal Navy, and like many shanghaied sailors they subsequently made it their living. Yet they had never taken to it in the way a gentleman does who makes it his career. A young lad of a high family who becomes a midshipman, lieutenant or captain will speak of the sea reverently and of his ship as if it were the Ark of the Covenant. To sailors like Danny and Striker the sea was a wasteland of water and the ship 'a bloody old lime barrel'. They did not hate the ocean or vessel: they were indifferent to them.

'Well, here we are, lads,' said Abe, looking up from his steak. 'Down under and off to be as rich.'

Danny, the small elderly Irishman, said, 'I'm eager to be slopin' off to the diggings, lads, that I am.'

'Well,' replied Striker, a willowy Cornishman who had previously been a tin miner and knew what hard work lay ahead, 'you can be at it soon enough, an' we'll stand and watch.'

Danny made a face, but he was full of humour tonight. Not far away, just a bit of a walk, were the goldfields of Sovereign Hill, where the three of them expected to make their fortune. The fact that thousands of others also expected the same, and there was only so much gold in the ground, did not dim their enthusiasm. They had the glint in their eyes, the fever as men called it, and it would take many months of hacking through clay to diminish it. They had read the reports in *The Buninyong Gazette and Mining Journal* of wild riches being found, and they believed every word. This was one chance in a lifetime and these three chancers were not going to miss it.

They finished their meal, paid for it with the last of their coin, and collected Bessie with her load. On Bessie's hump was their stake. The spare mainsail from the *Comet* and the sail from the skiff. Canvas was at a premium in the gold-fields, having its uses as tents, shaft covers, buckets and roofing for cabins. They could sell the canvas, keeping a little for their own use, and live comfortably for a good while as they set about mining. Hopefully there would be enough to purchase a shaft. There was a great deal of canvas in the mainsail of a man-o'-war.

When they reached the goldfields they were dog-tired and the sight of so many lamps dispirited them. Lights were scattered on the hillsides like fallen stars. There were shafts and winches; as many as trees in a forest. The whole landscape looked like a battlefield, with piles of earth and slag every few yards. Up on the main hill were shacks and false-fronted buildings. One of these was an alehouse which the three sailors entered, not to buy more food and beer, but to sell some of their canvas. As expected they had more buyers than canvas to sell, and very soon their pockets were lined with money. One man even sold them an old shaft he had worked for enough canvas to cover his current shaft and winch. He did not tell the sailors it had been worked down to a layer of clay beyond which gold had never been found.

'Look at the likes of this humanity,' Danny said, wonderingly, as they stared around them. 'Every shade of people.'

There was indeed every type of person the world had to offer on the goldfields, from Chinese to African, from British aristocracy to beggars in rags, from hatchet-faced women to hussies in flounce. What amazed Danny, Abe and Striker, though, were the would-be prospectors straight out of the schoolroom. Dozens of boys still wearing school uniforms had dropped their books and headed for the glory holes of Ballarat, hoping to strike it rich. The street and surrounding landscape were seething with prospectors, all with hope in their hearts. As they left the saloon, the three sailors found the smells were ripe too, and awful, for sanitation was primitive here. And these were men who had lived in the closest proximity with humanity on shipboard.

'I an't goin' to be able to sleep tonight,' said Abe. 'Who's for going to our claim and tryin' our luck right now?'

The other two men agreed.

So they found the shaft Abe had purchased and Striker winched Danny and Abe down the narrow hole to the bottom. There they lit candles and placed them carefully on the earth shelves that had been cut for the purpose. They found themselves ankle deep in water and soft mud. Striker lowered the canvas bucket and before long they had removed most of the water. Abe began clawing at the mud with his bare hands, slopping it into the bucket. Within a few inches they hit dense clay, which required more than fingernails to shift.

Striker sent them down two small shovels. Not knowing any different, for they were complete novices at the gold-digging game, Abe and

Danny began to cut through the clay, slicing it with their shovels and taking out pieces as if it were a cake of marzipan. Any seasoned prospector on the fields would have stopped right there and left the mine to nature, as the previous owner had intended before he had been confronted by three gullible sailors straight off the ship. But they were ignorant of the lack of possibilities and so dug away.

Gold deposits obey certain rules, which knowledgeable prospectors are aware of. Gold is the heaviest metal on the earth and finds its way to the bottom of softer material. But, occasionally, just occasionally, there is a quirk of nature. Sometimes a nugget exceeds all others in size and weight. Sometimes it is so large that over a period of time it sinks down even further into the dense thick clay.

Danny's shovel hit a hard object with a *clunk*.

'Somethin' here,' he cried.

Abe went down on his knees and began clawing again, using his sailor's strength to work around the rock. He cleared and cleaned a single knob on the boulder, an ovoid about the size of a goose egg. Danny kneeled down with him, a candle in his hand. Together they shined it on the stone. The flame reflected a yellowish hue.

Abe could hardly get the word out. 'G-g-gold!' he shrieked. 'We struck gold. We're rich, boys, rich!' He continued to scrape away the clay from the monster beneath.

'No, no,' replied a worried Danny, 'it can't be

gold – it's too big. It's as big as the bosun's head – bigger, even. No gold, this.'

'I tell you we've struck rich,' yelled Abe, angry with his partner. 'This is a nugget. A damn giant nugget. Look – see.'

Up on the surface, Striker was running backwards and forwards, only stopping to look down into the hole every two seconds.

'Is it really gold, lads? Are we rich, boys? Is it a nugget for sure, Abe? We've only been here not more than four hours. How can it be? Others have spent months! Shall I come down there and assist?'

'Don't be daft, man,' cried Abe. 'How would we get it out? Here, we've cleared it now. Try to lift it, Danny-boy. If you can lift it, it's not gold, for it's only as big as an iron bucket. Lift it, and I'll allow it's not gold – but lift it, man, and I'll kill you, for I'm anxious to be rich.'

Danny could not move the thing. It was indeed a nugget. Now the elderly Irishman let out a shriek of joy that pierced the ears of distant men, who came running in the darkness, waving their lamps. Suddenly the whole region was afire with the word. Riches had been found. A nugget the size of a bullock's head. The earth had disgorged its old wealth and paupers were suddenly elevated to the status of kings.

Only one man for ten miles around was not excited. The man who had sold the earth's bounty for a strip of canvas. All he could do was bury his face in his hands, and curse the fact that his deal had been made in a crowded saloon with witnesses all around, into whose faces he had smirked and winked, being such a clever fellow as to outwit some stupid sailors.

Oh, that Lady Luck, she was both princess and whore.

Two

1860, New Zealand

Captain Jack Crossman and three soldiers of the 88th Connaught Rangers were among the landing party. They were accompanying a naval party of some 60 bluejackets. Captain Cracroft, the commander of the bluejackets, was bringing his men ashore as reinforcements to assist in the defence of New Plymouth, which it was feared was about to be attacked by Maoris. However, once there was sand under their feet, firing could be heard away from the town. Cracroft decided to divert his men in that direction. For Crossman it was a rude welcome to the recently acquired colony known as New Zealand: he and his men had been thrust immediately into fresh conflict.

'Captain Cracroft,' said Jack, 'do you need us?'

Jack and his men were laden with their kit, unloaded from the *Niger*, the ship that had brought them to New Plymouth.

'We need all the men we can get,' replied the naval officer, who looked a little harassed. 'Are you willing, Captain?'

21

'No, we an't,' said Private Wynter, a one-eyed pale individual, from behind his commanding officer. 'I've still got the sea sickness on me. I an't a well body.'

Sergeant King, his NCO, snapped, 'Keep your silence, Wynter, or I'll bring it on you myself.'

Jack nodded at Cracroft. 'We're with you, of course. It sounds like quite a battle up there...' He cut his sentence short as a lieutenant-colonel leading a company of soldiers emerged hurrying from a woodland area ahead of them. The firing could still be heard, so the battle was not over, yet here were soldiers heading in the opposite direction. Captain Cracroft hailed the colonel.

'Where are you going?'

The other officer looked anxious and seemed upset.

'I have to return to New Plymouth by dark. My orders.'

'But isn't there fighting up there?'

The lieutenant-colonel looked uncomfortable as he urged his officers and men, most of whom appeared disgusted with their commander, onward towards the town.

'Yes, the Taranaki Rifles and militia are attacking the Kaipopo *pa* – but I have to get on. Colonel Gold's orders, not mine.' He looked anxiously at the darkening sky. 'Not mine,' he repeated. Then, seemingly as an afterthought, the lieutenant-colonel added, 'I have sent some men to assist.' Then he hurried away, waving his small force on with his sword.

'A bunch of civilians,' snorted a midshipman

standing alongside Cracroft, 'and he's leaving them to it?'

'Let's get on,' ordered the naval captain, 'before we can't see our hands in front of our faces.'

Wynter started whining again. 'What about our kit, sir?' he said, addressing Jack. 'If we leave it here, it'll get stolen for certain. You know what these darkies are like.'

Corporal Gwilliams growled, 'Not everyone's got your morals, Wynter. Some folk respect private property, darkies or not.'

Sergeant King said, 'Pile it up at the base of that palm tree...'

'This ain't no palm, Sarge, this here's a fern,' corrected Gwilliams, dumping his kit. 'Ancient plant, the fern. Older'n history.'

'Thank you for that botany lesson, Corporal. Just heft your Enfield on your shoulder and we'll be on our way,' King said, with a touch of asperity in his tone. 'Come on, catch up with the officer, you two. Move your backsides. And don't give me one of your looks, Wynter, or I'll knock it through to the back of your head.'

Sergeant King believed discipline had to come from his fists, which were indeed heavy and hammer-like objects. Normal means of correction were too slow for him. His small command of two spies and saboteurs was always on the move, often in enemy territory. To place a man under arrest was not feasible when in enemy country and needed consideration of rules and laws, and required paperwork. This method was

23

far too slow and indeed impossible when one was crawling through the bush, surrounded by insurgents. Physical threats were swifter and more effective. Sometimes King actually needed to carry them out, taking his man out of sight of the officer and flattening him with fists that had been formed in the forge of his father's blacksmith shop. Gwilliams had been thumped soundly. So had Wynter, more than once. Gwilliams had learned quickly, but Wynter was one of those men who forgot his pain in a very short time. Moreover he seemed to be able to absorb punishment like a sponge takes in water, and still ask for more.

As the column marched through the wooded slopes, a young midshipman, not much more than twelve or thirteen years of age, came running to the four soldiers. He was clutching three cutlasses.

'Beg pardon, sir,' he said breathlessly to Jack. 'Captain's compliments an' says you might need these.' He stared for a few moments at Jack's left wrist, suddenly realizing he was offering the cutlass to an arm without a hand on the end. 'Sorry, sir,' he said, blushing. 'Didn't see.'

Jack smiled at the boy who seemed in a high state of excitement, told him not to fret, and ordered King to take the cutlasses. Sergeant King handed the broad-bladed weapons around. Gwilliams swished his through the air, slicing the atmosphere with satisfaction.

Wynter looked at his broad-bladed cutlass in horror. 'Whaddo I want this for?'

Sergeant King replied, 'Obviously we're expecting close-quarter fighting.'

'Can't I use me bayonet? I an't never used one of these things.'

'Stick it in your belt then,' came King's reply.

A short time later, the firing became louder as the column reached the front line. Sprawled on the ground and under cover were the British militia, firing at a man-made hill ahead of them. It was Jack's first sight of a *pa*, an earth-and-timber fort built by the Maoris. There were rifle pits dug in and around the tiered earthworks, and a wicker palisade around the whole. It reminded Jack vaguely of Maiden Castle, an Iron-Age hill fort in Dorset. The *pa* looked formidable. Jack had attacked and overrun fortified positions in the Crimea and such attacks were often very costly. He wondered if a frontal assault was going to be ordered here, since progress could not be made by simply exchanging fire. His stomach tied in a knot at the thought. Jack was no coward, but dodging bullets as thick as a swarm of bees, while running over open ground was one of the most terrifying experiences in warfare.

Suddenly a huge man appeared above the palisade, his brown body gleaming with sweat. His long black hair flowed in the wind as he raised a muscled arm and shook his fist at the militia. Jack found his spyglass with his good hand and flicked it open. Putting it to his eye he observed a magnificent specimen of a handsome warrior with a tattooed face, arms and shoul-

25

ders, muscles standing out like iron ridges from his body. The warrior stuck out his tongue the length of his chin and then yelled: 'Come on, pakeha. What are you waiting for? Come and fight like men or go home to your wives.'

Dozens of shots rang out as the militia and navy sought to rid the skyline of this open target. But they were unsuccessful. The Maori had ducked down again, laughing as he did so.

Sergeant King said to a sailor next to him, 'Was that the chief?'

The sailor shrugged and replied, 'Might have been.'

'But he was so big – and strong-looking.'

'Brother,' said the sailor, 'they *all* look like that.'

'Shit,' muttered Gwilliams, 'we got ourselves a war then.'

''Ow many of 'em is in there?' asked Wynter of a Taranaki Volunteer, who was lying on his back, reloading his rifle.

''Bout five hundred.'

'Five hundred bleeders the size of that last one?' exclaimed Wynter. 'Why, we're all dead men then.'

The exchange of fire continued until the light began to fade and the landscape was drifting into gloaming. Captain Cracroft gave the order to prepare for a frontal assault. Jack drew his sword. King and Gwilliams gripped their cutlasses. At the last minute, Wynter also decided the blade was better than his rifle and bayonet. On a given signal they rose up out of the grasses

26

and from behind trees, charging over the open space between relative safety and the Kaipopo *pa*. Men went down under a fusillade from the rifle pits ahead. This was the last Maori hail of shotgun and rifle fire, answered by those on the run before they tossed away their firearms. Now it was sword, club and hand-axe.

The air was full of wild yells and battle cries. In the half-light the Maoris fought vigorously, hacking at the pakeha with the untutored skill of a warrior nation to whom warfare was almost a sport. Sailors and militia waded in with cutlass and rifle butt. Maori strategy was usually to cut and run once the enemy were within the walls. This they did now, slipping away into the falling darkness. The engagement was sharp and decisive, and was over within minutes. One naval man, coxswain from the *Niger* and first into the *pa*, pulled down the Maori flags.

The dead were counted as the darkness descended. Almost fifty Maori bodies were found, though only a fourth of those had gone down in the frontal attack. There were fourteen dead amongst the volunteers, militia and the navy. When the column marched back to New Plymouth, Jack learned of the animosity between colonists and the military. The colonists despised the Maori, while the soldiers knew they were fighting against a brave, resourceful and intelligent enemy. The Church had taken sides and fought for the rights of the Maori. The governor, one Thomas Gore Browne (or 'Angry-belly' to the Maoris), a seemingly indecisive

27

man, was caught between the factions.

It was the age-old problem of land. The colonists were hungry for it. They wanted to purchase land: lots and lots of it. Understandably many of the Maori were reluctant to sell their heritage. Under the Treaty of Waitangi land could only be acquired by British colonists if they purchased it from its owners or from the government. But ownership was often a misty and vague thing: sometimes land might be owned by one Maori, sometimes by a family, sometimes by a whole tribe. He who sold it might be only a part owner; even no owner at all. Even folklore had been known to come into it. One Maori maintained that a particular parcel of land had been first owned by his ancestor: a lizard that had lived in a cave above the plot.

This particular fight had been over a stretch of fertile land known as Waitara, down in the bottom left-hand corner of North Island. It had supposedly been bought from a sub-chief of the tribe that owned it, but the head chief disputed the sale. Jack learned that these purchases were often subjected to great arguments which led to outright war. Wiremu Kingi, the Maori leader involved in this dispute, had been declared a rebel, but many clergy and soldiers felt the governor was being unjust.

Jack and his men were billeted with the 65th Foot, where he had learned much of this from a lieutenant of that regiment: Brian Burns, who hailed from Kilmarnock in Ayrshire. As they sipped whisky in the mess, Burns filled in a little of New Zealand's recent history for Jack.

'We've been here since the late seventeen hundreds,' said Burns. 'The Maori have been here longer, of course, by about five hundred years. No real fuss when we first arrived. No guns. Just bits of paper. The Maori accepted us, but of course there were only a few colonists then. In 1840 the Maori and us signed the Treaty of Waitangi, which gave us sovereignty over all New Zealand. That's when the bother started. The two languages of the treaty didn't quite match up. Not surprising, of course – different languages never do. So the Maori interpretation is at variance with our own. Not wildly different, but enough to cause trouble when it comes to who rules whom, or the purchase of land.'

'Why did they bother? I mean, why did the Maoris sign in the first place?'

'Och, there was some talk of the French invading, so the Maori chiefs handed over the protection of the islands to us.'

'But they never did. The French, I mean.'

Burns took a swallow before replying. 'No, but it was a genuine fear, the French were indeed ready to invade. Since then we've had five or six governors, I can't remember exactly, but the best was George Grey. Unfortunately Browne isn't fashioned of the same material. Are you a Scot, Captain?'

The last question caught Jack by surprise. He was indeed a Scot, or half of one. His father was a Scottish baronet who had seduced an English maid and then turned her out once the child had

29

been born. That child was christened Alexander Kirk. When young Alex discovered his father's deception, he left home in high dudgeon and joined the army under the assumed name of Jack Crossman, which so far as the military was concerned he still bore. Since that time his father had been reduced to a mindless idiot by senile dementia and his older half-brother James had assumed control of the estates. James was a good man, far better than their father, and he was something of a hero to Jack.

'Yes, I am. Half, anyway.'

'I thought I detected something of an accent.'

'It's been ironed out. I was sent to school in England, then the army – you know. It's never been very broad.'

'No need for apologies – accent never made the man. Now where was I – aye, the governor. He tries his best, of course, but he has no vision.'

'Tell me,' asked Jack, 'why did the Maori retreat tonight? You would have thought they would fight to keep their fort. It must have taken a lot of work to build it.'

Burns laughed. 'They can fling up those things in a matter of days. Brilliant engineers, the Maori. It was bewildering at first, the way they simply melted away from their *pas*. But that's the way they fight, the way they've always fought. First it was tribal warfare, but now they've got us to battle against. They've modified the *pas* of course – added rifle pits – but essentially they're the same forts they used before we came on the scene. Bloody difficult to penetrate with ordnance. You can rain cannon-balls on them and they just absorb them. It's nearly always a frontal attack because they always have the sides and rear blocked. Earth-works like the *pa* are impenetrable.'

'Aren't frontal attacks a bit expensive in manpower?'

Again Burns laughed. 'We get slaughtered. Today we were lucky. I guess the Maori got a bit confused in the twilight. But others have not gone so well, Captain. There's been a few mis-takes here and there – a few arrogant com-manders who have been put in their place. Ah, here's Williamson. Colleague and friend. Stacy, Captain Jack Crossman, of the 88th. Jack, Cap-tain Stacy Williamson of the 12th.'

Williamson, a heavy-browed man, shook Jack's hand and then sat down in a vacant chair, heavily. In fact he exuded heaviness all over. He was big-limbed and bodied, with a large head and thick broad shoulders. An Aberdeen Angus bull of a man, except that when he spoke it was not from north of the border. It was pure country Suffolk.

'The hand?' asked Williamson, signalling one of the mess waiters with three fingers. 'India?'

'How did you know I came from India?' asked Jack.

'Oh, word travels. I heard there were 88th coming. Irish map-makers I was told.'

Jack's team were indeed map-makers, especi-ally the redoubtable Sergeant King, but they were also something else.

'Correct. That is, correct about map-making, but not about the hand. I lost that in the Crimea.' He paused before adding, 'And none of us is Irish, though the regiment was formed there of course.'

Jack's left hand had been crushed by a siege ladder and then amputated. He was now quite used to working round its absence. He could load his revolver by tucking it under his elbow. A rifle was more difficult, but being an officer he was not required to carry one. Of course he could not present in battle like other officers, with a pistol in one hand and sword in the other, but then battle was not his normal stamping ground. He was more used to sneaking around in the bush, blowing up enemy emplacements, and relaying intelligence to generals.

'Ah, the Russians,' murmured Williamson, 'a more pedestrian enemy. Down here we fight a more colourful enemy under different skies, different stars. Do you know what the locals call New Zealand? Land of the Long White Cloud. Poetic, don't you think? You should listen to some of their stories, too. I have. There's a chap down at the quay they call "Speaker for the 7th Canoe". His ancestors passed down the history of their migration to these islands to him. Memorized the whole voyage and told it to a grandson. Marvellous memories. Don't borrow money from them and expect them to forget it.'

Jack smiled. 'I have no intention of borrowing money from anyone, least of all a Maori.'

'Oh, they'd lend it to you all right – generous to a fault. Now where's my three fingers of gin...?'

While Jack was comfortably ensconced in the officers' mess, his men were down at a beer tent, swilling ale. Wynter was on his third jug and Gwilliams, the barber from North America – the United States or Canada, no one really knew which – was not far behind. Sergeant King was with them, though he could have been in the senior NCO's tent. King did not drink. He was trying to write a letter to his son Sajan, avoiding slops on a rickety table. Sajan was a child King believed he had fathered of an Indian mother. The biological connection was doubtful, but King had declared himself the parent and that, as far as he was concerned, was enough. Sajan was now in England at a Board School in York-shire, an exotic pupil amongst mill workers' children.

Gwilliams was thinking there were an awful lot of naval men around, but when he asked one of them why, he was told they were actually army. Apparently they had discarded their red coats in New Zealand and were wearing blue serge jumpers and blue trousers. It made a lot more sense to wear muted colours, since in this environment they were not fighting in neat lines, but battling through bush country.

'Well, soldier, what do you reckon on this territory?' Gwilliams asked of the man. 'Farm-ing country?'

'Sheep pasture,' replied the soldier, leaning his elbows on the table. 'When I get done with the army, I'm like to settle here for good. Rolling hills, meadowland. It's a paradise, man. You only got here today, but you wait till you get out there and see the main of it. Hot springs, too. Lakes the size of seas. Yes, sir, I'm going to send for the family and settle.'

'A long way from anywhere, though?' argued Gwilliams.

'Everywhere's a long way from anywhere, if it an't home – but if it is, you got the best of it here. No wild beasts. No snakes. When the Maori came there was only birds in the forests – and what forests they are! Hardwood trees the size of cathedrals. Down in South Island they got mountains with snow on top, and glaciers, and them Norwegian inlets, what are they called...?'

'Fjords?'

'That's them,' said the soldier, tapping the table now to emphasize his approval. 'Man, you got everything here, right on the doorstep. I'd be as happy as a king if I had the missus here. Plan to get her out. Bay of Islands – prettiest piece of land and sea you ever saw.' His face darkened for just a moment when a loud guffaw rent the air. 'Only trouble at the moment is them damn colonists. Bunch of ruffians.'

'But,' Gwilliams pointed out, 'if you settle here, you'd be one of 'em.'

'Well, you hope they've been diluted by then, so to speak. Fact is, soldier, at the minute they're

34

the dregs. Not all of 'em, of course, but quite a sizeable lump of 'em. Ex-cons from New South Wales, drifters from the whaling ships, foreigners thrown out from their own countries. I can see the day we get a better class of citizen here – some good honest ones have come already – but there's also a lot of riff-raff on the make.'

By the bar, a big sawyer was lifting two men up by their collars and shaking them like dolls, asking those around him to wager how far he could throw them. The barman seemed afraid to intervene. Gwilliams did not blame him. The sawyer was twice the size of any man in the place. Wynter slammed down his ale jug and stood up. He was a thin wiry creature, pale and bent-looking though still in his thirties. One of his eyes had been pierced by a bush with three-inch-long thorns in India. There was a burn-crease in his temple where he had tried to shoot himself and missed. This poor creature looked like a straw that would break in a draught.

Wynter caught the attention of the whole tavern by rolling up his sleeves and roaring out, 'Now who's the biggest bastard in the room?'

The sawyer, his black hair falling round his dark face, dropped the two wriggling men he held as if they were fish.

'I am!' snarled this giant of a man.

'Right,' replied Wynter, stepping forward, 'you an' me'll fight any two others.'

There was a moment's silence, then the whole tavern erupted in laughter, and Wynter got the slaps on the back he expected. The sawyer invited him to partake of drink with him, but at that point Gwilliams decided to leave. He knew by the end of the evening Wynter's temper would turn nasty under the influence of the drink and he was tired of wading in to help the private get rid of the venom in his veins. Gwilliams quietly finished his ale, said good-night to the soldier, and weaved towards the door.

Three

Fancy Jack Crossman believed his primary duty was spying and his secondary role was as a saboteur. Here in New Zealand the gathering of intelligence was carried out by Maori loyal to the government, and sabotage, which usually involved digging, was the province of the sappers. He could not, as yet, speak the language and was therefore fairly useless as a spy and there were no magazines, storehouses, railways or ships to blow up, as in the Crimea or India. Way down the list of Jack's duties was mapping, and here in New Zealand there was a rugged wilderness that needed good maps. Colonel Lovelace, his boss, had decided Jack's team would chart this unknown landscape of volcanic activity, mountains, braided rivers, fjords, glaciers and islands.

When Jack had protested to a senior officer that his primary function was the gathering of intelligence, that officer had replied, 'Exactly what is intelligence, Captain?' 'Why, information, sir.' 'And that's exactly what we require in New Zealand, Captain, information. Cartographic information.' Jack bowed to the system.

The trained mapper amongst them was Sergeant King, who had never really accepted his role as a spy and saboteur. King, a terrible shot with a firearm, was best with coloured pencils in his hand. He owned and used a vocabulary which included such words as: theodolites, Gunter's measuring chain, perambulators, quadrants, spirit levels, plane tables, barometric levellers – and many others. A lexicon that made Jack's head spin. Jack had had triangulation up to his ears and it pained him grievously to have to hand over the main duty of the group to King. He was the officer in charge of something he did not fully understand; he would never be as proficient as his subordinate NCO. He mourned the loss of his former dashing position as the leader of a forward action group.

Captain 'Fancy' Jack Crossman was not a fancy dresser, nor did he pomade his hair. He had been given his nickname by the troops when he was a sergeant amongst them. Being obviously from aristocracy he was at that time distrusted by both officers, and rank and file. The former wondered what a member of their exclusive club was doing parading as a common soldier. The latter believed him to be an officers' spy in the ranks, there to monitor any insurrection or mutiny. Jack could have, of course, asked his father to buy him a commission, but chose instead to work his way up without the assistance of his hated father's influence and money. Now he was a captain of foot, the old epithet remained with him, leaving others to wonder if the 'Fancy' referred to his way with the ladies.

He was indeed a handsome man, despite his

disability, but his interest in women stopped with his wife, Jane. Jane Mulinder of Derby, who would have been his cousin had his mother been his father's wife, was a tall beautiful female, daughter of a merchant.

Jilted by her former fiancé, Jane met Jack in the Crimea and they fell in love. Since then he had only window-shopped other women. He could still be aroused by a lovely female, naturally, but his fear of hurting his beloved Jane always curbed those wayward instincts. Jack believed that though she *might* forgive an indiscretion, especially as they had been apart for most of their married life, things would never be the same between them if he were to stray. He wanted them to be the same. He loved being exclusively loved. Jane was his anchor, his sanity during the insane bloodlettings of several wars. Without her devotion and regard he knew he would collapse under the horror of it all.

So, on a clear day when the New Zealand hills looked like green baize over soft mounds, Jack gathered his men together to brief them. They sat at a table outside a shack near to a parade ground where troops were being drilled. It pleased them all, but especially Wynter, that they did not have to be part of the army system. They were a unique unit, responsible only to themselves. It was a grand situation that made them special.

'I'm sorry to have to tell you,' Jack said, 'that we are not here as spies and saboteurs.'

'What?' said Wynter. 'We an't goin' to go

regular, are we?'

'No, we an't,' replied their commanding officer, mimicking his only private soldier. 'We're to concentrate on map-making.'

There was a stunned silence, then Sergeant King stood up and threw his cap in the air, shouting, 'Hurrah!'

'A little dignity if you please. You will take your seat again, Sergeant, and behave in a manner more becoming of a senior NCO.'

'Yes, sir,' replied King, grinning. 'Gladly.'

'Well, then, you've got your wish at last, Sergeant. I can only stand by and give you advice on army matters if you require it, but for the operations themselves I shall hand over to you.'

'You'll be told the areas, sir, where we're to work?'

'Oh, yes. I have *that* much control over you still. Well, perhaps not me, but the army. You'll have to instruct us all in the art and craft of it, Sergeant. I don't mind getting my hands dirty. That theodolite thing you seem so proud of. Do we need to carry it everywhere? It's a heavy creature.'

'Essential I'm afraid, sir. As are the measuring chains.'

'Then we shall need packhorses and perhaps even a cart, which won't make for easy travelling in the wilderness. I would have liked us to travel as light as possible, so that we could sneak about without being noticed, but I suppose that's not to be. Now, this is important –

many of the Maori tribes are friendly, don't forget that fact. Wynter, I don't want you blasting away at someone just because of the colour of his skin. There will be no shooting unless we're shot at first.'

Gwilliams protested here. 'That ain't right. We'll be on the back foot the whole time.'

'Orders I'm afraid. You may challenge anyone we see, but do not fire first.'

'Oh, good,' said Wynter in a sarcastic tone, 'I'll just ask 'em, "Are you a friendly Maori, or one who likes to kill pakehas?" and if he says, "Well, now, soldier, I'll just tell you the answer to that question after I've loaded and fired me weapon," I'll wait patient-like to be shot dead.'

'Be sensible, Wynter...'

There was a civilian passing them at that precise moment and this man suddenly stopped in his stride and swung round at the sound of Wynter's name. He was a well-dressed individual, if rather tasteless in his choice of attire. There was a tall black stovepipe hat on his head that shone with a silky gleam in the morning sun. His boots were clean and also gleaming. A white frill-fronted shirt nestled under a black frock coat with larger buttons than were fashionable in Auckland or New Plymouth. He looked like a man who was struggling to find a compromise between dandy and businessman. The effect of the expensive clothes, however, was offset by a horrible fork-lightning scar striking down at his chin, disfiguring the wearer's lean hard features.

Private Harry Wynter stared back at this tall figure. For a moment the two men remained with eyes locked, then Harry Wynter shouted in amazement and surprise, 'Is it you, Abe?'

The man's expression became a sidelong smile.

'Young Harry! What, the army has sent you here, eh?'

Harry Wynter jumped up and cried, 'It's me brother – me long lost brother, Abraham. Sarge, sir, it's me next oldest kin!'

Jack groaned and whispered, 'There's *two* of them?'

An excited Harry ran to his sibling and threw his arms around the man. Abraham extricated himself very carefully without returning the affection in any way. Instead he held Harry by the shoulders at arms' length and looked him up and down.

'My God, Harry me boy, what 'ave they done to you? You've got less meat on you than a gypsy's lurcher.'

Harry looked puzzled for a moment, then realized his brother was referring to his physical condition. He shrugged. 'Ah, well, you know – diseases and such. I got a terrible ague up there in the tropics. An' I lost the eye to a bloody great thorn bush 'cause them buggers over there din't get me out in time.' Gwilliams scowled and Sergeant King opened his mouth to protest, but shut it when he saw Jack shaking his head slowly. 'Me hair went white at the same time. Listen, I marched from Russy to the Indian continent, I did, an' even the officer thinks that's a great feat and saps the life-strength from your body. Stuff like that.'

'Remind me never to join the army,' replied Abe. 'Not that I ever wanted to. Navy was bad enough.'

'Where'd you get that scar then, Abe?'

Abraham Wynter touched the crease in his face with his right forefinger.

'This? From a Lascar, a shipmate, in Liverpool. I gave him a worse one back, you can be sure, brother.'

Harry now stepped away from his big brother and looked him up and down.

'But Abe – now look at *you*. Fine clothes. Fat as Christmas. You an't in the navy still, that's for certain.'

'No, I an't in the navy, nor ever will be again, thank you very much. I come out of the navy, all legitimate, up there in Austrailee. Me an' two pals went to the goldfields in 1851 and struck it rich. We found a nugget as big as a sucklin' pig. Now I'm as rich as crows is, Harry. I'm a respected citizen now, a landowner, and gettin' richer all the time. I own more land in New Zealand than the railways in England, and it an't long and thin like theirs, it's good prime sheep grazin' land, some of it bottom land and good for plantin'. I'm sittin' pretty and like to be the biggest man in this new country afore very long.'

Harry took off his forage cap and threw it into the air.

'You hear that, lads?' he screeched. 'My brother's a rich man. *My* brother.' He tried to put an arm around Abe's shoulders, but his brother slipped skilfully aside avoiding this clearly unwelcome display of filial affection for a second time. 'My brother Abe. Rich as crows is.'

'That's Croesus,' muttered Gwilliams, the classical scholar, who had winced when it was mispronounced the first time. 'Croesus.'

'Who the fuck cares?' cried Harry. 'Me an' my brother is rich – rich, rich, rich. No more bloody army for me. You can keep your skulkin' and conniving, Captain Crossman. I'm off with my brother Abe, to assist him in any way he needs me to.'

Private Harry Wynter had been through a whole war in the Crimea with Jack Crossman supposedly as his tyrannical sergeant. Then through the Indian Mutiny with Jack as his despotic lieutenant. Now he was still with the same slave-driving officer in New Zealand in the Maori wars. But clearly Harry thought enough was enough. Here was an end to his time under a British satrap. The years of bloody Fancy Jack Crossman lording it over him were past. He had found a rich brother who would take care of him. He started to remove his coatee.

Abe stepped away from his younger brother and brushed non-existent dust from the shoulders of his fine coat with a pale hand.

'Now, now, Harry boy, we've never been *that*

44

close.'

Harry's expression revealed his bewilderment at this remark.

'What I mean to say is,' said Abe, gently, 'we 'aven't been near each other in twenty-odd years. I wouldn't want to claim you as one of my own at this late date, old chum.'

Harry stared with uncomprehending wide round eyes. 'But – but we're brothers, Abe.'

'Well, yes – but, in actual real-life fact, do we properly know that? Half-brothers, maybe? Yes, that's most likely. You know what a strumpet our mother was. Who knows if we had the same father, Harry? An' fathers is what's important, in the family line. The paternal is what it's all about, Harry, not mothers. Mothers is just coincidental.'

Harry Wynter spat on the ground in contempt as his anger rapidly passed the white-heat stage and into bitter disbelief. Had he a rifle in his hands before that moment had gone, he might have shot Abraham Wynter where he stood. It was lucky for both of them that his weapon was in the hands of Corporal Gwilliams. Abe would have had a hole between his eyes and a fratricidal Harry would be heading for the noose.

Harry spoke evenly and carefully, despite the terrible emotions that swirled inside his heaving breast.

'You are my proper brother, Abraham Edward Arthur Wynter, and you God-damn well know it.' He came down like a blacksmith with a hammer on the words 'God-damn'. There were hot tears in his eyes. 'We was the youngest of eleven babes, you an' me, me bein' the total youngest, all the rest girls. By the time our mam got to us she was wore out and as wrinkled as a dry prune. No other man would've looked at her except Pappy, who loved her dear. I'll give you three God-damn days to come to your sensibilities. If you don't, I'll write to our mam and tell her what you said about her bein' a trollop. An' the rest on the family – our sisters. It's a blamed good job for you our beloved pappy, God rest his gin-soaked soul, an't alive to hear your blaspheming. But I'll tell all our sisters what you said and how you're treatin' a *real* properly conservated brother of yourn. You'll never be able to show your face in England again.'

Abe laughed out loud. 'And I care? Me the richest man in New Zealand? I an't never goin' home, Harry. Not in a million years. You just keep on armying. That's what you're cut for.' His face changed to a savage expression. 'My money's my own. I don't owe nobody nothin', not even kin. What did you ever do for me, boy? Not a blamed thing. So that's what I'm goin' to do for you, not a blamed thing. I need every penny I got. I an't goin' to be poor again, that's certain. You just keep bleatin' – that's all you're good for, boy. You was born bleatin' and you'll die bleatin'. You're a bloody billy goat, Harry Wynter.'

With that the wealthy gentleman turned on his heel and strode off towards the town.

Harry Wynter looked as if he had been struck

by lightning. He stumbled back to the table where the others were still sitting, having witnessed this terrible humiliation of one of their own kind. Gwilliams was inclined to side with Harry Wynter. He could not imagine any of his family – he had two sisters but no brothers – brushing him off in the same way as Abe had brushed off Harry. Jack, though he privately agreed with the 'bleating' accusation, thought that Abraham Wynter must be a callous and unfeeling kind of man. Sergeant King was stunned by this show of meanness on the part of Abe Wynter, but did not entirely disagree with the older brother. King did not believe that individuals should inherit wealth as a matter of course. He felt every man should earn his own living and receiving unearned riches only turned someone's head for the worse. In his opinion it ruined the sons of rich men, whose wealth came too easily to those who followed after.

'Can you credit such a hard man?' snarled Harry. 'Can you believe it could happen? What would a thousand or even a couple of hundred pounds be to a man what discovered that much gold? He didn't give me a penny. Not even a blamed farthin'. I got to live in this man's army till I die now, which most likely will be sooner than later seein' as how my bodily condition an't healthy at all.'

The others released sounds of sympathy.

After briefing his men Jack had a meeting with Colonel Gold in his office, a shack attached to the local Quaker Meeting House. The colonel was uncomfortable with this close proximity with pacifists, but building space was limited in the town. He liked the plain speaking of Quakers, but privately was horrified by the lack of a hierarchical structure. The Quakers, or Friends, had no ministers, leaders or layers of important officials. Decisions were reached, not by vote, not by a chairman or president, not even by consensus, but by a clerk gauging the 'feeling of the meeting'.

The colonel tried to imagine the army working in the same way and shuddered.

'We're like two exact opposites,' the colonel explained to Jack as the captain sat down in the proffered chair. 'On one side the warriors with written rules, regulations and where everyone knows his place – and on the other side of that wall they are pacifists who have nothing written down and whose organization is a total mystery, even to its members. Yet we manage to live together tolerably well. I tell you one thing, they don't make a great deal of noise. They're peaceful neighbours all right.' The colonel let out a raucous laugh, as if he had just made a great joke.

Jack stared at the colonel, unable to join in the laughter.

The colonel sighed. 'Their meetings for worship consist of an hour of silence,' explained the colonel.

'Oh,' replied Jack. 'No hymns or sermons?'

'The occasional quietly spoken piece of advice or query, so I'm given to understand, never interrupting the silence for more than a few minutes at a time.'

'And how do they settle disputes, sir?'

'Through conciliation and negotiation, apparently. They call it "conflict resolution". Not our sort of people at all, Captain, but each to his own, eh? Now, to business. I need you out in the field. I want you to produce some good maps of the Waitara district, to the south of New Plymouth. How are you fixed? Got all your equipment ready?'

'My sergeant deals with the logistics. Yes, we seem to be there.'

'Then leave as soon as possible. I'm giving you a Maori scout. His name is Ta Moko. You can trust him. Ta Moko is from a tribe to the far north, near the Bay of Islands, but he knows the country hereabouts. Shall I call him in?'

'Just one moment, sir. Could I enquire about something?'

The colonel looked surprised. 'Of course.'

'Do you know a man by the name of Abraham Wynter?'

'Know of him. He's in thick with some of the governor's men. A common sort of fellow, but he struck it rich in the Australian goldfields. Why? Had a run in with him?'

'No, nothing like that. One of my men is his brother. There was a confrontation between the two just before I came to see you. Basically my private thought his brother would purchase his release from the army, and the brother refused. Point blank. Abraham Wynter seems reluctant to part with any of his new-found wealth, even for family.'

'That sounds like him.' The colonel tapped a pencil on the table in front of him, before adding, 'Some of the more dubious land deals have been made in his name. Wynter has purchased land from Maori who have afterwards been proved not to own it. Yet his claims to legitimate contracts have been upheld by the government. He has someone in his pocket, that's certain. I don't like the man. I'm no snob, Captain, but there's the stink of bribery and corruption about him.'

'Thank you, sir. Now your Maori scout. May I meet him?'

The colonel shouted the name and a man in European trousers and shirt, but barefoot, stepped through the doorway. His broad face was a maze of tattoos and his hair was as black as a raven's wing. Jack had never seen such wide shoulders on any man before. They were huge and muscled, as were the rest of the visible parts of his body. He looked immensely strong. He stepped forward and Jack felt his good hand being gripped by powerful fingers. Brown eyes stared into his. They were bright, warm eyes, with amusement not far away.

'How do you do, sir? My name is Ta Moko.'

'So I understand. And mine is Crossman – Captain Jack Crossman.'

'Good. A cross and a man. I am also a Christian. Are you a Christian, sir, may I ask?'

'Yes, though I have to admit, I have not been

a practising one of late – but I was born so.'

'You may borrow my Bible, if you need it. We Maori always carry a Bible, since it is new to us. We don't know it by heart yet.'

Jack did not say there were very few British soldiers who would know the Bible by heart, if any at all. Once outside the hearing of the colonel, Jack was able to talk to Ta Moko more freely. Not that he had anything to say that was contentious, but the presence of a senior officer always inhibited the captain. There were still those around who were suspicious of the kind of work he did. It was not so long ago that senior officers in the army despised spies of any kind, even their own, and considered them to be less than gentlemen.

'Ta Moko,' he said, as they walked along, side by side, 'has that any special meaning?'

'My full name is Tohunga Ta Moko. My grandfather was the maker of tattoos. That is what Ta Moko means.'

'Ah, but you no longer follow your grandfather's art?'

'No, I am a warrior, and also pathfinder for the pakeha.'

Jack hesitated before asking the next question, but he felt he needed to know.

'Can I ask why you scout for us? The pakeha?'

Ta Moko shrugged. 'Why not? You have come here. We have accepted you. In the beginning there was no trouble – only in the last few years has trouble come. I have been to London and to Vienna. I have seen what power you people have in your machines. And there are so many of you. If it had not been the British, it would have been the French, or the Dutch, or the Portuguese. One or other of you. I myself own no land. I have nothing to sell. So I earn a living by what I can do.' He paused. 'I used to be a fisherman, but when my father died I lost my love for fishing. We would do it together. Now it is not the same.'

Jack took Ta Moko to his men and introduced him. Gwilliams, once a scout himself, gave Ta Moko a friendly nod. King shook the Maori's hand. Wynter typically stared at the newcomer sourly, but wisely kept his peace. Ta Moko was left in no doubt where he stood with each of the men he was to take out into the bush. He knew which one he would leave behind, if it became a necessary thing to do. Ta Moko knew also that there were men he came to regard and men he came to despise in all walks of life. Wynter did not bother him. He was aware he could crush the private like a flea if there was any problem with him.

Once the packhorses were loaded, the group set off southwards to skirt the edge of Mount Taranaki. As they left the camp Jack was aware that more soldiers were arriving from the ships. He recognized the colours of 40th Regiment, and the 13th, who were due in New Zealand. There were more Royal Artillery too. The military were building their numbers in New Plymouth.

When Sergeant King looked up at Mount

Taranaki, he saw a dramatic volcanic cone with a white snowy peak. It was a huge powerful presence dominating – no, domineering – the landscape. King could not help but be affected in a spiritual way by this beautiful physical force. Dozens of streams, which later became rivers, ran down the sides of the volcano, watering a vast array of wild flowers, shrubs and trees. An awe-inspiring sight.

Ta Moko saw by King's face that he was affected by the scene.

He rode up alongside Sergeant King. 'Do you want to know more about this mountain?'

'Yes, I do,' replied King, expecting and of course hoping to be told something of a geographical nature. He was after all a map-maker, whose principal interests were in the formation of the landscape and in the nature of earth movements.

'Well,' said Ta Moko, 'this volcano once lived with three other volcanoes – Ruapehu, Tongariro and Ngauruhoe – but Taranaki fell in love with Tongariro's lovely wife, a beautiful small volcano named Pihanga. He was caught with her and paid the price of stealing dark love. His penalty was to be cast out from the tribe and Taranaki went west, towards the setting sun. As he travelled his feet cut a groove in the land, which we now call the River Whanganui.'

A disappointed King said, 'Thank you for that story. I am most obliged to you, Ta Moko.'

'You do not believe it?' Ta Moko asked.

'Oh, it's not whether I believe it or not – I

53

thought I was about to hear something different.'

Ta Moko shrugged, wondering why his tale was not fascinating to this man. Other Englishmen, especially the members of the clergy, would write his stories down when he told them, eager to listen. Even the bishop himself was keen to hear tales, especially about Maui, the wonderful demigod who delighted all Maori children. Ta Moko sighed. The old gods were worshipped no longer: at least not openly. Some Maoris clung to them, of course, but most had become Christians. Being a Christian was probably special, but it could be quite boring. Did Jesus ever change heads with his wife and walk through a village to terrify the inhabitants? Maui did. Were there any giants in the Bible like Flaming Teeth, who would replace a charred stump in his mouth with a newly cut-down tree? Not that Ta Moko knew. And Little Wave and Big Wave, and the Eel-man, and tree goblins, and ... oh, so many gods and creatures. The Bible had stories too, of course, but none quite as exciting as the Polynesian tales told to Ta Moko by his grandpa.

And this sergeant seemed unimpressed by them and thus Ta Moko was also disappointed, because he had already decided he liked Farrier King more than any of the others in this group of pakeha.

The patrol continued through lush rainforest in the foothills of the mountain, past forests of rimu and kamahi trees. Above them were dwarf forests, with trees of stunted growth, their trunks and branches gnarled and hanging with moss and parasitical plants. If Ta Moko had asked Jack what he thought of the scenery around him, Jack would have regaled the Maori with an enthusiastic and resounding approval. Jack was beginning to fall in love with New Zealand. Probably, if he searched his heart, he would have discovered that what he liked about it most was the lack of people. Solitude was attractive to his soul. There were other places he had been – the jungles of India, the hills of the Crimea – which had been isolated and empty. But they had seemed lonely; here he was not affected by the loneliness, only the quiet beauty.

The packhorses carried supplies for the map-makers, but Ta Moko had brought his own food, which he ate separately from the others. Jack asked Ta Moko to join them, but for reasons he did not divulge the Maori preferred to eat alone. Once the tents were up, Jack was able to take in his surroundings. This was a rocky area, with some trees, but mostly shrub.

The bird life was many and varied. The only type he recognized was the kingfisher, because of that electric flash of blue when it zipped over the water, but he did not know the specific name of this kingfisher, nor was he greatly interested in labels. It was enough to have the evening come in with these familiar winged creatures around him, reminding him of England and Scotland.

Wynter and Gwilliams spent the twilight

cleaning the party's weapons. They were wrapped in blankets as they worked. During the day it had been around 55 degrees Fahrenheit, but now that the sun had gone down the temperature had dropped dramatically. It was no longer chilly; it was cold. Clouds had gathered in the twilight, and it started to rain about mid-evening and the group dispersed to their tents. That night it rained heavily, and the next day, and the day after that. It was April and winter was closing in on the land. When the sun finally came out and allowed them to emerge, the ground was like a bog, covered in casual water, and any movement stirred mud.

Nevertheless, King got to work that day, getting Wynter and Gwilliams to lay out his chains to form the base line for the triangulation. Jack watched and waited to be given a task. He was finally given a pole to hold which King called a 'calibrated stave' while King used a levelling instrument to measure the rise and fall of the ground ahead employing a method known as 'horizontal sightings'. It was all gobblede-gook to Jack, and though King tried to fire his interest, Jack would have been much happier taking the theodolite to bits and putting it back together again. He had a clockmaker's mental-ity.

Ta Moko watched with concern. He had seen maps before, of course, and knew they threat-ened the way he earned his living. It occurred to him that if the British managed to produce enough maps they would no longer need Maoris like him. When he said as much to Jack though, the officer shook his head.

'It'll be a long time before we have this country mapped, be assured of that, Ta Moko. And even when we do, we will always need guides like you. Maps won't tell us which rivers are likely to be swollen when the rains come or the snow melts, and the alternative path to take when they are. Or the quickest track through the bush. Maps won't tell us which plants to eat when we run out of food and where to hunt edible birds. Don't worry, even when we're all dead and gone, white men will be clamouring for guides in the bush.'

'You are not just saying this to make me help you with the maps?' asked the Maori.

'I never just say things. I try to tell the truth.'

'Good. Though many men try to tell the truth and cannot.'

Jack said, 'You have to ask yourself whether my words make sense.'

Ta Moko nodded. 'I will think about them.'

The mapping continued, with King scribbling down figures and words in his notebook, running from one instrument to the other to check levels and heights, and the others dragging their feet when he wanted them to run alongside him. As Jack had guessed it would, from past experience, the mood in the camp deteriorated. Sergeant King was the only one who knew what he was doing. Others simply did his bidding and were uninterested in learning anything further. It upset King that other men were so indifferent to his chosen profession. He did not expect them to be as violently enthusiastic as he was himself, but he did expect a degree of interest which was not there. With that apathy came mistakes, because his helpers did not pay close attention to his instructions.

'Wynter! That heliotrope is a very valuable instrument. Will you please not swing it around in that fashion?' yelled King.

'Keep your hat on,' grumbled the private under his breath. 'Can't do much harm to wave it about a bit. Air an't like a solid wall, is it?'

King switched his grievances to the corporal next.

'And, Gwilliams, you have left that measuring rod out in the sun. Do you not see that there is a thin brass wire running along its groove? Did you not know metal expands when it is hot? These measurements need to be accurate to a hair's breadth. Must I have to lecture all the time? It is most aggravating – most aggravating. What must I do to make you people realize the importance of accuracy in these measurements? Lord, give me men about me who know the difference between a coffer and a truss...'

Gwilliams' answer was to look away and spit a huge gobbet of tobacco juice in the direction of the distant adulterous mountain.

By noon on the eighth day Jack could stand it no longer. He had reached the point where he had a mind to strangle his sergeant while he slept. So he saddled his horse, took Wynter's Enfield, and told Sergeant King he was going out to shoot game.

'What? Oh, sir, you are needed here.'

Gwilliams and Wynter looked at the officer enviously, jealous of the privilege of rank that allowed him to escape this purgatory.

Sergeant King knew why Jack wanted to get away and was upset with himself for being so tetchy. He tried to entice his officer back into the camp with long overdue praise. He took hold of the horse's bridle. 'Sir, I have to thank you for yesterday's work. It was most satisfactory. Really. Most satisfactory. Over the first 700 feet the remeasurements have shown a difference only of 0.013 of an inch. Isn't that superb?'

'Sergeant,' said Jack, coldly, 'I have to confess to you that I have absolutely no idea what that means.'

'It means, sir, that if we were to measure from the top of India to the very bottom tip, we would be accurate to within six feet!' the sergeant cried, trying to instil some of his enthusiasm in the officer.

'Amazing,' replied Jack, unable to keep the irony out of his tone. 'Now if you please, Sergeant, I wish to ride out.'

'Oh, sir.'

The plea fell on deaf ears. Jack could stand it no longer. He urged his mount forward and cantered off into the bush. Once out of the camp he relaxed a little. The atmosphere he had left behind had not been pleasant. There was only one happy man in that camp. Even Ta Moko, who had been given tasks, was no longer fascinated by the brass and glass instruments and the coloured pens of the map-maker.

Now Jack could let his thoughts dwell on the countryside around him, which King had robbed of all interest by reducing to feet and inches. It was a wide expanse of wonderful wilderness, to be enjoyed not measured, and he was going to make the most of his brief freedom. When he came to a wild river, which tumbled and danced in high fashion over its rocky bed, he simply sat on the bank and gazed. An hour later, when the sun was almost vertically overhead, he shot a bird he could not name but which looked plump enough for the pot. It was a duck of some kind, but of a blueish hue and not like any in Britain. Before long he had half-a-dozen of the same bird and had tied five of them by their legs to hang them from his saddle. The sixth he plucked.

With the horse idly grazing nearby, Jack made a fire, let it burn down to cinders, and then roasted his bird on a spit over the glowing charcoal which remained. It smelt delicious and tasted like heaven. He realized of course that lighting a fire in enemy territory was dangerous, but he had seen neither hide nor hair of Maoris since they had begun their mapping and was inclined to think that they were all in their *pas*, or villages, and not out roaming the bush. Why would they be? There was little out here and the land was at war. All respectable Maori warriors would be gathering around their clan chiefs, awaiting attacks by the pakehas, or making preparations for the next battle.

It was perhaps the roaring of the river that hid the sound of their approach, but before he knew it he was being shot at from only a few yards away. Looking up he saw about a dozen Maori running at him, only one with a rifle, but the rest carrying hacking weapons the shape of small canoe paddles. Jack dropped the bones of the duck, which he had been lingering over, and leapt for his horse. With only one hand it was never an easy thing to mount a strange beast. Jack was not a natural horseman like Gwilliams or King, and the creatures knew it. This one shied away on being grabbed. Jack actually managed to get into the saddle, but, snatching at the reins with his good hand, he missed them, and thus the animal bolted, sending Jack tumbling to the ground.

He fell badly on his left foot and knew instantly that he had damaged his ankle in some way. There was some thought in his mind to draw his revolver from the inside pocket of his coat, but before he could do this a coarse-skinned brown foot pinned his wrist to the earth. Looking up he could see a grinning face staring down at him. Jack waited for that paddle-thing to split his skull in two. But the man's right arm simply hung by his side and there was no attempt to brain him. Through the open legs of his attacker Jack could see the other Maoris going through his kit, taking his kettle, the leather belt he had removed while eating, and of course the Enfield rifle propped on a log.

'What else in your pockets?' said the Maori above him, releasing his arm. 'Empty them.'

Jack took out some money, a handkerchief, the key to his quarters, and a letter from Jane. He wondered if he could reach his Tranter revolver, knowing however that it only held five shots. He counted thirteen Maoris milling around his fire, including the one who stood above him. He decided against lunging for it, hoping it might remain undiscovered and he could use it later. Something in his demeanour though, must have given him away. In the next moment the Maori had reached down and found the firearm, taking it from him.

'Ah, you would kill me?' cried his captor, and turned and said something in his own language to his companions.

There was laughter from them.

'So,' Jack said, sitting up in the dust, 'better get it over with then.'

'Get what over with?'

'Whatever it is you're going to do with me.'

They all crowded round him now, huge muscled fellows, their brown eyes devoid of pity. He waited for the blows to come, hoping one would be kind enough to hit him on the head and kill him instantly. Finally one of them raised a club and struck him on the temple and blackness entered his brain.

Four

When he woke, Jack was in a different place. It was not, as he expected, either the kingdom of heaven or even the bleak caverns of hell. He was still on earth and much the same earth as he had left. The river was gone though, and he was in some trees by a pool. It was a little while before his splitting headache would allow him to deduce that he had been either dragged or carried some way from where he had been attacked. Here they had dumped him, still alive. His head hurt. He touched the wound and felt encrusted blood. But worse was his ankle, which throbbed with live pain. Thirsty and unable to walk, he crawled to the pool and drank from its fly-dusted waters.

'What now?' he asked himself, sitting up and rubbing his ankle. It was swollen to three times its natural size. 'Make myself a splint?'

But he soon realized that would do him no good. A splint is fine on a broken ankle of normal size, but the pain of strapping wood to such a tender spot made him nearly pass out twice. He knew he would have to wait until the swelling went down, if it ever did. Instead, he put his foot in the cool water of the pool, to obtain some relief from the agony.

He sat there until nightfall, annoyed to find all his pockets completely empty. He had deliberately left his small brass compass in one of those pockets, when told to turn them out. Without a compass he was going to have to wait until daybreak to go anywhere. The sky was opaque and no stars could be seen. Jack needed the sun to be able to tell in which general direction New Plymouth lay. He had absolutely no chance of finding the camp. It was while he was bemoaning his lot that the skies opened and the rain came down in torrents. His misery was just about complete as he found himself wallowing in mud. For the next four or five hours there was no respite from the flood. It rained, it then rained harder, then still harder. Lightning cracked across the heavens, filling the world with evanescent light, then longer periods of darkness. Sleep was impossible, even when he crawled to the base of a giant tree, and tried to shelter in the hollow of its buttress roots.

In the morning it continued to rain. Jack dragged himself out of the wood and tried to get his bearings, but from a sitting position this was hopeless. Even when he found a branch and got himself into an upright pose, he could not see through the dense downpour. He slid back down to the ground and sat there shivering, hoping for a miracle.

The miracle turned up on two legs. He saw the figure coming, just a silhouette in the sheeting rain, like a dark phantom, and though he prayed it was one of his men, he knew from its build the figure was more powerful than any of his soldiers. It could have been Ta Moko of course, but it was not. It was the fellow who had stood over him while his companions had robbed Jack's camp. The fellow who had struck him with a bladed weapon.

The man had on a sodden jacket now, no doubt to protect his bare torso against the cold. It remained unbuttoned and looked far too small for the big Maori. The temperature had dropped very low and Jack's visitor was visibly shivering. Jack noticed the Maori was carrying the Tranter 5-shot revolver he had stolen.

'Come back to finish me off?' croaked the captain.

The Maori shook his head irritably. He tossed the Tranter down at Jack's feet.

'Came to give you this.'

Jack snatched the weapon up, but the Maori smiled grimly.

'It's empty. That's why I'm giving it back. I can't seem to get the bullets to fit it. Not the right calibre anyway.'

The revolver was indeed light enough to be out of ammunition. Jack tossed it aside. It made a splash on the muddy ground.

'You're not going to kill me?' It was a matter-of-fact question.

Again, the Maori looked annoyed. 'Why would I do that now?'

Jack admitted, 'I don't know.'

'I tried to kill you back in the bush, but you

65

have a head as hard as a steel pan.'

This was rather puzzling to the British officer. 'You didn't just try to knock me out cold?'

'No – I tried to kill you. If you could see your wound now, you'd know I did. Your skull is split open. I can see the white bone.'

Jack shuddered at these words. Gingerly he reached up and touched his head with the tips of his fingers. There was indeed a crevice there, beneath the coagulated blood. His scalp had been hacked open with a less than sharp blade. Indeed there was a flap of skin with hair on it, hanging to one side. He tried to replace it, like a divot flung from a lawn by a pony's hoof, but it fell to one side again. The knowledge of the wound made Jack's brain swim and he almost swooned away. He felt an ocean swell of nausea roll through his stomach and he might have thrown up at the Maori's feet if he had not lain back on the ground, with the rain forming a puddle around his supine body.

'Quite frankly,' said Jack, miserably, 'I believe I would prefer it if I had died under the blow.'

The Maori laughed. 'Is this the British humour?'

'No, this is the British irony. I don't think you would understand.' Jack was still lying on his back, looking up at the sky. One or two stars were beginning to show in the heavens above. The clouds were obviously clearing and letting through their light. 'I still don't understand something myself – why was there no second blow? Why not finish me there and then?'

The Maori found a sodden log and sat on it, staring down at Jack.

'In the old days, I would have done. If you had been a warrior from another tribe I would have caved your head in just like that. But the old ways are gone. We can kill them in battle. But we must – what is that word Bishop Selwyn uses? *Succour*. Yes, we must succour the wounded, not bash their brains in. That's why I have come back. To give you your pistol.'

In his right hand the Maori had a wooden staff, flattened to a broad blade at one end. He changed this to his left hand so that he could reach inside his coat. He pulled out something wrapped in muslin.

'I also bring you food and drink. Well, drink you have, from the rain. But here is some food. And I will patch your head for you, when the daylight comes.'

The Maoris, Jack realized, took the teachings of the Church literally. In the heat of battle, of course, a man would go down under such a blow and probably stay down. He would be a fool if he did not, for Jack was in no state to fight. This Maori had decided after he had struck him that the captain was out of it, and therefore entitled to live under these new articles of war preached by the clergy.

'Can I know your name?' asked Jack.

'It is Potaka. And yours?'

'Crossman. Jack Crossman.'

'Pleased to meet you.'

Potaka stuck out a hand and Jack reached up

67

from his ridiculous lying position and shook it. Then went back to staring at the stars. He had decided he would not move until the morning. If his skull was fractured, as it might be, he knew he still might die. It was better he did not hasten this state of mortality. Limited time was better than no time at all. A man will do much for a few more seconds, even at the end.

'You are an honourable enemy, Potaka.'

'I hope so. I try to be. Most of us try to be. There are a few sly ones among us, but I'm sure you find the same.'

Jack thought of Wynter. 'Indeed.'

Potaka took off his coat and rolled it up, placing it under Jack's neck.

'You will be more comfortable that way.'

'Thank you.'

Potaka nodded at Jack's empty wrist.

Jack said, 'In another war.'

'Ah, my brother has only one leg – also another war. Does it bother you still? My brother's lost leg still hurts him. He keeps looking for it, in the place where it was chopped off, hoping to find it and tend to it, so the pain will go away. He thinks his enemy ate it.'

'Ah, the old ghost limb. Not me,' admitted Jack. 'I used to feel it still there, but there was no pain.' Jack paused for a moment, finding a more comfortable position for his head, then added, 'And nobody would have eaten it, unless they like minced meat.'

'You have many battle scars on your face, soldier.'

'Who can tell with you? The tattoos hide everything but your eyes.'

Potaka laughed. 'Better to get some sleep now.'

'I think you're right.'

In fact sleep came very easily.

The following morning Jack woke to the sound of crackling wood. Potaka had lit a fire and was cooking something. After a while he came to Jack with a piece of flat wood and started to spoon a substance out of its shell.

'Breadfruit,' explained Potaka. 'You will like the flavour.'

'Not bad,' said Jack. 'What's that stick you carry with you all the time? Do you need something to support you?'

'This?' Potaka held up the six-foot-long staff. 'This is a *taiaha*, a fighting stick. But it was this that I hit you with.' He showed Jack a carved-greenstone bladed club hanging from his waist by a cord. 'My *patu*.'

'And don't I know it,' said Jack, whose head was still very sore and ached all the way down to the roots of his neck. 'That stick – our people used to fight with staves once, but that was long ago. As a boy I liked to play single-stick with my brother, but just for fun. I got quite good at whacking him around the legs.'

'The *taiaha* takes many years to master – it is no ordinary fighting stick. My whole childhood was taken up with learning the art.'

'Oh,' replied Jack, feeling he was being taken to task for bragging.

Once he was fed and watered, Potaka washed the wound on his head, which was a painful business, then inspected it.

'I think the skull is not broken right through, just dented a little,' muttered the Maori. 'I am going to put the piece of skin back and tie it down with a strip of cloth. It should take. I have no needle to sew it, so you must keep it still for a few days until it grows back on.'

'Grafting. We call it grafting.'

The business was soon done with a strip of Jack's shirt serving as the bandage.

'Now,' Potaka said, 'we must look at the ankle. Do you think it is broken?'

'No, I think I've torn something.'

'Good. Better than a broken bone. Ankles are terrible things to heal, if they're broken. Can you stand on it?'

Jack tried but went down like a felled tree. Potaka did nothing to stop him from crashing to the ground. He simply stood there with his hands on hips and said, 'No, you cannot walk on it.'

Jack muttered, 'I think I've hurt my head again,' and started to put his hand up to feel the wound, but Potaka arrested it, saying, 'You just jolted it. It has started bleeding again, but you must leave it alone. I do not want to have to change the dressing yet.'

Jack allowed himself to be ministered to. He felt he was in the hands of some capable female nurse, like Mary Seacole who tended him in the Crimea. Yet the man who tended to his wounds

70

was a heavy-set warrior who could have broken Jack's back in two halves if he had a mind to. The situation was very strange: the man who had wounded him was the man who now seemed intent on keeping him alive. Jack guessed it was a matter of work pride. On the one hand Potaka had tried to kill him and had failed, but now he had decided to doctor a patient, he was determined Jack would survive. It would be a job well done, to wipe out the stain of the botched killing.

Jack did believe, however, that the Maoris now took Christian ethics very seriously. Whatever their religion before now, they seemed even more fervently Christian than the arriving white settlers. The bishops, who frequently took the side of the Maoris in land disputes, had something to do with that, but there was something else going on too.

'Do you have a particular god you worshipped, before we came?' asked Jack later, as they huddled round a campfire together. 'I'm interested in your beliefs before.'

Potaka gave Jack a hard look. 'We knew how to give mercy, if that is what you mean.'

'But what about these old gods of yours? Where did they come from?'

The Maori shrugged. 'They were born, like you and me. There was Tangaroa, god of the ocean...'

Over the next hour Jack was given a whole pantheon, few of which he would remember. Two characters however seemed vastly more important than the rest. Tiki, the divine ancestor of these people, who always sat at the head of a canoe, and Maui, a wonderful trickster god. The powers of the gods were many and various. Some were just small gods, like Rongo-ma-tane, god of the sweet potato. Others had far more exotic positions in the pantheon, such as Hine-nui-te-po, goddess of the night, darkness and death. What was clear to Jack, though, was that the Maori had a complex culture of myth and folklore which belied the simplicity of their everyday lives. An intricate, multi-meshed culture, as tightly connected and webbed as a fishing net.

'We used to eat long pig, of course,' finished Potaka, 'which Jesus would not have liked. So we stopped all that.'

'For which I am eternally grateful, being quite attached to my thighs and liver.'

Potaka stared, licked and smacked his lips – then openly grinned with malicious pleasure. 'Just joking.'

'So, how did you find these great islands?' asked Jack. 'I mean, how did you discover them? You have no great sailing ships, like the British. Was it an accident? A fishing canoe blown off-course? Something like that?'

'There was a man called Kupe,' Potaka began explaining in a storytelling voice, 'who lived on an island far away. The name of the island was Raiatea. One day Kupe was out fishing when an octopus stole his bait. He was angry and set out in pursuit of the thief, which led him to these islands. In those days we could not write, so everyone had very good memories. Kupe remembered everything about his voyage, from the colour of the waves, to the direction of the swell, to small islands on the way. I am told by your navigators that Raiatea is 2,500 miles away, but Kupe described how to get to the Land-of-the-Long-White-Cloud by sailing to the left of the setting sun in November.'

Potaka paused for effect, then said, 'So we came. We brought our dogs and pigs, our taro, sweetbreads, sweet potatoes, and other seeds and plants. We did not mean to bring the rats, but they came with us anyway, as rats always do. When we arrived there were only birds. Many, many birds. There was a big one called a moa, twelve feet high, but we killed all the moas before you came here.'

Jack was impressed. 'That's quite a story. How many people in each canoe?'

'Perhaps a hundred or more. They navigated by the star paths and sea and land birds. There were blind navigators, feelers-of-the-sea we called them, who knew which part of the ocean we were in by its temperature. Some were just nature's tricks. Did you know if you throw a pig into the water it will always swim towards the nearest land, even when that land is out of sight?'

'Something to do with the scent of the soil on the wind, I expect. I must remember, next time I am lost at sea and have a pig handy.'

Potaka stiffened and stopped poking the fire

with a stick. 'You are making fun of me.'

'Only a little. Actually, I have a great admiration for a people who travelled thousands of miles over open ocean, while my own nation were still coast-hugging in far more seaworthy ships.'

'Your navigators are good now though, with their charts and brass instruments. Captain Cook was such a man.'

'I have heard of one of yours whose ancestor was Speaker for the 7th Canoe.'

'He is my cousin,' said Potaka, proudly. He grinned again. 'But then, most Maori people are my cousins.'

Following this conversation, Jack was allowed to rest. Potaka showed no signs of leaving him to his fate. The Maori made a camp, collected wood for the fire, cooked Jack's meal and changed his dressing. Their exchanges were not always as pleasant as their talk about migration. At times the festering anger which many Maoris felt regarding the influx of strangers in their land burst through and Jack was subject to a tirade. Why had the white men come here? They had not been invited. Why did they keep coming? When would it stop? When they had taken all the land there was to be had?

On the one hand Jack sympathized with Potaka's complaints. Had this been Scotland or England, with strangers arriving by the boatload every few months and establishing themselves on the landscape as if they had owned it since Adam, he too would have felt great resentment.

On the other he knew the settlers would continue to arrive until they were stopped, either by the government or by a natural law such as a dearth of jobs and land. He felt it would be better for the Maori to integrate themselves and try to assimilate the new culture which had been thrust upon them, than battle against it. As in all other colonizations by Europeans, so far as the natives were concerned the resources of the army they were fighting were infinite in terms of men and equipment. They would keep pouring in until the fight was won – by the British. Jack hesitated to call his people invaders, since they had not stormed the beaches of New Zealand but had simply arrived in batches until there were too many here for the Maori to ignore.

'Isn't it better to have established a rule of law here, Potaka, than for your people to have to suffer the dregs of our society?'

Jack was referring to the first settlers, who tended to be escaped convicts, sailors who had jumped whaling ships, and tough, rough traders. Not the cream of British society, to say the least. They had introduced prostitution and grog-shops, sex and drink being their raison d'EAtre, and all the vices and violence that went with them. Jack was not sure why the Maori had put up with them, but he guessed it was because they had not been a huge threat to their way of life. These were pockets of men, living on the edge, and of no great importance. If one or more killed your brother, you took lives in return, but these whalers and convicts were only dangerous when they grew in numbers. And of course they did. They grew until they were unmanageable, and then the British authorities had an excuse to come in and manage them.

'No,' came the emphatic reply. 'If we had known what trouble it would cause, we would have wiped them out ourselves.'

'Well,' said Jack, sighing, 'it's too late now – now that gold has been found in South Island and elsewhere you haven't a hope in hell of getting rid of us. We have to learn to live with each other.'

'You have no right to be here.'

'There's such a thing as right of conquest, which both our nations recognize.'

'Hmmm,' Potaka said. 'If a Maori tribe conquers another Maori tribe and captures his land, the land still belongs to the first tribe.'

'That surprises me, but let me ask you – do you ever relinquish that land to its former owners?'

Potaka raised his eyebrows. 'In truth? Not often.'

It was during one of these conversations that Potaka suddenly stopped in mid-sentence, threw a look backwards into the bush, and promptly disappeared in the opposite direction. A few minutes later a group of soldiers emerged from a hollow. They were led by Lieutenant Burns. King, Gwilliams and Wynter were among them. Burns greeted Jack with a salute and asked him how he did.

'Tolerably well,' said Jack, who was sitting

with his back against a tree. 'My head was split and my ankle twisted, but both seem to be on the mend now.'

'Thank the great good Lord we've found you, sir,' said Wynter in a voice that hovered on the edge of sarcasm. 'We thought you was a goner for sure.'

Jack decided not to rise to the bait. 'Thank you, Private Wynter, God has indeed received my thanks several times over the last few days.'

'Well, we wrote you off good and proper. I was just sayin' to the corporal the other day, the captain owns a good six-feet-by-two of New Zealand land now, and is become a lifelong settler. The corp says to me—'

Lieutenant Burns interrupted him. 'Will someone shut that man up? Sergeant?'

Sergeant King rapped the back of Wynter's skull with his knuckles. 'Wynter – you heard the officer.'

'Ow! That hurt.'

'Not another word, Private, or it'll be my boot.'

Jack was assisted to his feet.

Burns asked, 'Shall we make you a litter?'

'That'll take time and this is hostile territory,' said Jack. 'Just give me a couple of supporters. No, not you, Wynter, damn you! Gwilliams and King? Thank you. One either side, if you please. Let's get back to New Plymouth before I'm banged on the head a second time.'

They did indeed make it back to the barracks without further incident. Jack learned that they had been sending out search parties every day. A friendly Maori had told the commander of the base that Jack was still alive but in Maori hands. The man did not know where Jack was being held, but the word which travelled through the bush said he was still breathing. King and Gwilliams had not given up hope either and had been persistent in their demands that each new day a party went out over new ground, despite the obvious dangers. In fact the Maori had left them alone, for reasons which did not seem clear but had something to do with Captain Crossman himself. It would seem there was little honour in attacking a party of men who were retrieving a wounded soldier. The Maori were strong on their own code of honour.

Jack was taken to a regimental surgeon, who took a look at his skull wound and rebandaged it.

'Nasty crack, that,' said the surgeon. 'Lucky to be alive.'

'Don't I know it.'

'Who dressed the wound?'

'Man who gave it to me.'

'Funny chaps, these Maoris. Bash you one minute, arm around your shoulder the next.' The surgeon looked wistfully at his range of saws, one or two of them with rusting teeth. 'They don't like you taking off anything, either.'

Jack raised his eyebrows. 'Do any of us?'

The surgeon, a young man of about twenty, laughed at this.

'I suppose not. But you know, the rot will

creep up a limb until it stops your heart. Better to have no hand –' he indicated Jack's left wrist – 'than a stopped heart, eh? Who did that for you, by the way?'

'A Frenchman.'

Without invitation, the young surgeon inspected Jack's stump.

'Nice cross-grain action,' he said. 'Obviously an experienced sawyer. Some of these Frenchies are artists with a saw. I've seen 'em in Paris, practising on mahogany table legs. Mahogany, you know, has about the same density as human thigh bone? Not so, my colleagues. I've seen chums hack 'em off while discussing last night's rum-swilling. Leave a stump looking like a tree with its branch torn off in the wind. What you want is your nice rounded smooth stump – bit like the end of a scullery maid's copper stick, if you know what I mean. Nice white bump of a thing.'

'Yes, well, I can't stay here all day discussing amputations,' Jack said, wryly. 'Have you finished with me?'

'For now, Captain, for now. But don't be a stranger. You may need my services again soon.'

I damn well hope not, thought Jack as he fled the hut.

Five

Over the next few weeks Jack Crossman's men continued to survey areas indicated by Colonel Gold. The triangulation methods King had begun using were abandoned in favour of rougher results due to the inordinate amount of time needed for precise mapping. Gold had told them he simply wanted an aid to finding their way through the wilderness, not pinpoint a particular two-by-four rock to within twelve inches. All they had to do was pathfind their way to the enemy and provide the journey back again. Sergeant King fell back on his old standby, the linear route map, which he sketched on a yard-long pad showing a ribbon-like route with reference points either side. For the army this type of map was often good enough: they got the troops to the point where their commanders wanted them – and back again.

Jack's ankle mended relatively quickly, but his headaches gave him problems for a long time. During the worst he would go for long slow walks seeking solitude and quiet. He became, as many men did, enamoured of the scenery and landscape. Some of it reminded him of the Lake District of Northern England. Other parts, of

Devon and the West Country. It truly was a wonderful island. After a month of convalescing he was convinced that New Zealand was the place to settle with his wife Jane. Here in this land of contrasts they could happily raise a family. He wrote to Jane, telling her to take a ship out to Australia, and thence to the farther-off New Zealand shores. *Go to Auckland,* he wrote, *and I will meet you there.*

The thought of being reunited with his beloved Jane after so many years apart filled him with joy. The flora and fauna of New Zealand looked like Eden to him once he had dispatched the letter. In the meantime he could apply to become a resident army officer. If that was unacceptable to the government then they could keep their commission and he would find employment elsewhere.

It was on one of his walks that he met Abraham Wynter again, as that man came up against him on a bridge. Abe Wynter was surrounded by a gang of friendly Maoris, all well armed. Jack guessed he paid these men to protect him against hostiles. As before, Abe Wynter was dressed in expensive clothes, including a shiny black stovepipe hat. This he doffed as Jack stood aside to let the men pass him. As Jack stared down into the tumbling waters of a braided stream below him, a thought came to him. He called after the group of men, who all turned at his cry.

'Mr Wynter,' Jack said. 'Do you have a moment?'

'Ha, you know me name. Yes, yes – I remember. You're that cap'n, an't you? Can't recall the name, but I know you're me brother's officer. Please-ta-meetcha again, Cap'n.'

'Crossman. Captain Crossman. Have you been out buying land again, Mr Wynter?'

The lean, sharp-faced man stuck his thumbs in his waistcoat pockets and suddenly glared.

'What if I have?'

'No, don't misunderstand me. I'm just curious. You see, I'd like to purchase a plot myself. A small farm would be enough I think. Perhaps five hundred acres? Something of that nature.'

Abe laughed, turning to invite the Maoris to share his humour, which they seemed to decline, remaining with stony expressions.

'Five hundred acres? That's a piddlin' backyard, that is, Cap'n. Five thousand's what you want, more like. Do you know that in Australia they have single farms bigger'n England and France put together? *Farms!* That's what you want. Somethin' as big as two countries. A small farm would be the size o' Holland or Belgie. It's true this an't Australia – New Zealand is a country the size of the old country – but you can do better'n five hundred acres, old chum.' I'm not your old chum, thought Jack, but he did not say so. 'Do you want me to get it for you, Cap'n?' Abe continued. 'Seein' as how you look after me little brother, I could do you a deal you wouldn't get nowhere else. There's coves out there all linin' up for land, and you'd be at the back of the queue, just now. You just tell me where you're lookin' at, and I'll see what I can do for you.'

Jack glanced at the Maoris, who were lounging around at the end of the bridge, smoking pipes. They were dressed in woollen jumpers and trousers, and one or two wore caps. All carried rather scarred, elderly shotguns, which they leaned on like crutches. None of them had the magnificent build of Potaka or Ta Moko, but one or two were wiry rather than pot-bellied. They all looked tough and able.

'Admirin' my Maori, eh?' said Abe Wynter. 'Proud sort of fellahs, an't they? Me an' them get on just fine.' He winked. 'We got somethin' deep in common, see.'

'Something in common?'

'Ah, can't tell you, Cap'n, or you'd know all me secrets, wouldn't you? Now, what about your problems, eh?'

'You think I would have trouble finding land?'

'Know it, old chum. It's premium, an't it? But I got ways of jumpin' the queue, if needs must. Come an' share a pot o' beer with me. We'll discuss it. How much money you got? Honest now!'

Jack told him as they walked along. Abe nodded thoughtfully.

'We can do somethin' with that, certain sure.'

Jack felt very uncomfortable in the company of Private Wynter's brother. Jack was no snob and Abe Wynter was often in the company of far more exulted persons than a captain of foot, but there was too much of the Harry about Abe for

Jack to feel easy.

However, it would be nice if he could build a farm on his own land before Jane arrived so that he could surprise her. The more he thought about it, the more excited he became. And Abe Wynter was a legitimate agent, recognized by the government. What harm could there be in using him to purchase the land? Certainly Jack had not the time himself to deal with the negotiations and bureaucracy involved.

'I don't think I need to tell you, Mr Wynter, that I require everything to be legal and above board.'

Abe Wynter wore a shocked expression.

'Cap'n Crossman, 'ow could you think otherwise of me? What need have I to be underhand or chiselling? I'm a rich man already.' He leaned forward as they sat at a table outside the alehouse. 'Listen, I admit it – I jumped ship. But I've made amends for that with the navy. Paid a proper fine and all's forgiven, so far as they're concerned. Steep fine, mind you, but I accept that, to clear my name. Why would I want to besmirch it again? Not on your life. I'm a man with gold in his pocket, but I like somethin' to do, in the way of business, see, gold or no gold.'

'I can understand that. A man should be busy in this world or he feels useless. By the way, what happened to your two partners? Are they in New Zealand?'

'Eh?'

'You told your brother you had two pals with you ... when you discovered the gold...'

Abe Wynter stuck two fingers up at the waiter and, having made his order, bent down close again.

'Ha, there's a sad tale, to be sure. You see, after we sold the nugget we didn't know about this fine business. The navy was after us and they came to the goldfield, looking for deserters. We didn't know what to do. We was scared if we turned ourselves in we'd be lashed or hung and the money took from us. So we did the only thing we could do – we run. We run off into the outback of Australia.' He paused. 'We went what the natives there call *walkabout*. 'Cept we run instead of walked. Truth to say, we was lost almost afore we started. That there outback country is the very devil. It all looks the same. I swear I saw the same white broken tree a thousand times, yet it was different ones. There's nothin' but dry creeks, dust holes and bloody snakes and lizards out there, I can vouch for that. Water? We didn't see a drop for days. We roasted under a blisterin' cruel sun, our skins as red as soldiers' coatees. Our mouths cracked and slimed over. Danny, he went stone blind with the sheer hard whiteness of the light comin' off the sand.'

Abe Wynter licked his lips and looked long-ingly towards the doorway through which his cool beer would appear.

'Then one day some Abos found us. They took us to a creek and dug us out some muddy water. It was a bloody blessin', I'll tell you that, Cap'n. We drunk our fill, but the Abos vanished the

85

same way they come, and though we stayed a week by the waterhole, we was startin' to starve. I tried catchin' them lizards, but they was quicker'n roaches when they wanted to be. Anyways, we knew we couldn't stay there for ever, so we started walking again, this time usin' our canvas hats to carry some water with us. Ol' Danny, he didn't make it though. Died of the sun on his neck, he did. Went down like a felled tree and cracked his head open on a rock. We left him there, Striker an' me not knowing if we was next for the Lord's back pocket. He was on our side, though, Cap'n, 'cause we found a dirt track that led to a farm, and so providence delivered us two poor unfortunates back to the livin'.'

Jack recalled that Abe's brother Harry had walked from the Crimea to India, to help quell the Indian Mutiny. A hellish, desperate march that had cost the lives of most of those who had started out. But Harry Wynter had survived, and once again he marvelled at the Wynters' fortitude and resilience. This was obviously a family of survivors. Not without complaint though, because Harry at least never ceased complaining. The stamina in these two brothers was nothing short of remarkable. Others fell away, but they dug in, carried on, refused to go down. Both were scarred and ravaged men, with haunted eyes, but they were very much alive.

'That's an extraordinary story, Mr Wynter. And where is Mr Striker now?'

'Striker's his nickname. His proper name was Strickland. Oh, he's back in England somewhere. He don't like this part of the world and who can blame him. It's not a place for home-lovin' men.'

The beer came and Abe Wynter immediately ordered two more, despite Jack's protests.

Jack said he would send Abe Wynter a map of the region he preferred for his farm. Wynter said he could not promise anything, for many Maoris were 'dead reluctant' to sell. Jack repeated his warning that he wanted nothing that was illegal or even illicit. He might have added 'immoral' to his list, except that he guessed Abe Wynter would not really understand the meaning of the word. The two men parted with a shake of the hand and, his head thumping again – probably due to the ale he had consumed – he returned to his quarters.

Later, an incensed Harry Wynter requested to speak to him. Jack came out of his quarters. 'What is it, Wynter? Can't the sergeant deal with it? I'm very busy.'

'You bin to see my brother,' accused the private.

'I wasn't aware that you still speak to him, after his treatment of you, but, yes, I ran into him on a bridge and we spoke.'

'You had a jug or two with 'im, so I'm told.'

'Your spies are very efficient, Wynter.'

'It's our trade, an't it, sir? Well, what's it all about, eh? What're you two cookin' up 'tween you?'

'My conversation with your brother is confidential. And if you don't want to end up in the guardhouse, Wynter, I suggest you moderate your tone. Rest assured, it has nothing to do with you. This is purely a private matter between myself and Abraham Wynter. Now, was there anything else?'

Harry Wynter's eyes narrowed. 'Just this, sir. If you think you can trust Abe, you'd better think again. He's got no more soul than a snake – no more'n what I have, and you know that an't much, Captain, you an' me 'ave bin together quite a bit. I wouldn'ave nothin' to do with him meself, if I weren't his baby brother. He's a back-stabbing bastard, is Abe, and you couldn't trust him with nothin'.'

'Thank you for the warning, Wynter, but I'm well able to judge a man's character for myself.'

'Well, don't say I din't tell you.'

With that the private ambled off, towards the huts used by the rank and file, a bent, mean-looking man bearing many grudges.

The call to arms came on an early winter morning in June. Jack's head was at its worst, but he knew he had to do his duty. It had been raining a great deal and the ground around the camp, and presumably further afield, was layered with thick sticky mud. These conditions had not seemed to deter Colonel Gold, who ordered Major Nelson, the senior army officer at the army camp, to attack a *pa* known as Puketa-kauere. During the planning of this attack Jack had suggested that scouts were sent out to examine the ground before any assault took place, but his suggestions were ignored. His senior officers were not men to take notice of army captains who were in New Zealand merely to draw maps of the countryside. Why, this Captain Crossman did not even have a company to command! All he led were three rather dubious-looking soldiers, one of whom was a damned North American, if you please!

Jack's head was thumping as he made his way to the mustering point. A Maori woman had given him some powders. He had taken one in a glass of water, which had at least dulled the pain to a throbbing ache. He had no idea what the powder contained, but he was grateful for anything to relieve the agony.

The rebel chieftain, Wiremu Kingi, had built two more *pas*, not fifty miles away, but each within *one* insolent mile of the British camp at Waitara. There were, as usual, trenches and rifle pits guarding the approach to the *pas*, but what protected the flanks was swampy ground. Even as Jack and his men joined the assault troops, Jack recalled at least two battles in which swamps had played a significant role to the detriment of the most powerful army: the first was the Battle of Marathon, where the overwhelming numbers from the Persian King Darius's army were driven into flanking mire by a headlong charge of around ten thousand Athenians; the second was the Battle of Agincourt, where bogs devoured many of the French knights who charged Henry's archers and were forced to split to right and left of their target. Jack was sure there were many others, but battles between nations are as numerous as the stars, and no man knows them all.

Major Nelson set out that morning at the head of around 350 officers and men. These included Commodore Beauchamp-Seymour and 60 men of the naval brigade. The sky was an ominous dark grey colour, with streaks of cirrus like paintbrush strokes running through it. Shrubs and trees were dripping with recent rainwater as boots splodged through the tacky mud. Miserable-looking birds watched the troops pass. It was difficult to decide who looked the more disconsolate: the wildlife or the men marching by. Jack could only hope the Maori enemy, towards whom they were heading, felt just as morose as he did. Certainly there was no confidence in the air: no spring in the step, no martial songs coming from the mouths of the troops, no fife and drum music to cheer the lads on to victory. It was one of those mornings when everyone felt they should have stayed in bed.

Jack looked at his pocket watch as he trudged along. It had just passed seven o'clock. A heron passed overhead. A mile is only a mile, but when the ground is as adhesive as it was that day, it seemed to take ages. Eventually though, the Puketakauere *pa* loomed through the gloomy silver mist of the day, a lumpy man-made hill that looked deserted from a distance. The idea that the Maoris had vacated their fortress cheered the troops. Perhaps they would be able to go back to their beds after all, without an early-morning battle.

'What d'ya think, sir?' said Corporal Gwilliams. 'Have they flown the nest?'

Jack replied, 'It does look like it.'

'Back to the bacon and eggs,' muttered Wynter. 'I like it.'

Just at that moment a shot rang out and one of the soldiers at the head of the column crumpled like an empty sack.

'No such luck,' Sergeant King said. 'Here we go again.'

But Jack's men were held back. The naval brigade was at the head of the attack, both sailors and marines. They charged in, hampered by swampy ground, only to find that the enemy had not withdrawn to the *pa* as expected but were in the outlying trenches. The Maoris were armed with double-barrelled shotguns. These they discharged with devastating accuracy and effect, chopping down the attackers in swathes. Jack noted the quickness of the Maoris reloading. They were adept at this exercise, which took place at great speed. The air was full of deadly shot and those who ran in to face it were met by swarms of metal bees. Men were blasted skin from bone, while they were lodged up to their ankles in sucking mire. Shotgun fusillades were followed by *patu* charges. Maoris ran forward to hack down encumbered attackers with their honed stone axes. It was a dreadful sight for the troops at the rear and at times Jack turned away, sickened by the slaughter.

'Take those trenches,' cried the officers, who led their men from the front, one of them the gallant Beauchamp-Seymour himself. 'Into them, men! Into them!'

Eventually, some of the naval men managed to capture the first trench, but there were two more behind it. Although the artillery detachment was raining howitzer fire on these two trenches, it had little effect on the Maoris, who were well dug in and who commanded the field.

Jack saw Major Nelson looking anxiously around him and asked him what he thought.

'Eh? Well, we should have the reinforcements here shortly. Colonel Gold has promised to out-flank the Maoris. But I don't see them, do you? I don't see them. The signal has gone up, of course?'

It was an anxious question, and a lieutenant standing near the major looked startled.

'What signal, sir?'

'The rocket, man, the rocket telling Colonel Gold the attack has begun. It surely went up. I instructed the sergeant myself.'

The noise of the shotguns and rifles made conversation difficult, even from that distance.

The nervous lieutenant shouted in Nelson's ear. 'I saw no rocket, sir.'

Harassed, Nelson turned to Jack.

'Nor I,' said Jack. 'That's not to say it wasn't sent. But I didn't see it.'

Ahead of them the men in the captured trench were undergoing heavy fire. Each time they put their heads above the parapet, a hail of shot and rifle fire threatened to decapitate them. Whoops and triumphant screams were coming from the Maori trenches, and from the *pa*. They knew they had the British troops at a huge disadvantage and this time they were going to teach them a lesson in warfare.

'Where the hell are those reinforcements?' cried Nelson. He seemed about to tug his hair out. 'They should be here!'

Finally, the major realized that his attack was not going to succeed, and that reinforcements were not coming. The withdrawal began, under the umbrella of the howitzers. King, Gwilliams and Wynter were heartily glad they had not been forced to take active part in this fiasco. They were pleased to be called 'mere map-makers, of no material worth in a battle of this kind'. Jack too was not sorry he had been held back. He watched as Commodore Beauchamp-Seymour (known as 'the Swell of the Ocean' by his men) was carried wounded from the field. The commodore had a leg wound which looked rather grisly.

If the march out had been disconsolate, it was nothing compared to the forlorn return home. They plodded through the mud carrying the dead and injured. A few had been left on the field, unable to be reached by their comrades. In all 64 men out of the 350 who had set out had been either killed or wounded. Major Nelson was still gnashing his teeth and asking where the reinforcements had got to. They met no other force on their journey back to the camp. If there had been reinforcements they were safely in their barracks now. Jack reflected on the age-old tendency of modern armies to underestimate a so-called 'native' enemy. The British soldier was a superb fighting man, but he often met his match on the field when faced by an enemy to whom battle was a national sport.

Later King and the others talked over the day's disaster.

'I heard that Colonel Gold started out when he heard the shootin',' said Gwilliams, 'but when it went quiet again, he turned his men back, thinkin' it was all over.'

'He'll get hell from someone,' prophesied King. 'The army doesn't like defeats.'

'Who the hell does?' muttered Wynter. 'Anyways, they're all a bunch of no-hopers, them officers. Don't know their arse from their elbows. Some bleedin' general will come here from Australia, you see, to kick somebody's backside for this. Me brother says they got this electrolocal telegraphic wire in Aussie now, runnin' from Sydney to Melbourne. It's as quick as that –' he snapped his fingers – 'to get a message.'

'What a debacle,' said Gwilliams. 'Never seen the like.'

'A debacle?' Wynter questioned. 'I thought that was some kind of boat made of animal skin?'

Gwilliams grunted, 'You would, you bloody ignoramus.'

'I never had no schoolin',' Wynter shouted

back. 'How am I s'posed to know stuff if no-body tells me?'

'You could try readin' a book.'

'I an't got no books. Books cost money.'

'I'll borrow you one.'

'You bastard, you know I can't read.'

'Well, that settles that then, don't it? Let's go and get a drink. You comin', Sarge?'

King replied, 'No, I think I'll stay here and recalibrate some of my instruments.'

'You might want to recalibrate your head at the same time,' sniggered Wynter, taking familiarity just a little bit too far for comfort, 'eh, Yankee?' He nudged the corporal, who remained stony faced as the sergeant's head shot up.

King said sternly, 'I'll recalibrate your face for you, if you make another remark in that vein.'

'All right, all right – testy, an't we?' grumbled Wynter.

'You take it back now!' said King.

Wynter grudgingly did so, but he also added that people lost their sense of humour once they got three stripes on their sleeves. He and Gwilliams then left the hut and went to the local alehouse. There they had a peaceful two or three drinks, before Wynter took issue with something a Catholic Irish sailor might or might not have said. The sailor carried a shillelagh, with which he laid out the incensed Wynter in three seconds.

Gwilliams was impressed by the way the sailor had wielded his national club and struck up a conversation with him.

'What do you call that thing again?' he asked.

The Irishman told him. 'This here's oak,' the sailor added, 'but some prefer blackthorn.'

'Does the job though.'

Gwilliams invited the man to have a drink, which the sailor accepted without hesitation.

'You must excuse my comrade here,' said Gwilliams, nudging Wynter's inert body with his toe as it lay amongst the slops of beer. 'He's one of life's unfortunates.'

'Flash temper – foights over nothin'?'

'That's about the size.'

'Sounds loik meself,' the sailor said with a laugh.

'But I'll wager you ain't a complainer,' Gwilliams said. 'This one is – never stops complainin'. Wears a man down like a rough road wears down the sole of a shoe.'

'We have one of those. Every army or navy has one of those.'

'Not like him.'

'Oh, yes, I'm certain sure, just loik him. We have a boatswain name o' Desmond Cartwright. Always complaining, never stops for a minute. You know what we call him?'

Gwilliams was quicker than many.

'Desdemona,' he said, promptly.

'That's roight!' exclaimed the sailor. 'Des-de-moaner. You're a quick one, you are, boy. Where're y'from? Americy?'

'Sometimes. Other times from Canada. I keep 'em guessing. I was a barber. Used to shave and cut hair – that was my profession. Still do it for the captain, who's lost one of his hands and ain't so steady with the razor no more. I've shaved Kit Carson, the famous frontier scout, along with others like Jim Bowie.'

'Jim Bowie? Did you know, fellah, that we have a man here from the Mexico wars? Eh? Name of Major von Tempsky. Colourful bastard. Company commander of the Forest Rangers. Wears this red sash and carries a long knife invented by that other fellah just mentioned – Jim Bowie. Makes 'em for his men too, if they ask for one.'

'He carries a Bowie knife?' said Gwilliams. 'Ain't seen one of them in years. Wouldn't mind one meself.'

From the floor there came a groan as Wynter sat up and rubbed the huge egg on the side of his head.

'And here's Harry-De-Groaner,' said Gwilliams.

The Irishman shook his head. 'Doesn't work the same,' he said.

'Nah, you're right,' agreed Gwilliams. 'Pity though – I'd love to find something that does, just to get his goat.'

They both took swallows of their whisky as they watched with mild interest Wynter's failing efforts to get to his feet.

Six

Just when Jack thought his headaches were leaving him, they began increasing in ferocity and frequency. It meant he had to confine himself to his quarters for a few weeks. He found himself more and more dependent on the mysterious powders given him by the Maori woman and often took to his bed. His quarters were in a building that had been built by whalers to store their equipment: ropes, harpoons, spare sails and masts, and other paraphernalia. The shed, as it was, had once been a huge open barn-like structure with coffin-shaped storage boxes fixed to the floor, but was now sectioned off into small rooms to quarter many of the officers arriving from Britain and Australia.

There were now 2,600 officers and men in the region of New Plymouth, including nearly 900 militia. Another thousand men were scattered over the rest of New Zealand in towns like Wellington and Napier, the largest group being stationed in Auckland, all under the command of a General Pratt, who had just arrived from Australia to take command. Jack had never heard of General Pratt and for once knew absolutely nothing about the man in charge.

Jack was forever finding artefacts left by the whalers, many of whom had been from American ships. When he first moved into his room he discovered one of those teak coffins in the corner, which had been nailed shut. The previous occupant, a young ensign, had used the box as a bedside table, but the boy had been devoid of curiosity and had not opened it. Perhaps the shape of it deterred him and he had been afraid of finding bodily remains within. Curiosity soon had Jack prising the lid open, however, and inside he discovered a treasure trove of small objects. There were some beautiful scrimshaws carved out of whale ivory by some idle sailor whose profession belied his artistry; a knife with a handle fashioned from a sperm-whale's tooth, which still had dried blood on the blade; rope; harpoon flukes of varying shapes; letters from home countries, in Scandinavian and other languages, as well as English; and one or two books.

One of the books was an American novel about whaling by a man named Melville. The book's title was *Moby Dick* and one of its readers had marked the margins in various places with such phrases as 'Knows his stuff' or 'Got it wrong, here'. During the periods when his headache was not thoroughly in command, Jack read this novel and was amazed by the skill and imagination of the author. He had never read anything like it before in his life.

He was lying on his bed absorbed by *Moby Dick* when a newspaper reporter came to see him. Jack had only a curtain for a door and the man had knocked on the partition and then held the curtain aside. Since the noise in the whalers' shed was always at a high level, with officers coming or going, having friends in for drinks, or – on the far side but still well within earshot – some untalented fool of an elderly naval surgeon squeaking away on his fiddle, Jack had not heard the rapping the first time.

'All right to come in?' said a rather round, fat face.

Jack was annoyed at having to move his head, for he found if he kept it quite still the pain was bearable.

'What do you want?' he asked, testily.

The man entered without invitation. 'How d'ye do? Sorry to disturb. My name's Strawn, Andrew Strawn. Civilian.' A hand was extended. Jack's natural good manners made him reach out and shake it, but it caused him to wince in agony. 'Oh, so sorry,' said Strawn. 'Heard you were laid up with a head wound. Hurt, does it?'

'Like hell.'

'You should take something for it.'

'I've got these powders from a local woman,' Jack said, indicating some little parcels of folded newspaper about the size of a postage stamp. 'They seem to work a little.'

Strawn frowned. 'You want to watch these local witches – they're liable to poison you with slow-killing banes.'

'I'm sure this one is not a witch,' stated Jack, but he could not help feeling a twinge of concern. His headaches were getting worse and more frequent all the time. 'Look, I'm not in any real state to receive visitors. What is it you want?'

'Oh, yes – well, I'm from the *Te Pihoihoi Mokemoke I Runga I Te Tuana.*'

'What the deuce is that?' muttered Jack, irritably.

'Newspaper. You won't have read it. Published in the Maori language. Title means: The Lonely Sparrow On The Rooftop. Mouthful, ain't it? Not sure where the relevance lies, either, but there you go. I'm just a lowly reporter and don't have a say in these matters. There's this other Maori rag called *Te Hokioi*, which extols the virtues of Maori kingship. We were sort of brought into being to counteract articles which appear in the *Te Hokioi*. You know the sort of thing, one gives a battle one sort of slant, the other the opposite. Similar to Whig and Tory papers – different political bents.'

'I'm not sure I'm someone who can give you what you want. I'm not at all politically minded, you know. William Russell gave up on me in the Crimea. Told me I was a born soldier because I had no political bent and was prepared to fight for whoever was in government. I told him I fought not for Whigs or Tories, or even Independents, but for one person only – the Queen – whereupon...'

Strawn held up his hand to stop Jack's rambling, and said in a hushed, awed tone, 'You know William Howard Russell? Russell of the

Thunderer? Why, he's my hero. I would like to be just like him – a fearless man with the pen. *The thin red streak tipped with steel.* Had I written those words, I would have laid down my own pen and been happy. He is a god amongst mortals, Captain Crossman.'

Andrew Strawn, whose torso followed the same contours as his face, sat down on Jack's coffin box making it creak at the seams.

Jack was slightly embarrassed by the man's worship of Russell. 'Yes, well, be that as it may, I'm still not good at politics.'

'That's all right, old boy – not here for politics. Doing an article on Mr Abraham Wynter. Understand you've got a soldier who's his brother?'

'Private Harry Wynter.'

'That's the man. What's his background?' Strawn took out a leather-bound notebook from his tweed jacket pocket. 'Poor as a church mouse, I understand.'

'Most private soldiers are,' said Jack, placing *Moby Dick* by his pillow. 'For some reason army life doesn't attract wealthy gentlemen. It's probably the weevils in the bread which puts them off or the worms in the pork and cheese.' He warmed to his theme, hoping to alienate this unwelcome visitor. 'Or possibly the thousand-mile marches and the diseases which kill them off like flies—'

'Ah,' interrupted Strawn, 'sense of humour, eh, despite the debilitating injury? Good, I like that. I see you're a reading man? What's the work? *Ordnance For Boys*?'

Jack smiled, in spite of his mood. 'Touché. No, I wish it were so. It's a novel – *Moby Dick*.'

'Never heard of it. Must have had poor sales, because I read like a man possessed. Anyway, back to the Brothers Wynter. I understand you have employed Abraham Wynter to buy you some land? Good move, if you want to jump the queue. He's very good at what he does.'

Jack coloured and lied. 'Well – I wasn't aware I was queue-jumping.'

'Oh, don't worry about it. Settlers are mostly rough-heads and rogues in any case. You don't want to stand in line with that lot. Employ an agent by all means, if you can afford one. As land agents go, Abe Wynter is one of the best. He knows how to use the army to shift the Maori. Would do the same myself if I had the blunt.'

Jack's earlier misgivings rose to the fore. Did he really want a man like Wynter as his agent? It was true he wanted to surprise Jane with an established farm when she arrived, knowing how pleased she would be with him. His vision of their meeting again made him feel like a small boy, needing praise from a woman who had become almost a stranger in his head. Indeed, in the last few years it had even become difficult to picture her face, and he knew things would be very awkward between them for a while. It was those thoughts which spurred him to cut corners, though he knew the morals of doing so were dubious to say the least.

'I'm a little bewildered by Wynter's influence,' Jack said. 'I mean, I'm aware of his riches. Does he buy politicians?'

Strawn looked uncomfortable. 'That I do not know.'

'And the army? Why are they in his pocket?'

'Oh, well, that's easy. It's the old back-scratching thing. You know he's a captain in his own right?'

Jack sat up abruptly, making his head pound madly. He suddenly felt sick and likely to swoon.

'A captain? How's that?'

'Why, he purchased himself a commission in the Honourable Artillery Company. He did it by mail, he tells me. He's quite proud of the fact.'

'Is-is that usual?'

'*Highly* unusual I understand. He employed a member in London to grease the wheels. It's one of the reasons I came to see you. I was told you had a cousin in the Honourable Artillery Company. Abraham Wynter himself doesn't seem to know an awful lot about the company – says he doesn't need to know, just needs to be in it.'

'Who told you? About my cousin?'

'A Lieutenant Williams – you spoke with him about your cousin in the mess the other evening. You seemed to know a great deal about the HAC. What can you tell me? When it was formed?'

Jack's English cousin, Sebastian Whente-worth-Carter, was indeed a subaltern in the HAC, and had talked with Jack extensively regarding his good fortune on becoming a member of that unique military establishment.

'What can I tell you?' mused Jack, settling back down on his bed. 'Well, the company was given its Royal Charter by Henry the Eighth, somewhere in the mid 1500s. I forget the exact date. It began life under the name of the Guild of St George – better known as the Gentlemen of the Artillery Garden – and its members were supposed to be adept with the long-bow, cross-bow and hand-gun. The HAC has always had a strong connection with the City of London, but so far as I know has no battle honours. I understand it had the unique role of fighting on both sides in the Civil War. The company hasn't seen active service abroad yet and seems to operate more like a private club than a regiment.'

'Really?' said Strawn. 'Do go on.'

'The head of the company is known as the "Captain-General" who at the moment is Prince Albert, but it's actually run by a body called the Court of Assistants. It sits more or less monthly and conducts the company's business and civil affairs, but there are nine committees which sit under the Court.'

'It even has its own church, so I'm given to understand?'

'Ah, yes, strange title. Can't remember exactly.'

Strawn flipped back a couple of pages in his notebook.

'I have it here, from Wynter himself. It's a chapel, actually – St Botolphs-without-Bishops-gate. He did know that much, which is strange for a man who hates the clergy here for their stance in the Maori situation and professes to have entered a church only once in his life, when his mother took him to be christened. Wynter seems to like the quirky aspects of the company. There's a Vellum Book apparently, which bears all the names of the members of the regiment.'

'I don't know about that,' Jack said, 'but if you are chasing quirky, my cousin has always been particularly taken with the regimental toast, called the Regimental Fire. It takes the form of a ninefold shout of the word "Zaye!" accompanied by sideways movements of the right hand, and ending with an upward movement on the last zaye. Guests, of which I was one before I left London to go to India, are toasted with the Silent Fire – eight silent zayes, followed by a single audible last zaye which comes out with great force.'

'As you say,' murmured Strawn, scribbling in his pad, 'the sort of thing that exclusive clubs employ. Good fun, really. Nine zayes, eh? Wonderful stuff. Where do they get 'em from?'

'Well, I asked the same question of course, and I was told it's supposed to stem from the movements and timing required to light the fuse of a grenade, but who knows?'

Strawn, with extravagant gestures, dotted a couple of i's and crossed one or two t's, then said, 'That should be enough. Thank you, Captain. And I'm sorry you're ill.' He stared intently at Jack. 'You do look very pale, you know. I would check on those powders, if I were you. Don't trust these natives. Some are all right, but others ... well. I would get the stuff analysed if you can. Do you know any chemists?'

Jack snorted, impatiently. 'Yes, Mr Strawn, they're two a penny out in the bush.'

'Sorry, yes. Silly thing to say.' He stood up and made ready to go, but then said, 'Oh, one last thing. What about this sergeant of yours – what's his name?'

'King? Sergeant King?'

'Yes, the farrier chappie. How long has he been lost? I was going to do a short piece on him too, when I knew I was coming to see you.'

Once again, Jack sat up. 'Lost?'

'Why, yes, went off into the bush to do some mapping and never came back. He's been in there two weeks now. Shouldn't think he's alive, would you?'

Jack was stunned. Why had no one told him about this? Where was Corporal Gwilliams? This was monstrous!

'Ah,' said Strawn, 'you look shocked – didn't know about it, eh? Sorry to be the bearer. I'll leave you now.'

The newspaperman left without another backward glance, having got what he came for.

Jack rose from his bed and dressed, before going on a search for his men. He found Gwilliams in the sickbay, laid low by some fever or other contracted (they thought) through drinking water from a stream where sheep had been wading. Gwilliams was aware enough to tell Jack what had happened. When Jack finally tracked down the last member of the group, Private Wynter, he found him still half-drunk from the night before, sleeping in a ditch. On being roused and doused with cold water, Wynter admitted he knew that Sergeant King was lost.

'I din't come an' tell you, 'cause I knew you was sick and din't want to make you worse,' said the private, indignantly.

Jack was blazingly angry.

'That's not the reason – me being sick – is it, Wynter? The fact is you hate Sergeant King and you couldn't give a damn whether he's found or not? Tell me the truth, that's it, isn't it?'

Wynter shrugged, knowing it was useless to deny it.

'Gwilliams, your NCO, gave you an order, to report the matter to me – you disobeyed that order, Wynter.'

Wynter looked up, sharply, the wake-up water still dripping from his mean-looking face. Disobeying an order was a serious crime. The punishment could be just as serious. Wynter did not want a flogging. He had had several such punishments in his army career, but he was not as strong as he had once been. The venom he had once had in him had provided enough backbone to metaphorically spit in the eye of the man who wielded the lash. Lately though, such vitriolic energy had been drained from him. He was haggard, half-blind, grey-haired and old before his time. Even though only in his thirties he looked fifty.

'I was tryin' to save the captain bother. Me bein' the only rank what wasn't sick, the decision was up to me, I thought. So I give an order to Ta Moko to go look for the sergeant. He come back this mornin', sayin' he couldn't find the bleeding ... couldn't find the sergeant. You was sick, sir. I made me decision an' I stick by it.'

Jack realized Wynter had a point. Although he was at the end of the command chain, the private had been the only man who was not ill and therefore however bizarre the situation he was nominally in charge of matters to do with the group. Jack was relieved to know that he had sent out the Maori to look for King, but concerned to learn that Ta Moko was back without finding the sergeant.

'You get cleaned up, Wynter. Be ready to leave for the bush. I'm going to speak to Ta Moko.'

Another hunt and he was rewarded with the Maori, who was just sitting down to a meal of pork and beans in an eatery.

'Sir, I did not find the sergeant. I think he must have strayed into Waikato country. If I go in there I will be killed. The Waikato tribes are very fierce and they do not like my tribe. I will go in if we take soldiers with us, but you will need to find another guide if you go in alone.'

'Thank you, Ta Moko. I like a plain-speaking man.'

Jack went in search of a senior officer. He found a major, who told him there were no troops to spare. Everyone was on alert, either guarding the town, out on patrol or fighting.

'The sergeant's probably dead by now, Captain. You need more than just a patrol if you're going up to the Waikato – you need a whole company. And I ain't got 'em, Captain. I've been depleted of men for some time now. If you're going to do it, you'll have to hire some civilians from the town. But if I were you, I wouldn't. Most of them have no idea of the bush. They're townies, or at best farmers. Take the roof away from their heads and they get frightened by the stars.'

'Thank you, sir,' Jack said. 'I like a plain-speaking officer.'

It was only when he was on his way back to his quarters that Jack realized his headache was gone. His brain was as clear as crystal. Whether it was because he needed to be worrying about something or his brain needed to be busy, he did not know. He was just relieved that the pain was gone, even if only temporarily. He felt guilty for doubting the Maori woman, whose powders had finally worked.

He bathed, dressed in bush clothes, armed himself, then went in search of Wynter again. Jack found the soldier ready to go. Wynter had already been to stables to saddle and bridle two horses. He had been given a little trouble by the NCO in charge of the stables, but Wynter had told him his captain had ordered it. The pair then went to the stores and begged provisions for a journey into the bush. Finally, they went down to the alehouse which was frequented by friend-ly Maoris and Jack asked if any of them knew of a man called Potaka.

At first he was greeted by sullen looks, but after buying a round of drinks, one of the Maori said, 'You may find him at the old L-shaped *pa* – but do not go there, Captain, or you will be killed.'

Jack thanked the man, gave him a coin, then he and Wynter set out for the L-shaped *pa*, which had been the scene of an earlier battle in this war. Wynter did not complain, which was a miracle in itself. Jack supposed the soldier was anxious to redeem himself, but it was quite unlike Wynter to admit, even by inference, that he was in the wrong. In past times he would rather be burned alive at the stake than give any credit to rules and regulations. Here he was, however, silent and stoic, ready to ride into the halls of death for the sake of his captain.

When Jack and Wynter were three hundred yards from the *pa*, Jack dismounted and called, 'I wish to speak to a man named Potaka. Is he here?'

Wynter shifted uneasily in his saddle, turning this way and that, wondering from which direction death would come to him. In what form would it be? A rifle shot? A spear? A flung stone axe?

'Potaka,' shouted Jack again, as the wind soughed through the fern trees. 'A man named Potaka.'

The *pa* looked deserted. Jack could discern no movement within. The silence made the wait seem long. A hawk passed by overhead, letting out a wild cry. Wynter ducked an invisible missile.

Suddenly a voice rang out, which made Wynter start in his saddle.

'Go away!'

Jack had no intention of going away.

'I must speak with Potaka,' he insisted at the top of his voice. 'I have business with Potaka.'

There was another period of silence, then a young Maori woman stepped out from behind a palisade. She was beautiful. Long black hair tumbled over her broad, covered shoulders. As she walked towards Jack and Wynter, Jack could see her wide, brown eyes gleaming in the light which lanced through the trees. She was barefoot, wore a blanket wrapped tightly around her body, and the two men could discern a trim figure beneath its folds. There were some small square-keyed tattoos on her chin and at the back of her head were two tall eagle's feathers – dark with white tips.

The woman stopped not far from the two men and stared at them.

'Go away,' she repeated, 'or you will be killed.'

Quietly Jack said, 'I am looking for my friend, Potaka.'

'Does he know he is your friend?' asked the woman, tilting her chin.

'I think so. He kept me alive, at least.'

She smiled, wryly. 'That does not mean he will not kill you if he sees you again, Captain Crossman.'

'Ah – you know me. Potaka has told you about me. You have me at a disadvantage. May I know your name?'

'Amiri.'

'Thank you. Has it any meaning?'

'It means the East Wind, but knowing my name will not save you from being chopped in two by your enemies. The ugly skinny one there –' she nodded towards Wynter – 'they will use him for firewood.'

''Ere!' cried Wynter.

Jack said, 'Please, Amiri, will you take me to Potaka? I need his help. I have lost one of my men and if I don't find him, he'll die.'

She shrugged. 'What is that to us? You have killed many of our men.'

'Some of our men have died too in this smouldering unhappy war – but this is an unnecessary death. I can honestly say that if Potaka came to me, and asked for my help for a similar problem, I would certainly give it to him without a second thought.'

She stared at Jack again, with those fathomless brown eyes.

'All right,' she said, at last, 'follow me. But do not blame me if he shoots you. It will not be my fault.'

She led the way through the bush. Jack made Wynter dismount and they too went on foot, since Jack would have felt uncomfortable riding while a woman walked. The trail went through a bouldery valley and eventually led to a cave on a hillside. A lookout had seen them coming and

113

six armed men were waiting at the cave's entrance. One of them, Jack noticed, was Potaka himself. The woman Amiri strode ahead and called to the Maoris, 'I told him you would kill him on sight. Are you going to make me out to be a liar?'

One of the Maoris – not Potaka – raised his shotgun. But the moment he did this, Amiri stepped in front of Jack, shielding him with her body. Jack thought: why are women always so complex? First she virtually orders my death, then steps in and saves me from it.

'What?' said Amiri to the man with the shotgun. 'Would you shoot a man under a flag of truce?'

'What flag?' asked the shotgun man, lowering his weapon. 'I see no flag.'

'I am his flag,' Amiri said. 'Do you not understand? Potaka, am I not the white man's flag of truce?'

Potaka grinned and shook his head sagely.

'You are all things to all men, Amiri,' he said. 'Step aside. The officer will not be harmed. Jack, what brings you here? This is no place for a British captain. You are lucky to have reached this far. Come and sit by the fire. Your soldier too. Is he hungry? He looks half-starved. Do you not feed your men, you high-born officers? We all eat the same fare, whether high or low rank. Come, join us. Tell me why you have come here. I am listening. I am listening with my best ears.'

114

Seven

Once they were around the fire and were tucking into the roasted limbs of unknown birds, Jack was able to tell Potaka why he had come.

'I have a man missing. He may be dead by now, who knows, but I feel it my duty to find him. No one in New Plymouth, British or Maori, will take me up into Waikato country. You are my last hope. I am prepared to offer you a large sum of money to guide me through the bush.' Jack had been in such situations before and he knew the dangers when dealing with other cultures. 'I will not do so if you feel it would be insulting you. I merely mention it to show how serious I am about finding my sergeant. This sergeant is no great threat to the Maori nation. All he wants to do is make maps of Aotearoa's landscape. He is useless as a warrior and I'm sure he has been unable to shoot any game to eat, since he is the poorest shot with a weapon I have ever had the misfortune to lead into battle. I am prepared to leave this man –' Jack indicated Wynter, who was gnawing on the greasy thigh of his roasted aviator, shining hot fat running down his chin – 'as a hostage with your men, until your safe return to them.'

'Eh?' exclaimed Wynter, his head coming up fast. 'What? You an't goin' to leave me? What if you both get killed and don't come back?'

'Then you'll likely be executed,' Jack stated, and as he spoke he used his left stump to indicate a point, bringing his missing hand to the attention of the Maoris, who he knew would consider such a wound a battle honour, 'which will be a shame for you.'

'You'd be court-martialled for it, you would!'

'Since I'd be dead, I hardly think that's going to trouble me. In any case, I'd just tell the court you volunteered.'

'That's lyin', that is,' cried the incensed Wynter. 'If there's one thing I can't stand, it's a liar.'

'It seems to me,' Potaka interrupted, pointing at Wynter, 'that this creature is quite worthless, and therefore not a suitable hostage.'

'Eh?' said Wynter again, predictably.

'British officers have to value all our soldiers' lives equally,' replied Jack, 'however useless and pathetic the individuals might be. This man here is as valuable as a general, in human terms. Were I to murder him, which I frequently have a strong desire to do, I should receive the same punishment as if I had murdered the governor of New Zealand. Our law is equal in that respect. It's a shame because the world would be a better place without him, but I am bound by the codes set by my forefathers, as you are, and have to treat his life as more worthy than that of a garden slug, though we both know it is not.'

All the Maoris around the fire roared with laughter.

Wynter jumped up. 'I'm not standin' for this,' he shouted. 'I'm a man! You can't talk about me like I'm nuthin'. I'm a man an' entitled to respect...'

One of the Maoris was now staring intently at Wynter and now he too jumped up and faced the soldier.

'You have the same look as Scarface, the land stealer!'

Wynter was thrown off-balance by this sudden outburst.

'What? Who's Scarface?'

Potaka said, 'Yes, he does. He has the features of that pig Abraham Wynter.'

Wynter drew in a sharp breath. 'Don't you call my brother a pig, you bloody savage!'

'Careful, Wynter,' Jack said, soothingly, as the other Maoris began to get to their feet, gripping their stone *patus*, 'we don't want to upset our hosts, do we?'

Wynter looked at his officer and suddenly he became aware of the danger of the situation. He sat down and picked up his bird-bone. Jack could see the private was still too angry to talk without landing himself in more trouble, so he spoke for him.

'Abraham Wynter is indeed the older brother of this soldier, but as you see, this man is still in the army. If they had been close brothers, with the love for each other which brothers should have, this one would not be in the army but at

117

Abraham Wynter's side, would he not? Abraham Wynter has gold enough to purchase the discharge of a thousand soldiers, yet he lets his own flesh and blood rot at the bottom of the army's lowest rank. You cannot blame this one for the work of the other. He is not his brother's keeper, but a jealous and vengeful man who would work the downfall of that brother, if he could.'

Potaka nodded. 'What you say makes sense.'

'Well,' asked Jack, 'will you help me?'

'Leave the campfire flames to the Maori,' said Potaka. 'We will discuss it amongst ourselves.'

Jack and Wynter withdrew to the shade of a large tree. As soon as they were out of earshot of the warriors, Wynter complained bitterly about Jack's insults. Jack told him that humour had to be used to reach these Maori or they would be lost.

'We had to get on friendly terms with these men, or you and I might not see our comrades again.'

'You din't mean none o' that stuff, then? About me bein' lesser than a garden slug.'

'Of course not, man. Of course not.' Jack paused and then could not resist adding, 'You're at least as far up the Chain of Being as a snail.'

Wynter was actually sharper than he looked.

'You're joking again, an't you? Well, I'll think up somethin' for you, don't you worry.'

'Ah, there's the rub,' said Jack, sighing, 'you can't.'

Thinking the officer was impugning his

intelligence, he asked, 'Why?'

'Because I'm an aristocratic captain and you're what Wellington called the scum of the earth. If you were to make jokes about me, I would have to have you flogged.'

Wynter bristled. 'That an't fair.'

'Nor it is, but who said the army was fair? Oh, hello.'

Jack got to his feet as he realized Amiri was standing over them, looking down at him.

She squatted and Wynter's eyes nearly left his head like bullets from a gun muzzle as her skirt wafted up revealing much more thigh than any Englishwoman would consider proper. The soldier then had the good grace to look away, aware that his stare had been noticed. Amiri glared at him, and folded the skirt between her legs to recapture her modesty.

'Captain Crossman,' said Amiri, putting an arm around the stiff officer's shoulders, 'do you like me?'

It was Jack's turn to be taken aback. He was suddenly aware of a new danger. In India two Eurasian girls, the grown daughters of a corporal and his Hindu wife, had followed him around like doting schoolgirls, claiming to be in love with him. Jack had been flattered at first, as many men would be since the sisters had been quite beautiful. But they quickly became a nuisance. He was a handsome man and he knew it, though no one could call him vain. He was bound to attract women without meaning to, not the least because of his aloofness towards them.

Jack was the kind of man that women saw as a challenge, a remote region to conquer, a heart they had to reach and capture with their character and beauty. It was no good Jack telling them he was married, that only made him more irresistible to them.

'I'm married,' he blurted out.

'So am I,' she said, squeezing his shoulder lightly, 'but we are probably both unhappy.'

'Shall I go off somewhere and wait,' said an embarrassed-looking Wynter, 'so's you can make out?'

'That had better be your attempt at a return joke, Wynter,' snapped Jack. Then more softly, 'Amiri – I am not in an unhappy marriage. I love my wife and she, I believe, is quite fond of me...'

Amiri did not release him. She merely smiled disarmingly into his face with those huge brown eyes. He left the arm there, not shrugging it off because it felt so good, so very, very good. His blood was hot and racing through his arteries, making his heart beat faster than the battle-call tattoo on a drum. And she was a handsome woman. More than handsome: beautiful. She smelled of nut oil and frangipani flowers. One full warm breast pressed gently against his ribs. He had long ached for such company and her bare brown arm, with its flawless skin, looked good enough to eat. He would have made love to her there and then in the dust, thrown all thoughts of Jane out of his head, if there had been no others to witness his fall from grace.

When Potaka came over to him Jack tried to shrug her off, but Potaka took no notice of this compromising scene.

'I will come with you,' said the warrior. 'This one will stay here with my men. If we do not return, they will kill him.'

'That's fair enough,' said Jack. 'I thank you.'

'No, it an't,' growled Wynter. 'It an't fair at all, an' if you don't come back I may hope you roast in hell, sir!'

Jack and Potaka left the Maori camp on foot, leaving the horses there. Potaka said it was easier to track and navigate the bush without the use of mounts.

'The first thing to do,' said Potaka, 'is to question people we meet. You must stay behind me at all times, when we approach other Maoris. Even I am not safe from some. If a fight starts, then you must come to my aid, but otherwise keep silent and still.'

'You are the expert here,' Jack replied. 'I bow to your knowledge of the bush.'

Potaka took Jack off on a half-running, half-walking trek which tested the officer's fitness severely. They went through bush country, forest and open landscape, Jack struggling to keep up with the Maori. Fortunately, his head stayed clear and he began to hope that at last he had rid himself of the pain. Perhaps he had jolted something in there? A clot of blood? A piece of bone? Heads were such complex devices, being the boxes which carried the thinking machine. No wonder the Maori used their stone hand axes, their *patus*, with such frequency.

The rain stayed off, though several days into the trek black clouds gathered in towers over the Hauhungaroa Range, near Lake Taupo. Potaka said that it *always* rained in the Hauhungaroa, so that was nothing unusual. They had one night of fierce winds, which kept them awake with its noise and power. This was followed by a day of complete calm, during which not a ripple appeared on the still waters of the island, though of course there were torrential streams to cross. They did this by linking arms, for which Jack was grateful, since Potaka was more sure-footed than himself, especially since the stream beds seemed to consist of boulders and huge stones. There was always the danger of a twisted or broken ankle, with rocks you could not see.

Jack had hoped that Potaka could pick up a trail, but the Maori told him this was impossible. King had been missing for quite some time now and the rains had come and gone with regularity. Any trails would have been washed away. In any case they did not know where to start or which direction the sergeant had taken. To follow a trail through the bush you need definite early signs, which you know belong to the lost man and not to some other roving individual.

Indeed, they had to rely on sightings by other Maori, who may or may not have been hostile. In King's favour was the fact that the Maori were in general naturally curious men. They would wonder what a lone soldier was doing, wandering around the bush, scribbling on a pad.

They might just leave him alone, not approaching him in any way, to see what developed. Certainly a single man was no threat to a tribe or nation. If you kept a watch on him, he could do little harm. On the other hand if you killed him straight away, you might never find out what he was doing there. The Maori had seen surveyors before, of course, especially on land that had been sold to the whites. This one looked like a surveyor, but what was he doing on Maori land? So Jack hoped they might have left him alone, intending to rob King of his notebook once he looked like leaving the region he was charting.

The first two or three groups of Maori Potaka questioned claimed they had not seen anything of a lone sergeant. One group said they had encountered a patrol, further south, and had exchanged fire, but surely only an insane soldier would wander right into enemy territory on his own? This same group, a hostile bunch of warriors if ever Jack had seen one, was not the friendliest they encountered. They wanted to know what Jack was doing there, why Potaka was guiding him across their land, and they needed a good reason not to kill both intruders.

Potaka proceeded to give them several 'good reasons' none of which seemed acceptable. He then offered to do battle with the biggest of the party for the right to cross their territory. The largest warrior amongst them, a huge but amiable-looking fellow, declined to fight. His argument in essence was that he refused to get his head caved in over something as trivial as unsanctioned trespass. He was willing to do his bit when it came to full battle, but he was not interested in single combat. One of his companions called him a coward, which contrarily resulted in a healthy scrap between the accuser and the accused, making the big man's refusal to fight Jack somewhat nonsensical. The big man eventually flattened the smaller man with a hammer fist on the top of the head. Finally the party left, carrying the unconscious loser and wishing Jack and Potaka luck in finding the missing sergeant.

A weak winter sun shone on the day after this encounter. Potaka decided they would take a hill trail, which involved crossing chasms on fallen trees and fording wider and faster rivers than Jack had so far encountered. There were one or two rope bridges too, which had his heart fluttering in his chest. Potaka drove them at a mighty pace and once, while they were negotiating a six-inch-wide path on a slope of scree, Jack almost plunged to his death. Only a healthy right hand full of uncut fingernails saved him. He buried the hand into the scree thus arresting his slide down a steep slope to a ledge that went out into nothing but cool clear air. In those few seconds Potaka managed to get fingers on Jack's collar, eventually hauling him to safety. Potaka berated Jack for his carelessness.

They spent the night in an abandoned hut, only to find themselves in the company of three Maori when they woke.

More questions followed, this time with a

satisfactory outcome. Yes, the three men had seen a solitary soldier.

'He is off his head,' said a lean Maori with a pot belly and a tattooed skin that was a work of art worthy of wall-space in any London gallery. 'No one bothers him because he is a witch man, who weaves evil magic in the night. He talks to the moon, even when it is not there.'

King had probably been gabbling at them about his work and would have been regarded as 'speaking in tongues' or something like. Madmen, Jack decided, got away with their lives while sane men would have been cut down where they stood. He found that in India, during the mutiny. Officers and soldiers had been discovered wandering, often naked and filthy, talking away to themselves. Even though many of the locals they encountered had been rebels, the madmen continued untouched. In many societies it was considered bad luck to harm a simpleton, a man whose reason had left him. Such a person drew sympathy and pity, rather than hate and hostility.

Jack asked, 'Where did you see him last?'

He was amazed and delighted to learn that his sergeant was still alive. He honestly had not expected to find King with breath in his body. How had the man managed to feed himself, out in the wilderness? As a hunter he was absolutely useless. Indeed, Jack would not believe that King was still alive until he personally spoke to the man.

'What have you got to offer?' came the rejoinder.

Jack had indeed brought some money with him, some of which he distributed amongst the three Maori. They then led him and Potaka along a valley full of hot springs to a rock overhang. There they found a ragged Sergeant King fast asleep by the remains of a fire, his chin sprouting an unwholesome-looking stiff ginger beard. Jack picked up a pinch of the ashes, turning the dust over in his fingers. It was still warm. Jack was quite impressed by the campsite. There was no unpleasant smell of faeces, a shallow bowl in a rock had been filled with water from a nearby stream, and a fire had been lit, and obviously tended with great care. There were bird bones in a neat pile nearby. If King was off his head, he had retained all the habits of good army training. Indeed, here he was cuddling his rifle, ready to shoot any hostile beast or man who woke him.

Potaka's iron grip closed on the weapon and held it there.

King woke with a start and after a moment tried to wrest the rifle from the Maori, failing. He sat up. His face had a lean, haunted, ravaged look and his clothes hung off his normally square frame. Bloodshot eyes regarded the people around him. Finally they rested on Jack, who was standing half-hidden behind the three Waikato Maori.

'Oh, hello, sir,' he croaked. 'You found me then?'

126

Jack said, 'Yes, I've found you. You look half-starved, Sergeant.'

King attempted a grin. 'Half? More like nine-tenths.'

'You should be dead, if not from Maori spears, from hunger.'

'Ah, you're speaking about my ability with a firearm,' King replied. 'Well, sir, that was a drawback, I admit. But there's more than one way to kill a ptarmigan. You see, I'm pretty good at setting animal traps. I'll wager you didn't think of that, eh? Used to do it when a boy, out in the countryside. Used nets of willow twigs then, but of course, no willow here, so had to use another springy sort of tree wood. Only caught small birds, unfortunately, but they were better than nothing at all.'

'King, you amaze me.'

'I'm glad to do so, sir.'

'But you're supposed to be mad, you know.'

King looked genuinely surprised at this. 'Am I? Who says so?'

'These three men. It's why they allowed you to live. It seems it's unlucky to kill madmen.'

King stared at the three Waikato Maori.

'These might be they who I tried to recruit, to hold my survey poles. I cut some poles and marked them up for measuring. I was going to use the secant method, you know, sir?' Clearly his visitors were not going to get away without an explanation, and after a quick sip of water from his rock bowl, King continued. 'You can calculate distances north or south from a straight surveyed line. Then one corrects the straight line, using set mathematical formulas, to a legitimate curve. The position of latitude can be checked by astronomical observations. Of course, one can always approximate how the curved line should run, but one likes to be as accurate as one can be in the circumstances.'

'See!' cried the pot-bellied Maori, dramatically pointing with his *patu* at the sergeant. 'This is how he spoke with us. These incantations such as the church priests use, but –' he waved a finger in Jack's face – 'these are not Christian words! And there were magic spells and potions. This man is an unholy witch. He does things in the night, making offerings to the stars with his bowls of strange liquid. We have seen his magical instruments. Yes, yes, it is true. I have seen it. I have watched him boil his potions on the fire, then stir those potions with a glass wand which he then holds up to the light to test the strength of his devious sorcery...'

King said, 'Strange liquid? Oh, yes...' He croaked a laugh. 'My bowl of mercury, which serves as an artificial horizon – I use the reflecting surface to measure the altitude of the stars I need to observe. Yes, and the boiling of liquid? Simply water which I test with my thermometer to check elevation. The lower the water's boiling point, the higher the altitude. This is not magic, gentlemen, it is *science*.'

'Arrrggh! *Science!*' cried another of the Maoris, stepping back. 'The very word does not sound Christian.'

'I shall take this man back to the army,' Jack told the Waikato Maori gravely, 'where he will be put on trial for witchcraft.'

Potaka snorted. 'This man is no witch. This man is a *surveyor*. These things you speak of, they are the tools which help him survey the land.' He looked at Jack. 'They know what he is. They're not fools, Captain. Better to have it all out in the open, now.'

There was an uneasy silence amongst the Waikato Maori on hearing these words. There was a tightening of grips on weapons. Despite his explanation, Jack felt he had been betrayed by Potaka, the one Maori present he had trusted. Surveyors were regarded as only slightly less evil than the devil himself, assisting, as they did, the hated European land-grabbers. Jack's good hand edged towards the revolver, stuck in his belt. The silence was broken by an indignant Sergeant King, who climbed unsteadily to his feet and glared at Potaka.

'Surveyor?' he said, contemptuously. *'Surveyor?* I, sir, am a map-maker.' King stooped and reached down for his long pad, almost toppling over in the effort. He lifted it up with effort, for the pad was quite a heavy object for a man in his condition. He untied the ribbons that held it closed and opened the leather cover with reverence, then held up the latest map he had drawn for all to see. 'This is an accurate map of this valley, not a common *survey* chart. The two may not be spoken of in the same breath, if you please.'

Clearly this show of great indignation impressed Potaka, who immediately apologized to King for his error. The other Maoris, too, were affected by King's rhetoric. They crowded round the coloured map of the valley and pointed out various aspects, such as the contours of the surrounding hills, and the grid lines, and the course of the stream down below the rock hang. One by one they nodded and said, having seen other charts, that this was indeed a proper map. This picture was for finding a path through the wilderness of bush country, not for establishing the best place for farmhouses and farmlands. They asked King how long it took to be trained to make such maps, and whether he thought they were capable of learning such *science*.

King told them that of course they had the ability to do such work. He himself had been but a lowly son of a blacksmith in his own country, and his own intellect was not of an astonishing level. All it took was training and practice, he informed them. Any one of those present, probably even the British officer, was capable of learning the skills necessary to make maps, given the time and patience necessary.

Jack gave his sergeant a wry smile and said they needed to be on their way. King was given a little mashed breadfruit – not too much, for his stomach had shrunk – and once he felt ready they were escorted by the Maori to the edge of their territory. There they all shook hands and said it would be good if they met in battle sometime. It would do well to prove that letting an enemy return to his people was not a sign of weakness and that it was not for lack of courage that this act had been performed.

Potaka took Jack and his sergeant back to where his men were still holding Private Wynter captive.

'Thank God you've come, sir,' said Wynter, as they entered the camp. The private seemed to have made himself completely at home. 'This lot 'ave bin lickin' their lips and looking at me like I was dinner.' Wynter grinned: a grotesque-looking expression these days, with his scarred face and blind milky eye. 'I feared for my liver.'

Jack thanked Potaka and said he would now take the sergeant back to New Plymouth, to get him hospitalized.

'Why did you betray us, back there? Personally, I thought the Waikatos were convinced that Sergeant King was a witch?'

'Because it was not the truth,' explained Potaka, bluntly. 'I do not like to walk around with a lie on my back.'

'We might have got ourselves into a fight – unnecessarily.'

'So be it,' said the Maori man with a shrug. 'But we would have died with the truth on our lips.'

Deviousness was obviously an abhorrent trait to this man and Jack felt he understood a little. But he himself would rather not have tested the Waikato Maori. He and King were in the business of being devious. They were by trade, skulkers and dealers in mendacity. It was only

King's professional pride that had saved them from attack. If King had not puffed himself up with indignation at the idea that he was a common surveyor they might all be lying dead in that valley. It was a sobering thought. One different word, or inference, or emphasis, might have sealed their deaths.

Eight

Jack had just about enough time to hospitalize Sergeant King, when he learned that there was to be yet another attack on another *pa*. The commanders never seemed to learn. There were seemingly endless assaults on these Maori forts, which came to nothing. Men were being killed on both sides, but the war appeared to be bogged down by real mud and by politics. Both were as messy and sticky as each other. Jack disliked the thought of soldiers' lives going to waste, simply so that commanders could be seen to be doing something. If it was not constructive, not a positive move to bring about an end, then why perpetrate it? *Pas* were extremely difficult to penetrate, they were expendable to Maori, and these interminable attacks could go on for ever without any advancement of any sort on either side.

Jack's mind was also on the woman he had met. He found it difficult to dismiss Amiri from his mind. She was athletically lovely in the strong-looking way of many of the Maori women. It was a new experience for him, to be struck by the beauty of a woman other than his wife Jane. He found himself waking in the middle of the night, not with an image of an English rose, but a Maori flame-tree blossom.

It was not a picture he tried to dismiss from his thoughts.

He was in the officers' mess, enquiring about mail from England, when he saw a man enter the room with a great flourish. The officer wore knee-length highly polished boots, black breeches, a black silk shirt open at the neck, and a forage cap perched on long black locks. On his face was a magnificent bushy moustache. A sabre hung low at his left side. There were thin leather straps crossing over his chest that accentuated its proportions. He was indeed a broad-shouldered fine figure of a man, who moved with all the arrogance, panache and élan of a French cavalry officer. He did not simply speak – he announced. Every sentence was delivered with dramatic effect.

'Major Von Tempsky,' boomed the man, hand on sword hilt, bowing smartly to the officers at the bar. 'At your service, gentlemen. Who among you brave fellows will buy a soldier a drink? I have just come from an encounter with the so-called Maori kingmaker, Wiremu Tamihana. Unfortunately, this eel slipped through my fingers this time, but our future encounter – for there will be one, gentlemen, have no doubt on that score – will be different. He is mine, and mine alone.'

With that the gallant major swept towards the bar, where a number of officers were already reaching for their pockets. There was no doubt

Von Tempsky was popular amongst them, but he was a little too colourful for Jack's grey-grim Scottish Presbyterian upbringing. Jack always distrusted flamboyance, which he knew was stiff and awkward of him, but could do nothing to change. He watched in amusement, as the drinks flowed and the toasts were made, to the Queen, to the American President, to the Forest Rangers, to every regiment represented in the room – but he could not take part.

'Come on!' cried a drunken lieutenant of foot, waving his whisky glass. 'Let's take our ambergris on to the lawns outside, where a friend of mine is about to give a demonstration of an extraordinary weapon. Who amongst you here has heard of Mr Perkins' amazing steam gun? The Duke of Wellington himself was enamoured of this gun, and so he should have been, for it fires one thousand shots per minute! Think of it, chaps, the enemy will go down in droves, a thousand men at a time.'

Everyone began to troop outside, and Jack followed, as curious as the rest, but he noticed Von Tempsky had a frown on his forehead.

On the lawn near the flagpole stood Abraham Wynter, with two soldiers at his side, and a strange-looking device – a six-foot barrel with all sorts of paraphernalia projecting from one end – attached to what appeared to be a steam generator. This machine looked extremely ungainly and, since it was supposed to be a weapon, very impractical for lugging along mud-strewn ways to battlefields. Steam engines required fire and water to produce their steam. The steam pressure had to be raised to a level where it could exert great force. However, Jack was willing to concede that it could possibly be carried on the back of a cart and probably used from that position. However, though he loved inventions, he was sceptical about fancy ones. He had always distrusted rockets, for example, believing them to have more flash-and-bang about them than destructive power. They were like this Von Tempsky character, lost in their own charismatic performances.

Abe Wynter tipped his hat to the gathering officers, and began his rhetoric.

'This 'ere gun is bein' donated by me, on behalf of the Honourable Artillery Company, to any officer 'oo cares to borrow it for the purposes of chopping down Maoris by the dozen.' His thumbs went behind his coat collars, as he warmed to his theme. 'This marvellous weapon was invented by Jacob Perkins, in 1824, but thus far an't received any battle honours –' there was laughter amongst some of the officers present – 'which is a cryin' shame, 'cause it should do.' Abe picked up a stick from the ground and began to use it as a pointer. 'Just 'ere, at the back, is the hoppers which hold the balls, an' feeds 'em down to the chamber of the gun. These hoppers can hold up to a thousand balls, but for purposes of demonstration, we're keeping that to sixty.'

Jack now remembered reading about the steam gun in *The London Mechanics' Register*, but could not remember the details.

''Ere is what they call the throttle-valve, which means the steam is delivered from the gubbins at the back,' continued Abe, puffed up with self-importance, 'an' this 'ere is the swivel joint, which allows the gun its elevation and lets it be moved in any which way, so's the enemy can be walloped from whatever direction you choose. All right then, let's see our boys 'ave a whack at those planks up there!'

The two soldiers, who looked a little nervous, went down on the machine and made ready to fire. Just fifty yards away were some reasonably thick pine planks. Jack watched as the gun was fired with a rat-tat-tat-tat sound, the musket balls shooting from the barrel in an amazingly swift time. The targets exploded in a blizzard of timber chips, splinters spraying everywhere. Jack had to admit it was an impressive performance, and he felt he had cause to wonder at the ingeniousness of men like Perkins, who could produce such devices. However, he still remained unconvinced of the worth of the gun when it came to battle. Demonstrations were one thing, war was another.

There was chatter, and speculation, following the demonstration. Officers wandered up to the planks to inspect the damage and nodded their heads, approvingly. Von Tempsky, however, did not move or speak for a while. He simply stood with his glass of whisky staring down at Perkins' steam gun with a blank expression on his face. Finally he gave voice, waving his drink and spilling it over the lawn.

'Sir,' he yelled at Abe Wynter, 'this is a foul, monstrous machine which should never soil the hands of a real soldier. Why, it is worse than canister, which I detest above all things. Where is the need for a brave heart? Where is the need for selfless action, brother giving up his life that his brother shall live? Since these are the only real virtues of war, there being no others of any worth, war becomes itself a thing to be despised. I, sir, am a warrior, born and bred. I was made for fighting and fighting is what I do well. But this – this ugly disgusting device –' he nudged the steam gun with his foot – 'takes away all that is glorious in war. To kill a thousand men in one minute? Why, a battle would be fought in the time it takes to break for coffee! If one side has it, then the other side will get it too, for that is the way of war. Send five thousand men to fight an equal number, and in five minutes both sides will have annihilated each other. Where's the glory in that? Where's the excitement, the courage, the selflessness, the *fun*? I tell you, sir, this is a metal monster and I would throw it out. I would, sir! I would toss it away with the garbage. Good day to you.'

With that, Von Tempsky smashed his whisky glass on the steam gun's chamber, and strode off towards his horse, tethered on a rail outside the mess. Abe Wynter stuck two fingers up at the major's back in the contemptuous style of the English longbowmen at the Battle of Agincourt, when showing the French that they still retained

138

the arrow-fingers the French had promised to cut off after winning the fight. Wynter's face bore a sour expression, which turned sunny when the other officers returned from inspecting the planks. Wonderful, they told him. Excellent work. They would certainly be using the gun the next time they went out to meet the Maori.

Abe Wynter was still staring at Von Tempsky's back when Jack tapped him on the shoulder.

'What?' he snarled, spinning round, then seeing it was Jack his expression changed. 'Ah – you'll be wantin' to know about this land I promised to get you? Well, Cap'n, it's on its way, that's all I can tell you at the present. On its way. It's gettin' harder to get hold of, but I've got a piece in mind and things are movin', that's all I can say. Now –' he gestured after Von Tempsky – 'there's a man what don't appreciate a good invention, eh? But you do, eh, Cap'n?' He touched the side of his nose. 'I heard it from my own brother's mouth. Well, then –' he took Jack's arm and led him gently towards a wooden hut near a large house – 'come and look at this. It came on the same ship as the steam gun and it's a peach of an invention, I can tell you. Here, a gander.'

Wynter opened the hut door and presented Jack with a shiny new metal contraption, gleaming with copper and brass.

'Da-da!' exclaimed Abe, sweeping off his top hat. 'You know what that is? That's Joseph Bramah's pan closet toilet! Eh? Eh? Cost me a packet, I can tell you, not even countin' the bill for the passage, which made me eyes water, I can tell you.' He put an arm around Jack's shoulders. 'What I wanted to say is, you can use this anytime. Anytime.' He gave Jack a wink. 'So long as I'm not sittin' on it, consider it yours, Cap'n. I won't charge you a sou. There, what d'you say to that?'

Jack shrugged the arm away and replied, 'I would say nothing on earth would tempt me to enter that hut.'

Abraham Wynter stared at Jack for several moments, then gave a guffaw of laughter.

'You – you're a card, you are. My brother warned me about you. You said that with face flatter than a clothes-iron. Well, Cap'n, 'ave a good day, and I'll be gettin' back to you soon on that other matter.'

With that the rich gentleman walked back to supervise the boxing of his rapid-firing steam gun.

On that count Jack's feelings were in accord with Von Tempsky's. He did not like the major, but he agreed with his sentiments. This gun was a monstrous object, and it occurred to Jack that if it had been around since 1824, and was so amazing, why was it not in general use by the British army? Someone, several someones, had since decided it was not all it was cracked up to be. Jack wondered how many of the officers here, praising its capabilities, would actually use it. It would be an interesting study, if one had the time to wallow in study, which Jack had not, for General Pratt was anxious to get to grips with the Maori problem. General Pratt had the idea that the sappers could win the war for him by digging trenches and beating the Maori at their own game. Apparently the 14th Foot were on their way to New Zealand, full of zest and eager to dig as well as fight, but would take some 90 days to get there.

In October, Pratt ordered operations on three *pas* on the Kahihi River, which proved successful. The trenches aimed straight at the hearts of the *pas* were dug out under cover of bulletproof screens. The Maori defenders of the mud-and-timber forts had to watch in consternation as the enemy moved slowly towards them, unable to stop this snail-paced approach. However, the obvious answer for the occupants of a *pa* under such attack was to wait until the last minute, then vacate their fort and run off to build another one. Jack sort of agreed with the settlers that this kind of warfare got lost in itself, with neither side gaining any sort of advantage.

In November, with the promise of summer in the air, Jack took part in an engagement which took place at Mahoetahi, a point around two and a bit miles from Waitara and some few more miles from New Plymouth. A note had been sent from a Maori chief called Taiporotu to the Assistant Native Secretary, which went something like as follows:

Friend, I have heard your word – come and fight me.
That is very good.

Come inland and let us meet each other ...
make haste, make haste.

It was signed by Taiporotu, who claimed to be
speaking for several tribes in the region,
including the Ngatihaua, Ngatiamaniopoto and
other Maori peoples who supported Wiremu
Kingi. Taunts such as this one were common
with Maori chiefs, who had the same sort of
sense of humour owned by the British soldiers
who fought against them. One chief, having had
a reward posted on his head by the Governor of
New Zealand, promptly put up his own posters,
offering the same amount to anyone who would
bring in the governor, dead or alive. Another had
sent directions to his *pa*, in order that the British
attacking force should not get lost in the
wilderness on the way and would easily find his
fort.

Before they set out to attack the *pa*, which a
settler told Jack gleefully was rotten and falling
to pieces, there was the funeral of a local white
tradesman who had been murdered when he got
drunk and wandered too far off the safe limits of
town. He was found with a greenstone *patu* axe
still buried in his skull. It took two men to
remove the weapon, one of whom kept it as a
souvenir. Gwilliams had been on drinking terms
with the settler, though not on the night he had
been killed, and so asked if they could attend the
ceremony. Jack reluctantly allowed his men to
do so, going along himself.

It was not the dismal affair Jack expected it to

be, mainly because most of the mourners were half-intoxicated and not inclined to be miserable on behalf of their friend. There was the general feeling amongst the company that 'Bill' would have wanted a merry send-off. Moreover he had been a bachelor, so there was no widow in black or long-faced children to placate with false sentiment, though indeed a spotty-faced nephew of about 15 years was in evidence. A bottle was being passed from hand to hand behind the row of backs, even as the minister intoned the Lord's Prayer. Finally, as the coffin went down into the clay, a hastily formed band began to play. To Jack's astonishment a loud guffaw broke out amongst the mourners and broad grins appeared as whispers were exchanged with those who were not laughing.

'What's that all about?' Jack asked of Gwilliams. 'It seems to me to be in very bad taste, even at a wake.'

'You recognize the tune, sir?' replied his corporal, who had to bite his lip to stop sniggering.

Jack said, 'Well, that tone-deaf mob is murdering it, but I believe it to be Bach's "Sheep May Safely Graze".'

'On the nail, sir,' said Gwilliams with a laugh. 'You see, the man who was killed, he was the local butcher.'

Even Jack had to smile at that.

The following morning at 5 a.m., Jack, Gwilliams and Wynter joined a force led by General Pratt. The column consisted of over 650 regular troops and volunteers. Jack had maps drawn by

Sergeant King and he and his two men led the way. Major Mould followed on behind with another 300 soldiers. When they arrived at the *pa* they found it in poor condition with almost no cover for the Maoris. Despite the fact that several tribes had joined together for this battle, Jack realized there were only around 150 of them in the entrenchments ahead. The Maori were vastly outnumbered, facing overwhelming odds, but they stood resolute with their muskets and stone axes, ready to repel the onslaught.

A red sky illuminated the battle area. It was a fine morning; no morning for men to die like cattle.

'Sir, let me go and speak with them?' asked Jack of a major on the general's staff. 'I may be able to persuade them to lay down their arms.'

'I think not, Captain. The general is in no mood for conciliation.'

'But they don't stand an earthly. It would be slaughter.'

'Too bad. They should have thought of that before Puketakauere. It's our turn this time.'

It was true that General Pratt and some of his officers were thirsting for revenge for that earlier failure.

Jack insisted. 'These are brave men. Their pride will never let them surrender unless we give them an opening.'

The major's expression was like granite. There was nothing moving in his heart. He simply stared hard at Jack with blue eyes that showed nothing but contempt.

'Is it *their* welfare which concerns you, Captain, or your own?'

Jack stiffened. He said slowly and deliberately, 'Major, I have fought innumerable battles, in the Crimea, in India, and here. The last man who questioned my courage is now buried near Gwailor. Have a care with your accusations, sir.'

The major's eyes widened a fraction. He gazed into Jack's own for a full minute. It seemed that what he saw there prevented him from upbraiding the captain for his insolence. Finally, under Jack's fixed stare, he turned his head away and seemed to hear a call from the general's direction, because he strode off without another word.

'That's the way to tell 'em, sir,' muttered Gwilliams. 'I heard tell of that one. He don't know his arse from his head.'

This was praise indeed from his corporal, though Jack knew he should not comment further on the matter.

When the attack came, the Maoris did indeed stand their ground, even when the bayonet charge came. Pratt's soldiers charged up the hill to the *pa* and overran what entrenchments remained. The Maori muskets, once discharged, were thrown aside. Hand axes and spears came into play. But such weapons were no match for the rifles and bayonets of Pratt's soldiers. Colonel Mould's forces then arrived and attacked the flank of the enemy. Rifles blazed from two directions and the Maori at last vacated their ruined fort. The air was full of battle smoke and stank of burnt powder. Bodies remained draped over the rotten wood of the fort's palisade. A wounded Maori staggered along a ridge, finally falling over on the far side. An eager, excited militia volunteer chased after him only to reappear a minute later with blood pouring from the side of his head. Jack saw the pakeha's legs go from under him, and he pitched forward into the mud with half his scalp missing.

The Maori warriors scattered and ran for a river in the rear, flinging themselves into the water, swimming and wading across to the far bank under fire. Jack saw one big fellow flee, the water around him pockmarked by balls striking the surface. Then finally one shot hit him in the back of the head, just below the cranium, and he went down into the current. The body floated away downstream past a group of parrots who screeched as it bumped their overhanging tree. Their audacious chieftain Wetini Taiporotu, was one of those who remained on the hillside along with nearly forty of his comrades-in-arms when the British troops overran it. A dozen more were killed in or over the river and tens were wounded in the retreat to Puketakauere. One old man, later identified as a chief called Mokau, was about to cross a swamp when he saw an old friend dying in the mud. He bent down to rub noses in a gesture of farewell, but because of the delay he was then mortally wounded himself by a bullet straight through the heart.

Nine

For every Maori at war with the pakeha, there were two others happy to farm the land and provide the newcomers with food. Wheat was being grown by the ton and even exported to Australia. The sweet potato had been pushed aside to make way for the pakeha potato. Cattle, sheep and pigs were moving into the millions. Every tribe had its own flour mill now, sometimes more than one, and maize crops were abundant. Less than a century before Jack arrived in New Zealand, Captain Cook had introduced pigs to the islands, which were now both domesticated and feral, running through woodlands and pastureland. It did seem to Jack that the war was but a few wrong stitches in a tapestry that would eventually show a landscape at peace, Maori with pakeha.

'I am ready to settle down,' he told Sergeant King, who was now out of hospital, 'and become a farmer.'

King was astonished. 'But you're a soldier,' he said. 'How can you suddenly turn dirt farmer, sir? You don't know anything about farming, do you?'

They were sitting outside one of the usual soldier haunts: a tavern on a green that could have been in Surrey. Behind them, rolling meadows rose and fell like the soft green breasts of a giant maiden. Nearby, ducks and geese were milling around a pond while a young child was feeding them with breadcrumbs. It was an idyllic scene that might have turned Attila the Hun into a pastoral poet. King was not above being influenced himself, by the spiritual nature of the weather and the landscape, but to give up soldiering? Why that would have meant giving up map-making, for no other profession was interested in charting the topography of these new British possessions abroad.

'I could learn,' replied the captain, with some stiffness. 'I'm not a complete idiot, you know.'

'Yes, but, sir, I've been trying to teach you map-drawing since I've known you, and it don't seem to work. You don't like to learn new skills, do you?'

'Well, maps are one thing, farming another.'

The officer seemed to be implying that map-making was of lesser importance than ploughing a field. King could not take this view seriously. He began his standard lecture, even though he saw that Captain Crossman's expression had turned from dreamy to despairing.

'Maps,' said King, 'are just as important to farmers, as they are to generals. Look, don't sigh, sir – it's true. Every man who owns a bit of land wants to know what it looks like – its shape, its length and girth, its ups and downs, its borders. Think how delighted the first king was, who saw an accurate picture of his country on paper! What would he have known before that? What image was in his head? He would have had none, for there was no way to imagine the shape and position of his kingdom on the face of the planet. The king of the Eastern Angles, for example, would only know that his state extended from the North Sea to his neighbours in the west, to the Wash in the north, to the Thames River in the south – but he would have had no idea of its shape.' King took a sip of his beer, before continuing. 'You will need to know the contours of your farmlands, sir, and only a map-maker can do that for you.'

'I admit it helps to have a map to settle land disputes with neighbours.'

'Good.' King's face brightened. 'You admit it then.'

'I've been soldiering since I was eighteen, Sergeant. I've seen enough blood-and-thunder to last me the rest of my life. Colonel Lovelace, he's the sort of man you need to expend your argument on. He's a life soldier. This country is what I've been looking for. I've found it and I mean to stay.'

'You'll sell out?' King made it sound like a distasteful business.

'I don't need to. I didn't purchase my commission, I earned it.'

'Well, same thing. You're going to leave the army.'

'I think so. I've had enough of slaughter – and settling disputes with maniacal cavalry officers...'

'Ah, you're talking of that blaze you had with Captain Deighnton in India. He was a madman, sir.'

'Him and one or two others. I swear they don't get enough of killing on the battlefield, so they have to look for brother officers to shoot down between times. My own blood lust has long been satisfied. I need a rest, Sergeant. You'll be all right. You'll get some officer who's keen on your maps and you'll be in seventh heaven. Ah, here's the man who's going to get me my farm...'

King looked up to see Abraham Wynter, black-coated and high-hatted, striding in front of his personal army of six Maori. He saw Jack and waved to him, calling, 'We're gettin' there, Cap'n. Just give me a couple more weeks. Good piece of land goin' to the south. Just need a bit more time to persuade the current owner to part with it.'

This announcement was somewhat slurred in its delivery.

'No underhand stuff,' Jack called back, seriously. 'I want it purchased fair and square and willingly parted with.'

'O' course, o' course.'

Abe Wynter winked broadly, which did not settle Jack's fears in the least. The businessman looked quite drunk to Jack. Today was Saturday and no doubt Abe Wynter had been down to the marketplace making deals and sealing each one with a drink or two. It was quite difficult not to over-imbibe on such occasions, for the Maori

150

expected such rituals, and the settlers were also in the habit of quaffing a jar on a sale or purchase.

'I mean it, Mister Wynter. No land-grabbing.'

''Gainst the law, Cap'n.' Abe Wynter nodded slowly and solemnly to show how serious he took this warning. Then his face changed again, to that sly, greasy expression which made Jack doubt the wisdom of dealing with such a man. Abe continued, 'I'm now off with my Maori for a bit of roasted pork to settle the gin in me belly.' He nodded back at his half-dozen minders, all dressed in shirts and trousers, but shoeless. They leaned on their rifles and grinned when they were referred to by their master. 'We often share a bit o' pork,' he added, then rather more enigmatically, 'In the past, there's bin another kind of roasted pig we've indulged in, but not together, oh, no – them here, me somewhere else. But it sort of makes me like a brother to 'em, if you know what I mean.' He slung an arm around the neck of one of his followers, who grinned even more broadly. 'Me an' them 'ave got this thing in common, see. We're brothers under the skin.'

Jack tried to look under the words for Abe Wynter's true meaning, and thought he found something quite unpalatable. Did Abe really mean what he was implying, or was it show? Probably the latter. If he were to demand loyalty from his Maoris, Abe would need a connection with them. Perhaps he had invented one and made use of it. In any case, Abe's private habits were of no consequence to Jack. There were probably many unsavoury aspects to his character, but since Jack was not a friend he need not concern himself with them. Abe Wynter was merely someone to do a brief spell of business with, and then Jack need have nothing further to do with the man.

'What was all that about?' asked King. 'All that stuff about pork?'

'He's three sheets to the wind, Sergeant. I don't think he even knows himself what he's about.'

King said, 'I don't like that man.'

'Neither do I.'

'Yet you deal with him, sir?'

'I don't have to like a shopkeeper to buy an ounce of tobacco from him,' said Jack, puffing on his chibouk to emphasize his point. 'I might even despise the man I sell my horse to.'

'Still an' all, sir.'

'I know what you mean, Sergeant, but he's the only man around here who can get me my farm. I could try myself, but I'm not a good negotiator and I'm sure I'd be swindled. I would deserve to be, given I'm a flat when it comes to such things. I'm not happy about that, but it is a fact and therefore I'm having to swallow my dislike of the man. Personally, I think he's going to get shot by someone soon and we'll all go to his funeral and sing hymns, think him a fine fellow – or at least, we'll think he was not as bad as he was painted.'

'Not me, sir. I could see him dead tomorrow

152

and shrug it off.'

'Sergeant King, you're becoming as hard-metalled as our own Colonel Lovelace.'

King smiled. 'You could be right, sir.'

At that moment Corporal Gwilliams was seen coming up the dusty road, with Harry Wynter and Ta Moko in tow. The trio had been out with a scouting party. They arrived at the tavern looking tired and dishevelled. Jack asked them how they had done.

'Pretty well, sir,' answered Gwilliams, throwing himself down on to the bench with a thump. 'We found what we was sent for.'

'This one,' Ta Moko added, slapping the back of Wynter's head, not too hard but enough to jolt it forward, 'was dragging his feet.'

'Hey!' cried the private, rubbing his neck. 'You didn't ought to do that, blackie. I'm a soldier of the queen, I am. I want respect.'

'You call me *blackie* again and I'll throw you into the pond, Harry Wynter, soldier of the queen.'

Wynter squinted at the Maori, whose broad face with its tattoos and wide nose was fearsome enough. He knew Ta Moko could pick him up and snap him like a twig if he decided to, but Harry Wynter had never been put off by the threat of pain. His battered body, white hair and sightless eye attested to that. Harry Wynter could soak up punishment like a sponge soaks up water. He had done it all his life. It was the pattern of his world and he knew it would never change. Even now an insult was on the tip of his tongue.

Ta Moko remarked, 'Don't say it, Wynter. Better not.'

'It's said in my mind,' muttered Harry, 'an' that's as good as said out loud.'

'We've just had the pleasure of your brother's company,' King told Harry. 'He sends his love.'

'You're teasin' me, Sergeant. He an't got no love for me, that brother o' mine; otherwise he'd look after me like he should. I hope he rots in hell, damn his eyes and liver. One o' these days he's goin' to regret what he did to me an' what he din't do *for* me. It's not the money, that he's rich an' I an't got a sou, it's what one brother should do for another is what's important. I'll see him out yet, you wait.'

Harry Wynter was not finished on the subject. He continued for the next half-hour until the others were heartily sick of hearing about Abraham Wynter and his foibles. Soon after that King and Gwilliams drifted away, heading back to their quarters. Private Wynter followed on a short time afterwards. Jack and Ta Moko only were left to appreciate the gloaming, as evening twilight came in across the hills. The pair were silent for a long time, just enjoying the tranquillity.

It was Ta Moko who spoke first.

'The woman wishes to see you – tonight.' The big Maori did not turn his head when he said this, but there was no indication that he disapproved in any way. 'Shall I tell her yes?'

Two savage animals suddenly began an

intense battle in Jack's breast. The less admirable of the two finally won. He could not help himself. He hated the choice; he hated his feelings. He was being wrenched from his complacent mood and thrust into a state of mind unfamiliar to him. Jack could not look away from the scene in front of him. Words like loyalty and honour were swirling around in his head, but he ignored them in favour of passion and desire. His noble spirit wafted away and was replaced by a demon called lust. Amiri was remarkably beautiful. Her body was like a hot fire to the touch. He could not reject it when it was offered so willingly. Why should he? he argued. He had fought wars without so much as a warm embrace at the end of each one. And here was so much more, just rewards, enveloping him.

'Tell her yes,' he said, throatily. 'I–I would like that.'

Ta Moko nodded. 'I think she would like it also,' he said, sagely. 'She is a free woman. Her man was killed by another.'

But am I a free man? thought Jack. No, I am not. However, he did not voice these observations, but allowed the excitement, the anticipation of the meeting, to well up inside him and dispel any doubts. It was a feverish Jack Crossman who waited in his quarters for the visitor he expected to come just before midnight. Indeed, he was not disappointed, for at 11.50 there was a light knock on the door of his quarters.

Jack opened the door, saying, 'Ah, the East

Wind is early for the season...' but was stunned into cutting the sentence short by being confronted by his superior, Colonel Lovelace.

'Good God – Nathan?'

Nathan Lovelace gave Jack a half-smile, extended his hand to be shaken, and said, 'Are we into coded phrases now? I'm afraid no one told me tonight's password.'

Nathan, wearing the new insignia of a colonel, was immaculately dressed in his uniform at a time in the evening when most off-duty officers would be wearing mufti.

This was the man who had recruited Jack Crossman to the intelligence service when he was a sergeant and had taught him everything he knew about espionage. They had served together through the whole of the Crimean War and afterwards saw out the Indian Mutiny. Jack admired Nathan Lovelace a great deal, but also disapproved of his fierce ambition and dedication to his duty. He liked the man as a person, though he was often frustrated at not being able to see what lay beneath this enigmatic character. Nathan was responsible for Jack's progress in the army, from sergeant to captain. You had to like a man who did that for you, even if you did not wholly approve of his methods of working.

The Rifle greens fitted him tighter than a second skin. His highly polished boots gleamed in the light from the lamp. He was just about the perfect shape for a soldier: tall, barrel-chested, broad-shouldered, slim-hipped and strong-limbed, without an ounce of extra fat on him anywhere. The wide smile on his handsome face went only skin deep, but women loved that mysterious reserve in him. It told of secrets which they thought they might winkle out of him. It never happened though, for Nathan Lovelace was a strongbox of cryptic information that could only be accessed by Nathan Lovelace and God: and God was not particularly interested in the detailed affairs of soldiers. His blond hair and blue eyes belonged to an angel, but his heart had been passed to him by one of those creatures who live in the countervailing world.

Jack shook the hand of his commander. 'Nathan, how good to see you. What are you doing here? This is just a little backwater place for us spies. Not much of a war, either. The Maori fight like wildcats, but it's all very bitty – incidents rather than grand battles.'

'I know,' said Nathan, removing his cap and looking round for a chair in which to sprawl. 'I came to see General Pratt, but I thought I'd look in on you while I was here. As you say, not much of a war for men of our stamp. Would you like me to send you elsewhere? I'm sure I could find a more exciting place for you.'

Nathan found a wicker chair and sat in it, placing his cap carefully on the dresser next to it.

Panic rose in Jack's breast as he himself sank back on his cot.

'No, there is much for me to do here. I'm in deep now and want to see the thing out. You understand? It's gets personal after a while.'

'But I understand it's just mapping. I thought you hated all that stuff?'

'Well, Nathan,' said Jack, with a little laugh, 'there's a bit more to it than that. Have you had complaints about me? About my work? From the general or any of his staff?'

'No, no, they're quite pleased with your efforts. Pratt said the maps you were producing were a great help to him. Sergeant King's labours, I imagine? Yes, of course. But I presume you oversee his work and pick up bits of information here and there? Naturally you've formed a network of Maori spies?'

'It's well in the making,' lied Jack, realizing just how idle he had been since he had arrived in New Zealand. The place had enchanted him into becoming lax. He made a mental note to knuckle down and do just what Nathan was suggesting. 'I'm grooming a Maori chief called Potaka who's ... look, Nathan, I've no whisky here in my room. Can I take you somewhere and we can talk over a drink?' Jack looked at the clock by his bed, his stomach churning. It was ten past midnight. Any moment now Amiri would burst through his doorway.

Nathan waved a hand. 'No – quite unnecessary, Jack. Tell me about this Potaka fellow then. Is he in with the rebels?'

'He *is* a rebel, but I've gained his confidence – and that of – of a woman in his tribe. You know how useful women can be, Nathan. They're often ignored by warriors as they sit round and plan their next attack. The women walk amongst

158

them, fetching and carrying, and listening to the men's talk.'

'Oh, without a doubt. Women often make the best intelligence agents for those very reasons.' Nathan chuckled, adding, 'For some reason men who would not trust a woman with their best friend are quite happy to trust them with their war plans. I do believe most men think the women are not interested in "male games" and that plans and such go over their pretty little heads. What nonsense. Women are the most intelligent and devious of creatures on this earth, Jack, and the only thing they love more than collecting secrets is passing them on to a third party. Even when they're caught out they look as if butter wouldn't melt—'

The door suddenly flew open and to Nathan's astonishment a woman entered swiftly and slammed the door behind her.

'Jack...' she began, her brown eyes alight; then, seeing the visitor, she shrank into a corner.

'Speak of the devil!' cried Jack. 'Here's my informant now. Amiri, how are you?' Jack was shaking badly as he took her hand and pumped it as if he were meeting a comrade-in-arms. 'Have you been discovered? Is that why you're here?'

Amiri looked from Jack's face to the visitor's face, her expression one of wariness and puzzlement.

'No,' she said, after a while. 'No discovery, Jack.'

Nathan seemed to be waiting, expectantly, for

revelations, but then he stood up and took his cap.

'Ah, she won't want to speak in front of me, will she? She don't know me from Adam. Look, I'll see you in the morning, old chap. I just thought I'd make contact tonight, so that you could gather yourself together for a meeting tomorrow.' Nathan placed a large hand on Jack's right shoulder and looked into his eyes. 'So good to see you again, Jack. You look a bit peaky though. Been ill?'

'Took a knock on the head,' Jack said, rubbing the wound given him by Potaka. 'It's healed, but I still get headaches.'

'Ah, yes, heard about that. Nasty, eh? Understand Sergeant King's had a tough time of it too. Got lost. You found him though. I met Gwilliams coming out of the local inn on my way here. He was sober enough to fill me in on a bit of recent history. But you can give me the whole picture tomorrow. Well, goodnight, Amiri, is it? Now what could that mean in Maori? Let me guess. Something to do with the wind? The East Wind? There, your eyes show surprise, ma'am, but I'm not a complete dunce. Jack knows that very well, don't you, Jack?'

With that Nathan opened the door and stepped outside, only to be hit squarely on the nose by a wicker ball.

'What the hell...?' he exclaimed, but Jack had followed him to the threshold and said, 'There's probably a message inside. It's the picquets – they use wicker balls to pass messages to each

160

other and headquarters. You could give that to the orderly officer on your way.'

'Oh, right.' Nathan laughed. 'Thought someone was using me as a coconut shy. Night, Jack.'

'Goodnight, Nathan. I'll see you in the morning.'

'Who was that?' asked Amiri, as Jack closed the door carefully behind him.

'My boss.'

'Does he know? About me?'

'I think he's guessed. Not much escapes that man, Amiri. What he'll do about it, I have no idea.'

Jack felt deflated. His affair with Amiri now seemed rather sordid. If he sent Amiri away now he would feel no cleaner inside. She smelled of coconut oil and some other Maori perfume. The desire rose in him as quickly as the disillusionment with himself subsided. Lust was a very difficult transgression to reject when a woman such as Amiri stood there as a willing participant in the game. Jack's throat was dry with yearning. Amiri exuded passion and – yes – love.

'Can he keep a secret?'

'More closely than the Almighty keeps the secret of death.'

She moved into his arms. 'Then we can feel safe. *You* can be safe. I do not care what they think of me.'

Safe, but unsavoury, thought Jack. How long had it been since he had lain with his own wife? Three? Nearly four years? A man was not made of stone. But these were mere excuses. Should he not love honour more, as the poem went? A poem written by a Colonel Lovelace. Not his colonel, not Nathan, but another Colonel Lovelace, a soldier back in Tudor times. *I could not love thee, dear, so much, loved I not honour more.* But that was not about deception, but about war. About a knight who loved war more than he loved his mistress. Well, that was not Jack. War could go and hang itself for all Jack cared...

He sank with her, back on to the hard cot, her softness beneath him, opening for him. Jack's head swirled with a mixture of guilt and pleasure. Then the guilt swam away into the darkness at the back of his mind. A brown body, her tattoos tracing the contours of her body, one of them recently done for him. He ran the tips of his fingers along the lines, stroking her breasts on the way down, until he found the softest of places, the warmest, the most moist of crevices.

'Oh my God, Amiri,' he murmured in the back of his throat, 'you are so beautiful, my love.'

'As are you, my wonderful Jack,' she whispered in his ear. 'Now move with me – slow, slow – ah, you are my wonderful lover...'

The following morning Jack met with Colonel Lovelace in the officers' mess in the camp near New Plymouth. Nathan was in a cheery mood and he even patted Jack on the back as he spoke to him.

'Well, Jack, are you ready to move on?'

Jack was taken by surprise. 'Move on?'

'To pastures new. This was to be a short rest posting, wasn't it? I thought we agreed on that. There are areas where you'd be far more useful than you are here. Back in India, possibly. Or Burma. Africa? I can't leave you in a soft spot like this for ever, Jack.'

'But –' Jack was dismayed – 'I've only been here a few months, Nathan. And there's my wife, Jane.'

'Jane? What about her?'

'I've sent for her. I thought – well, I imagined we'd be here a year or two, till things settled down. Nathan, I haven't seen my wife for over three years. I was hoping we could be together for a while.'

'This is the army, Jack.'

'I know, Nathan, but surely and all, *three years*. That's longer than Jack tars spend away from their families.'

Nathan's face went a little rigid. He looked down at his boots and then up again to stare into Jack's eyes.

'Do you really want your wife here?' he asked, meaningfully. 'I'm only asking because it seemed to me that you were pretty comfortably settled.'

Now Jack's face went stiff and mask-like. 'Sir?'

Nathan's hand came up. 'I'm not prying into your private affairs, Jack. I'm not your moral guardian – I am no saint myself. I simply wonder whether you're on a course of self-destruction. You're a good officer, a man I know I can trust to do a good job. There will be openings for you – higher posts than the one you hold at the moment.' Nathan gripped his arm. 'Jack, intelligence in this man's army is in its infancy. There's no ceiling to promotion in the near future. With you at my right hand I expect to make general in a very short time – and the post would hold an enormous amount of power. We would be the quiet men behind the crown. I – we – would control a worldwide network of intelligence agents in every country in the British Empire. Now that generals like Raglan have gone, the new men at the top are convinced of the need for efficient spy systems. There's no longer any talk of "skulkers". I have spent all my time doing the convincing. This is the modern era, Jack. You and I are modern men.' Nathan paused and poured himself a glass of water from a jug on the mess table. They were alone in the room. Only an orderly could be heard clanking around in the distant kitchen. 'Think of it, Jack. This is a unique opportunity. Once in a thousand years. In another three or four decades it will become just like any other army unit, with several officers battling for the top spot. At the moment it's all free air, no devious rivals to screw things up – just a blank space to fill.'

Jack sighed, looking down at his restless hands.

'However,' Nathan continued in a less excitable tone, 'I could leave you here, if that's really what you want. You could see these troubles out and then – well, who knows what then? But I'll have gone on without you by that time. If you can't get on board now you'll have to run alongside the track with the others when the time comes.'

There was a long period of silence, then Jack said, 'Can I think about it?'

Nathan stood up. 'Of course. I can see you're in a bit of a spin at the moment. Think about it hard, Jack. I'm here for a week or so, and then I'm on my way back to Sydney on the *Triumphant*. Get word to me. If I don't hear from you, I'll assume you're bent on staying. In which case, I still expect you to do good work here. I know you will. Good luck, man.'

The new colonel shook Jack's hand, strode from the room, and left the mess to Jack and the saucepan-clanking orderly.

Ten

Captain Jack Crossman was in a quandary. His army career, which he once considered to be his sole reason for living, was in crisis. He knew he could not have everything. He certainly could not have two women and his removal from New Zealand would solve that decadent problem for him. But Jane was probably on her way out to the antipodes already, and what if she were to arrive and find him gone? What would be the level of her disappointment? Would she forgive him? To find her husband had chosen to leave her yet again for his other mistress – the army – might be the final straw.

Certainly he, Jack, could not even remember her face now, without looking at the miniature she had given him. Did he still love her? He was bound to say he did, even given his wayward behaviour of late. And Jane did not deserve to be humiliated by a husband who deserted her in favour of promotion. No, leaving New Zealand would not solve anything between Jane and himself. Would she understand the lure of women like Amiri on a lonely soldier? Possibly, but it would tarnish him in her eyes and he was devastated by that thought. Better she never knew, if it were possible to keep it from her.

But that was by the by. His immediate problem, which he seemed to have resolved, was whether to stay or join Nathan Lovelace. Nathan was of course destined for greatness; there was no denying that. And Jack could have clung to his coat tails and been there with him when that greatness was achieved. Or he could settle here, in New Zealand, and be satisfied that he had risen from private to captain on his own merits. Should he change his mind later, and wish again to pursue the dizzy heights, why then he could attempt that on his own merits too. He did not need Colonel Lovelace to help him along. The feeling of achievement without favour was much more exhilarating. Why, his own father had been willing to buy him a captaincy at one time, at which starting point he would probably now be a colonel himself!

'Do it on your own,' he told himself, 'if you wish to do it at all. Let Nathan look after Nathan, and Jack see to Jack. I would be forever beholden to the man if I went with him.'

He stared out of his window at the sheep grazing amongst the ancient ferns. His mind was made up. The old iron was re-entering his ferrous veins. Fancy Jack Crossman was in the ascendancy, reliant on his own talents. Nathan would always be a friend, but Nathan's focus was on one road which led to a single goal. Jack had several paths he wished to explore. Nathan had but one friend as far as Jack knew, and that was himself. Jack had many friends, a brother he loved, a wife he loved, and a father he had once hated. Nathan could not even afford the time to hate someone; sometimes a great motivation for striving for those goals and values one desired. Jack would be better travelling alone.

He wrote a formal note to his colonel.

Sir, I have considered carefully your very generous proposition and while I am fully aware that I am under orders, it is my request that I remain in New Zealand to assist my superiors here in any way I can. If this request cannot be met, due to exigencies of the service, I will of course be at your disposal. However, I would be greatly in your debt if you should see fit to allow me to follow my aspirations.

I remain your most obedient servant,
Captain J. Crossman.

Within an hour he received the following reply: *Good luck, Jack – Nathan.*

Feeling a little more relieved and in command of himself (though consciously aware he had one more enormous problem to solve), Jack sent for his men. Sergeant Farrier King arrived first, followed by Corporal Gwilliams and Private Wynter. Last to arrive was Ta Moko, whose shirts and trousers always seemed too small for him. The Maori came into the room stretching every seam.

Jack had commandeered a storeroom in a school for his office. Next door, children, and indeed army corporals with ambitions set on

168

being quartermasters one day, sat side by side chanting their times tables. This heavy drone was clearly audible through the walls. Jack's soldiers sat on boxes and awaited their orders. Wynter picked his teeth with a twig and seemed more interested in 'Six sixes are thirty-six' than what his captain had to say, for his ear was placed against the wooden partition and his lips were moving silently in unison with those beyond.

'Sergeant King, you will take Corporal Gwilliams and Private Wynter up the Whanganui River. You will chart that watercourse for as far as you are able. The Maori regard it as an essential waterway to the interior and so we must consider it important also. You will need tents, equipment and stores to sustain you in open country. I will also have assigned to you twenty soldiers of the 68th Foot – the Durham Light Infantry. These are good men, well versed in the war with the rebels, and they will be under your command. Ta Moko will be your guide on this enterprise, and you are to trust to his judgement when it comes to matters regarding pathfinding and retreat from hostiles. And Wynter, seven fives are thirty-five, not thirty-four. I can lip-read, you know.'

'Sir?' said Wynter, jolting upright.

'Pay attention, man, it may save your life.'

'I'm tryin' to advance meself, sir.'

'You will advance into *hell* if you don't heed my orders.'

'Yessir.' Then a very low mutter. 'Might even

169

like it better there, than in this bloody place.'

Captain Jack Crossman ignored this expected response. 'Right – any questions?'

Corporal Gwilliams stared at his officer. 'Beg pardon, sir, but you don't usually ask for such from the likes of us. It's usually do-this-or-else, ain't it?'

'Well, perhaps I'm becoming a bit of a democrat in my old age, Corporal. I just want to make sure you're happy with the assignment.'

Happy? That was a new one too. Gwilliams looked at King, who simply shrugged and tapped the side of his skull. The knock on the head their captain had received had obviously bruised his brain. His men wondered how long it was going to take before that injury was completely healed. Clearly any officer who worried about the contentment of his troops was unfit for command. You did as you were told and *that* made you happy, because anything that went wrong was not then your fault, but that of your commander. It would be a bad day when common soldiers had to take their own initiative. Of course, if things did go wrong, you might be dead, but in that event your worries were over anyway. Happiness could be said to belong to a soldier who died saying, 'It's not my fault.'

Once he had packed his men off on their mission, Jack then set about his own plans. Nathan had suggested a network of local intelligence agents. Jack thought about Potaka. He might be persuaded to aid them if Jack were clever enough. He had no qualms about turning a man traitor to his own kind. He viewed the long term and knew from experience that although the wars might go on for a while, eventually the pakeha would win. They always did in such situations. The manpower behind the British throne was almost infinite, while native nations like the Maori, small enough by comparison in the beginning, had been depleted by war and disease, especially the latter. The Maori, like the American Indian and Pacific Islanders, had no defence against illnesses that had previously been unknown to them. They had no immunity. They died quickly and easily of smallpox, venereal diseases and even the measles.

The captain knew for certain that the rebel Maori tribes would be vanquished. It was a given fact. Therefore it was his job to see that few soldiers were killed in the meantime. If he could help end the wars sooner rather than later, by using Maori spies, then he would do his utmost to recruit them.

Jack knew the way to Potaka's hideout now and wearing civilian bush clothes set out to reach it by sundown. When he neared the cave he saw Amiri. She was squatting on the ground with two Maori boys of about nine or ten years. On an exclamation from one of the children, she looked up to see him and her face turned sunny. He knew in that instant that she believed he had come for her, not Potaka. Chagrin was now a constant companion of Jack's and he bore it with fortitude.

'Amiri?'

She beamed from her brow to the tattoo on her chin, which resembled two companionable Hs. Despite her bright expression he had no doubt this woman could become a hellion if scorned.

'Ah, my beloved Jack is here.'

'It's nice to see you, my dear – but I'm really after Potaka.'

'Oh?' A shade of disappointment crossed her face, but she soon recovered. 'He is out hunting. He will be back soon.'

'Can I wait?' He propped the Enfield he was carrying against a handy rock.

'But of course, my darling man. How dashing you look! You are more handsome than Major Tempsky, with his silk shirts and tight trousers.'

'I compare favourably, do I?'

'Oh, you are superior, Jack.'

He laughed. It was pleasant to be in her company. Why, Jane would love her, if it were not for the fact that Jack had bedded her. But he had, and he knew he would want to kill someone like Nathan, of whom he was presently fond, if that man had seduced his wife. Sauce for the goose.

'What are you doing?' Jack asked.

'With the children? I'm telling them about Moeahu, the dog-headed man, who had a dog's head and feet...'

Jack realized Amiri was relating a Maori myth. The Maori had a vast range of tales in their repertoire; far, far too many for the recall of any ordinary European person, but the Maori had been without written language for much of their existence and their memories were phenomenal. They could recite whole genealogies, going back to great-grandparents in the mists of time. They passed on mental charts of long ocean voyages from one generation to the next. They carried in their brains an encyclopaedia of stories of their old gods, demigods, heroes and ancestors. It was an amazing national talent, shared by other Pacific islanders, which Jack found wonderful and inspiring.

Amiri continued, knowing Jack was listening. 'Moeahu was always barking like a dog, but he had the brain of a human. He could run like the wind and any tormentor could not escape him. He carried with him in his paws a *patu* club made of whalebone and a *taiaha*, and his home was in Turanga, in a forest.' Amiri cleared her throat before continuing with the tale. 'There was a Maori called Te Kowha who stole some fish that had been left on drying racks, so Moeahu felt it just to eat some of Te Kowha's chickens. Te Kowha was very angry and tried to spear the dog-headed man, but the Maori was clubbed to the ground. Te Kowha's three brothers saw what was happening and three of them ran to his assistance, but Te Kowha was dead. They attacked the dog-headed monster and set out to chase him from their region. Unhappily for them, they became strung out in the chase, and Moeahu suddenly turned and killed the leading brother. Then he waited for the second brother and killed him also. Finally the last of the brothers, the slowest runner, caught

173

up with his dead family and he too was slain by the monster Moeahu.'

Amiri nodded slowly and the boys murmured in appreciation.

Jack waited in vain for the moral at the end of the tale, but none was forthcoming and he supposed it was up the listener to make up his own mind as to whether justice was done or a wrong had occurred. He himself had no idea. The original theft of the fish was bad, and possibly the eye-for-an-eye stealing of the chickens balanced that crime, but for the end to result in the deaths of four men! He could not decide whether this was a warning against felony, a natural consequence of brotherhood honour, or simply a fatalistic view of life. The Maori mind was alien to him, as his must be to them, and he left it at that.

Jack did not have long to wait, before Potaka and his gang came back from the hunt. They had an enormous feral pig, a roly-poly squashed-faced *kune kune*, slung upside down with its feet tied around a carrying pole. It was still alive and was making a huge fuss, the mad beast struggling and screaming shrilly.

'*Tena koe, e hoa!*' cried Potaka, which Jack knew meant 'You there, O friend!'

Tena koe was the ordinary greeting used by the Maori, the 'O friend' had been added for Jack because a terse 'You there!' might sound ungracious to a pakeha.

The four companions of Potaka went off to the charcoal fire pit while Potaka stayed to talk

174

to Jack. He rubbed noses with Jack; a form of male greeting which always made the reserved Englishman squirm in his boots. It was the Maori who opened the conversation.

'Were you in the battle at Mahoetahi?'

'Yes,' admitted Jack, 'I was.'

'So was I. Several friends were killed. I swam across the river and went to Puketakauere.'

'I'm sorry – for your friends, I mean.'

Potaka nodded gravely. 'Did you lose a comrade?'

Jack shook his head. 'No – no, in fact we lost only four men. Two regular soldiers and two volunteer militia.'

Potaka raised his eyebrows. 'So few? We lost many men. Now, Captain, what do you want here? Your woman will visit you in your camp. You have no need to come chasing her into the bush, which is a dangerous place to be. If one of my men catches you, without me being there to stop it, he will try to kill you. It is best you stay there and she come to see you.'

'It is you I came to see.'

'Ah – then we must sit by a fire if we are to talk for very long. My bones will ache if I stand here in the cold wind.'

Jack was relieved when Potaka led him to the fire, which had been vacated by Amiri and the children, rather than to the charcoal fire pit, where his men were in the process of slaughtering the pig. Jack could not have spoken in front of the other men. What he had to say was only for the ears of Potaka.

Once they were sitting cross-legged on blankets before a restocked fire, Jack began the conversation.

'You say many Maoris died in the battle the other day?'

'Too many. We are few enough anyway.'

'Very true. It would be better for all concerned if these wars were to end as soon as possible. I would wish to do all in my power to hasten that end.'

'Go home to England.'

Jack smiled wryly. 'Yes, that would of course end it all, but you and I know that's not possible. The Treaty of Waitangi has been signed by all the chiefs...'

'Not all.'

'All right, not *all* the chiefs, but most of them – and certainly the important ones. The pakeha are here to stay and that's a given fact, Potaka. They won't leave now, ever. We must learn to live together on these beautiful islands which you call Aotearoa and we call New Zealand – were they not fish hooks which your divine demigod Maui raised up from the ocean floor? Something like that?'

Now Potaka smiled. 'Something of that nature.'

'Then your Polynesian ancestor, the great seafarer and Raiatean navigator Kupe, found them while chasing an octopus who had stolen his bait. He returned to his people and told them there were some beautiful islands which could be found by sailing to the left of the setting sun in November. A voyage of several thousand miles.'

'I told you that story myself.'

'They are wonderful tales, difficult to accept as fact, but nonetheless...'

'Nonetheless, as real as the Garden of Eden and Adam and Eve.'

'Granted.' Jack cleared his throat and scratched his bare wrist-stump, which he rarely disguised with a false hand these days. 'Potaka, the end of this war, these wars, is inevitable. The pakeha will win. We always win. In North America. In Australia. In India. It is sad but true. We have conquered and controlled nations of millions. The British are not the only Europeans to do so – the Spanish and Portuguese have taken all of South America, and the Dutch and French have taken lands too. If not the British, then some other European nation. Our weapons are superior, our military discipline and organization have been developed over centuries, and our numbers are immense. We might lose a battle, here and there, but in the end we always win the war. It is essential for the harmony of both our nations that we get on together. You and I must work towards that end.'

Potaka grimaced. 'You want me to turn traitor.'

Jack sighed. 'That's an ugly word. What I think would be expedient – what I would like you to do – is for you to join with me in ensuring this war comes to an end quickly. Not just you. It is my desire, my fervent hope, that you might form a secret society of Maoris wishing to assist me in terminating a war that will only lead to more deaths.'

Potaka was silent. After a long while he finally spoke.

'Captain, first the Taranaki tribes went to war against the pakeha. Now the Waikato tribes. You think if I spy for you I can help my people? I think not. You will be lucky if the Waikato tribes do not turn north and attack Auckland as I suggested they should. We will fight to the last man now that war has been declared.'

'I don't doubt your courage, not in the least. But is it worth it? Why all these deaths, just for...?'

Jack could not finish the sentence. He had made a hole for himself.

'Just for a *bit of land*?' said Potaka, grimly.

Jack hung his head. 'Something like that.'

'I must tell you, Jack, that I would die a thousand times for the land which belongs to me.'

Jack acknowledged this, saying, 'So would many farmers and landowners in Britain, but I have heard the 57th Regiment – we call them the Die-Hards – are on their way to New Zealand from India. They are very good at guerrilla fighting, Potaka. In India we had a rebellion, just like here, only there were many thousands of rebels, while here there are just a few. We put down that rebellion savagely. I'm not proud to be part of that, for I believe we went too far in our retaliation. There were horrible atrocities from which the so-called civilized British were not exempt. They did some bad things; we did some very bad things. I shudder to think the same thing might happen here. The trouble with war, an internal war, is that it escalates and individual horrors are tolerated. Insane thugs who would not normally be tolerated are let off the leash. God forbid we should have another Sepoy rebellion in New Zealand.'

Potaka said, stiffly, 'We are good Christian warriors. We succour the wounded, and we do not torture our prisoners. We do not kill women and children.'

'Not yet.'

'Never. Listen, Captain, I will not do this thing you ask. I cannot do this thing. Please do not drive a stake into our friendship.'

Jack realized he was not going to get anywhere. He shrugged his shoulders and sighed again.

'Well, I tried.'

'Will you stay and share our Captain Cooker with us?'

'No – I'm not that keen on wild pork, thanks, and I had better be getting back to my own people. Thank you for listening, Potaka. I respect your decision, though I believe it to be the wrong one.'

They now did a European thing: they shook hands.

Jack rode four hours back to camp to find a lieutenant sitting in a wicker chair on his veranda.

'Can I help you?' he asked.

The lieutenant, a young man with a rather large Roman nose, had been half-asleep and leapt out of the chair with alacrity, his feet getting tangled with his sword.

'Oh, sir – you startled me.'

'Well, I'm sorry for that, but you're on my veranda and using my chair without invitation, Lieutenant.'

'Baxter. Lieutenant Baxter, sir. Royal Artillery.'

'So I see.'

'You're wanted, sir. Colonel Smith-Williams wishes to see you. He's on the staff.'

'I know he is. Is it immediate?'

The lieutenant sorted his feet out from his scabbard.

'Yes, sir.'

'Lead on, McDuff.'

'Baxter, sir. Lieutenant Baxter.'

Jack rolled his eyes. 'Lead, man, lead.'

The youth led Jack to a building on the edge of barracks, knocked and entered. In a moment he was back out again and ushering Jack inside. The captain found himself facing a huge colonel, who was not fat, but packed with big solid bones that were overladen with thick heavy muscle. He was like a rhino in uniform. This powerful beast of a man looked up from sorting some documents on his desk. His sausage fingers finding it difficult to hold the flimsy paper.

'Bloody admin,' he grumbled. 'Wish I could

burn most of it. Sit down, Captain. No, not that chair – it's broken. It's got a greenstick fracture in the near hind leg. Take the one next to the door. That's it. Bring it over here, over to my left, my right ear's gone. Deaf as a post that side. Field guns did for it when I was younger. Ah, yes, the missing hand. Crimea, eh? You've got a few scars too, round the face.' The colonel seemed to have done his homework on Jack. 'Now, you're Captain Jack Crossman. Colonel Lovelace's man? Yes? Good, good. Don't want to reprimand the wrong fellah, do we? Could be two captains with only one hand. The army is quite proficient at producing cripples.'

'Reprimand?'

'Yes, 'fraid so, young man.' The colonel was not much older than Jack, but he seemed to have assumed a paternal role. 'I hear you've been rather indiscreet. In danger of being compromised, so I'm told.'

Jack feared his visits to Potaka had been observed.

'I think I can explain. You see—'

The colonel's hand came up. A massive appendage which blocked the light from the window.

'I don't want to hear any sordid details about what you do with your own cannon, Captain. I myself am a happily married man. I'm sure these *passions* which rule younger men like yourself are very difficult to manage. But control them, you must. How do you know this Maori woman isn't a spy? Does she ask you things – you know – in the heat of the moment?

It's easy to blurt things out when you're on the point of firing your weapon. Married I may be, but I know when my fuse has been lit it's hard to deny a request.' He chuckled. 'My own dear Emily has extracted many a promise of an expensive gown just at the point when the ball's on its way, travelling down the barrel.'

Jack's heart sank. 'How – how did you know about – about the Maori woman, sir?'

'Told of course. Colonel Lovelace. Expects me to put a stop to it. Now, I can't order you to stop seeing this native strumpet – well, I *can*, but I'm not going to. I expect you to look to your morals and begin behaving like a gentleman. Married man, ain't you? Start behaving like one, is my advice to you, Captain. These licentious manners might be all right in the back alleys of London, but they won't do for a British army officer. Lovelace mentioned your real family name is Kirk. Knew your father, by the way. Wonderful officer.'

Jack said, 'He wasn't licentious, of course.'

The sarcastic tone went right over the colonel's head.

'No, no. Very upright man, your pa.'

'Which makes it quite strange that I'm his bastard.'

The colonel immediately sat up very straight in his chair, making it sway and creak with the sudden violent shift of eighteen stone.

'What? Now don't you become insolent with me, Captain. That kind of language is not fitting in the office of an artillery man, whatever you might think. Colonel Lovelace has left strict instructions that you are to cease these clandestine meetings with this woman – for your own good, and for the good of the army. If you should reveal any sensitive information you could be shot as a traitor. No matter if it did come out while you were firing that howitzer between your legs. Get your priorities right, sir, that's my advice to you. Good morning.'

The colonel loved his euphemisms, that much was certain.

'Good morning, Colonel.'

Jack left the man's office seething. How dare Nathan do this to him? Why had Nathan not said something himself instead of humiliating Jack with this interview by a third person? Had Nathan wanted to punish Jack for his rejection of his future plans for him? Or did Nathan think that if he did the job himself, Jack would take less heed?

By spreading the story around, Jack was now bound to end the liaison. He suddenly realized Nathan had given him the excuse he needed to stop seeing Amiri. It was true that he had needed one. Well, Nathan had provided him with a coward's way out of his entanglement. And no doubt his friend, the ruthless espionage colonel, was thinking, one day he'll thank me for it.

Eleven

'That's *Captain* Wynter to you,' said Abe, in a friendly way of course, for he was speaking to a youthful naval officer. 'I 'appen to be a commissioned officer in the Honourable Artillery Company.'

'Oh, I didn't know that,' said the young man in blues standing before him. From his expression he might have added, 'And less I care,' but for the sake of civility was holding his tongue. 'In that case, Captain Wynter, I have to inform you that we have a passenger on board our vessel without funds. He has informed the purser that you will pay the bill for his passage from Sydney, Australia.'

'Does he now? Sounds a bit forward to my way of thinkin'. An' you, sir, I take it, is the purser?'

'I am indeed that very man.'

'Well, I can tell you straight out,' said Abe Wynter very slowly, twirling his cane, 'that there's about as much chance o' that as an elephant saying "How'd y'do?"'

'You have no intention of settling his debt?'

They were standing in the doorway of a coffee shop in New Plymouth, with passers-by glancing at them.

184

'Can you whistle?' asked Abe Wynter, then added rudely, 'I've been in the navy meself and I know you salts whistle all the time. Well, you can whistle for your money, sir, that's what you can do. Pipe the money aboard, why don'tcha?'

The young man straightened his back. 'There is no need to be offensive, Captain Wynter. I will inform the unfortunate Mr Strickland of your decision. He will likely rue your name from debtor's prison, for that's where he's going if he doesn't pay his charge. Good day, sir.'

The naval officer turned on his heel and was striding away when a pale-faced Abe Wynter called him back.

'Wait a bit – I meant no offence. It was just my little joke. Strickland, you say? Arthur Strickland?'

'That was the name he gave us.'

'Big man, hangs low at the shoulders, stoopin' like?'

'A reasonable description.'

'Scarred lip, 'ere?' Abe pointed to the right-hand corner of his upper lip. 'Nose sort of twisted sideways?'

'Captain,' replied the officer, impatiently, 'I do not have time to describe Mr Strickland from stem to stern. The colour of his underwear is unknown to me. We are speaking of the same man, I have no doubt. Now, do I tell him you have no interest in his plight, or shall we come to terms here and now?'

'Coffee shop.' Abe indicated with his cane, pointing with the end mounted with a silver hawk. 'You drink coffee?'

'I do indeed.'

'Then let's wash away the taste of last night's brandy-wine and settle this man Strickland's debts at the same time.' Abe entered the coffee house, followed by the young man. 'Now tell me all you know about Mr Arthur Strickland. 'Ow did he come to be aboard your ship, eh? And what's 'is story so far?'

Abe Wynter learned all he could about his old shipmate from the young officer, who once he had been paid was quite willing to impart as much knowledge as was required. Finally, the officer departed leaving Abe still swilling down strong coffee. Twenty minutes later a large man in ragged breeches entered the coffee house. He peered around the gloomy interior until his eyes settled on Abe Wynter. A sort of twisted grin, which went the opposite way to the direction of his nose, appeared around his mouth. He walked over to Abe's table.

''Ello, Striker,' said Abe, not moving. His face having turned to stone.

'Abe, me old shipmate. 'Ow are yer? No handshake for your pal? What? You an' me, we struck it rich together.'

Abe made no move, but nodded to the chair opposite.

'And you've gone and spent yourn?'

'Every penny,' said Striker, sighing.

'Don't tell me – cards and dice?'

'The very same.'

They both laughed loudly at this, making

heads turn in the coffee house.

Abe said, 'You was always one to gamble, Striker. You'd wager on a snail race, you would.'

'And have.'

The tension between the two men was a physical presence in the room and many people there were aware of it.

Striker was then overcome with a violent fit of coughing. He took out a piece of old sailcloth and filled it with phlegm, while Abe looked on – not in disgust, but in alarm. Striker obviously caught the look for he said, 'Yep, consumption. Me lungs are in shreds, matey. It was that trip we did around the Horn what was responsible. 'Ow you got away free, I don't know. You was always the lucky one, Abe.' He put the damp piece of sailcloth back in the pocket of his breeches. 'Australia was a bit 'arsh on the chest. I heard the air was good 'ere, in New Zealand, so I came.' Striker sniffed loudly. 'An' it is, too, ain't it? Nice clean air. Should put a couple years on what I got left.'

'So that's it? Dyin'?'

Striker's expression hardened. 'Not as quick as you might want, Abe – but gettin' there gradual.'

Abe tried to look shocked. 'I don't want you to die, Striker. Gawd 'elp me, you're my friend.'

'Yes, an' we share a dark secret together, don't we, Abe? But don't look so panicky, like a rabbit lookin' down a gun-barrel. I ain't goin' to say nothin' to no one.' He paused. 'I need you to stake me though. I need to earn a livin'. I don't want to be a leech on you, Abe, an' expect you to give me money when I want it. I ain't a beggar. I've always worked for me bread, you know that.'

'Of course I do. What is it? Gold prospectin'?'

'Fishin'. I'm from a fishin' family in Cornwall.'

'I thought you was a tin miner?'

'An' fishin'. Mining and fishing. Them was the two main occupations of my folks in Boscastle. I need a boat, Abe. Somethin' nice and neat I can handle. I'll get a local boy to assist. What do they call 'em here? Abos?'

'Naw, Maoris. Look, I'll get you a boat. You'll need nets and things, too, I don't doubt. Is that what you really want to do, Striker?' asked Abe Wynter, to whom fishing was a foul occupation. 'Fishin'? Won't the cold water bring on your sickness?'

'Good clean air is what I want. An' if it does bring it on, you won't be arguin', will you, Abe? Now, can you stand me a meal? I've a hankerin' to fill my belly.'

Abe stood up, his feelings in turmoil. It was a great shock, having Striker here on his new stamping grounds, but the good thing was that his old shipmate would not be here for long by the sound of his chest. Abe had good reason to want to be rid of Striker. He did not believe that fishing would be a healthful occupation for a man with consumption, so he was more than willing to stake Striker in this enterprise. One of his Maori aides was an ex-fisherman. He would give him to Striker to assist with his fishing. And if Striker were to linger too long in this world, why the man would be there, available, to give his old shipmate a nudge into the next.

It was while Abe and Striker were in the harbour-side eating house that Gwilliams and Harry Wynter entered. Abe signalled to his younger brother to approach their table.

'Harry, this is me old shipmate, Striker. He was one of them what was with me on the findin' of the gold in the Ballarat fields, along with poor old Irish Danny. Striker, this is me younger brother, Harry. He's an army man, as you can see. It's his long-term career, an't it, Harry? Goin' to be a sergeant one day.'

'Been one,' snapped Harry. He nodded at Striker, seemingly wary as ever, but obviously found it prudent to be polite. 'Pleased t'meecha. You stayin' here, now?'

'Yep, your brother has very kindly offered to stake me in the fishin' industry.'

Harry looked understandably surprised. 'But an't you rich like him?'

'I was,' said Striker, with a grimace, 'but I was unlucky at the cards. Misfortune follered me like a black dog and finally brought me down. Can't even afford a shark steak, which my ship-mate says he will kindly donate to me empty stomick.'

Gwilliams knew what was coming, just as much as Abe Wynter did, and he tried to steer Harry Wynter away. Harry was having none of

189

it. He would have his say.

'You stake *him*,' he yelled at his older brother, 'but you can't think to help your own flesh an' blood? I'm your next o' kin, I am – it says so in the paymaster's book. Next o' kin! But do you treat me like the family I am? No. You let me rot in this man's army. You're a fuckin' bastard, Abraham Wynter. I could kick you.'

'I'm also a bloody captain in this man's army, brother,' Abe yelled back. 'You have more respect for your seniors, you little twat. I'm an officer in the HAC. I could 'ave you court-martialled for insubordination. I'm thinkin' about doin' it, right now.'

'Go on then, arse-face. Do it. I'll tell 'em how you wet the bed when you was gone five or more. Yes, he did,' shouted Harry, turning to the rest of the diners. 'Proper little snot, he was. Had a punctured bladder. Wun't be surprised if he din't still do it, the wettin'. Cried like a babby when our dad belted him for it. Like a babby, he did.'

Furious, Abe was on his feet, his hawk-topped cane in his hand.

'I'll knock your fuckin' block off, you lyin' little squirt. Tell on me, eh? I'll swing for you, you...'

Harry lifted his rifle and aimed at his brother's chest. There was menace in his face and voice. His eyes glittered.

'Swing for me, would ya?' Harry said softly. 'I'll do the same for you, brother.'

'Jesus!' muttered Striker, his chair scraping as

he moved out of the firing line.

Gwilliams stepped forward, but Harry said, 'Back off, Corp. I got this one in me sights. I can drop him like a sack o' spuds before you get near me.'

Abe felt the cold sweat ooze to his brow. He stared into his brother's eyes. Who knew what went on in young Harry's prematurely white-haired skull? His younger sibling had always been crazy and a lot had happened to him in the army to make him crazier. Look at him, with his milky blind eye, his ugly scarred countenance and his broken-boned body! A quiet madman if ever there was one. Why hadn't the army got rid of him? Sent him to Bedlam where he belonged? But they hadn't, for here he stood, a long black weapon in his hands and a thin evil smile on his features. Harry Wynter was just as likely to squeeze that trigger as not, for the consequences of his actions were always so far back in his brain they more often than not failed to emerge until after the deed had been done. It was of no use to Abe that afterwards Harry would regret those actions. Abraham Wynter would be lying on the floor, blood gushing from his carcass, departing this world in terrible pain.

'Harry, Harry...'

'Don't you Harry me. You're as rich as a king, you are, an' you give me nothin'. Yet here you be, givin' this man who an't so much as a tenth-cousin what he wants while you leave your brother to the workhouse.'

'You an't in no workhouse, Harry.'

'No, I'm in worse. I'm in a bloody army what whips me when they got the notion an' tosses me in the clink when they feels like it. In fact –' Harry squinted down the barrel – 'I'd be better off dead. There's got to be a better place up there, where Harry can rest 'is weary head an' not worry about them who put upon 'im. A place o' peace and quiet.'

There was a deathly hush from the patrons of the eating house now. Forks full of meat and vegetables were poised on their way to open mouths. A little man with cracked spectacles on the tip of his nose put his fingers in his ears. A large woman behind Abe began sniffling softly, but the now audible clattering of crockery and utensils from the kitchen – whose chattering occupants had no inclination of the life-and-death struggle going on in their dining room – would probably be the last thing Abe Wynter would hear as he left the world.

After two full minutes Harry lowered the Enfield and shrugged.

'You an't worth it, you black-hearted sod.'

A sigh of relief went round the whole room.

Harry walked towards the door, Gwilliams joining him, and to everyone's amazement and indignation they were both laughing.

'Weren't even loaded,' cried Harry over his shoulder, as if the joke were priceless. 'Not even a pea up the spout. Nice t'meecha, Mr Striker, sir. Hope you enjoy your steak, brother. Don't let it choke you.'

Striker let out a sigh of relief. 'You was lucky

there, Abe – he's got junk in his attic, ain't he?'

Abe sat down still staring balefully at the doorway.

'I'll give 'im junk, the little bastard. There was a time when I used to punch his 'ead just for exercise. Now he treats me like an equal. Well, never mind all that...' He turned back to Striker. 'Let's get you sorted out with the fishin' industry. I got this Maori who's done a lot of that. He'd suit you fine as a helper.'

Striker gave his ex-partner a thin smile.

'You wouldn't be thinkin' of doing away with me, Abe, would you? I don't want this helper assistin' me to a watery grave. You really ain't got nothin' to fret about, you know. I'm as fearful of treading the planks of the gallows as you are.'

Abe tried to look suitably shocked. 'I wun't do nothin' like that, Striker, you know I wun't.'

'I don't no nothin' of the sort.'

But they left it at that.

'Now,' said Abe, after a suitable period of silence between them, 'let me get you a beefsteak. They do a good one 'ere, nice and bloody in the middle, if you arsk 'em.'

'No, thanks,' replied Striker, 'I only eat fish now.'

Abe looked sharply at his shipmate.

'No meat at all?'

'Can't keep it down.'

Abe shrugged and let out a shout of laughter that was not shared by Striker.

'Suit yourself,' he said, signalling to the

193

waiter. 'You can eat garouper if you want. Me? I'm 'aving a nice fat juicy wodge of beef as rare as you like.'

Later Abe took Striker to the Maori village on the edge of town. Striker was impressed by the native houses he saw there. He admired the carved doorways, support posts and rafters in houses constructed of wrought timber. Not all the houses were elaborate, but they were all solidly built of seasoned wood, and Striker had once been a carpenter's mate so he knew good workmanship when he saw it. He expressed the opinion that he would not mind sleeping in one of those dwellings himself.

'I'm sure that can be arranged,' said Abe, a little puzzled by his shipmate's admiration of the Maori architecture. 'Tarawa would probably take you in, if you asked 'im. If you want fishin' it might be better to build a little place near the beach. He'll help you with that, too, if you want.'

'Tarawa bein'?'

'This helper I'm givin' you.'

'Ah, yes. That fellah.'

They found Tarawa and the Maori was delighted to be assigned to 'Boss's friend' to teach him how to fish in local waters. They sat on the floor of Tarawa's hut and discussed the details. To his own surprise Abe found himself just as fascinated as Striker by the local fishing techniques.

'You like to fish with net or with line?' Tarawa asked Striker.

'Oh, line and hook. I'm not one for the nets.'

'Good – line is better for excitement.'

Before the end of the morning Abe had a list of things to buy for the pair, including the canoe, hooks, hand nets for catching the bait and various other items. Abe told Striker he would be fully equipped for his new profession and that no expense would be spared. Later the two white men went off to get drunk together while Tarawa set about purchasing the necessary equipment.

Over a drink Abe Wynter bragged to his old shipmate. 'I got a nice set-up 'ere, Striker. I'm a land-dealer.'

'So I 'eard. You always was a canny bastard, Abe.'

'That's me. An' you wanna know somethin' else? I got this steam gun – sent to England for it. Perkin's extr'ordinary steam gun. Fires a thousand shots a minute. Mow down a whole tribe, you could, if you wanted to. Might have to. Might have to, indeed. Dead stubborn, some of them. Hang on to their land like it was gold itself. But they got to learn their betters are 'ere. There's certain parcels of good bottom land just goin' to waste. I aim to get some of 'em, soon now. An' if I get stood in the way of, well, I know what to do, don't I?'

'You was always a ruthless bastard, Abe.'

Twelve

Over the next few months Jack was relieved to find that Amiri made no pressing demands upon him. They ceased to become lovers but met casually as friends. Jack was mildly upset by the fact that she did not seem to miss their illicit liaisons while he still yearned for her body. He knew he should have been glad of this lack of passion on her part, but he was a man, and a man's ego is ever capable of being wounded by seeming indifference. After a while he too came to accept that he would not suffer greatly from ending the affair.

A new governor arrived on the islands. Sir George Grey was reappointed to the governorship of New Zealand and Gore Browne was sent packing. Grey had already had some successful years as governor and many, including the Maori, welcomed his return. He was more level-headed than Browne, more ready to listen, and was regarded by both settlers and Maori as a man of intellect and good judgement.

Those same months saw the death of the old Maori king, Potatau (or Potato as the settlers would have it), and his son Matutaera took over the role of kingship, backed by the kingmaker,

Tamihana. However, a truce was declared which meant that trouble only came from roving bands of young Maori warriors. Their way of life had been disrupted by the wars which had taken them from their peaceful homes and flung them abroad, they harassed both Maoris and pakeha alike. They stole horses and goods, and some became bandits on the highways. One of the things they liked to do most was chop down pakeha flagpoles. They were costing the government a fortune in flagpoles.

This was an idle time for soldiers like Jack, who received a letter from his wife Jane saying she had not yet left England.

My father has been ill with the typhoid and though now recovered from the worst he is too weak for me to leave him for a while, my darling, but rest assured as soon as his health improves enough I shall be on my way to your arms.

This was not good news. Jack realized he could have accepted Nathan's offer of swift promotion and written to Jane to tell her to stay where she was until he was sure of a long-term posting. Now he was kicking his heels. Indeed, he was still waiting for news from Abraham Wynter that his land had been purchased. The waiting seemed interminable, though Jack was aware that these deals were long and drawn-out with much haggling on both sides.

This heel-kicking did not last far into 1863, for

there was an ambush of a party of two officers and seven other ranks of the 57th Regiment who were in the process of taking a military prisoner to New Plymouth for his trial. Only one man, a private, escaped the massacre. Peace was at an end. The war resumed after this action, but there were moves in the British parliament to remove all British troops from the islands. It was felt that the civilian population should look after themselves by forming a more effective militia. Once again Jack thought he would be moved from New Zealand if he continued to remain an officer in the British army.

The troops themselves were learning new songs that had drifted over from the American continent where a civil war was in progress. 'Dixie' and 'John Brown's Body' were heard in the valleys and hills of North Island, New Zealand, sung with fervour if not with an understanding of the sentiments that lay behind the words. The British soldier was not shy of borrowing new marching tunes from an ex-colony. And in a darkness lit by campfires, courtesy of an Irish fiddler, they listened to the minor key of an American violin tune that for some reason made them think of home and privately weep for their loved ones, though they had never actually heard the melody before that night.

'So which side would you be on in this Yank war?' Harry Wynter asked of Corporal Gwilliams one night. 'North or South?'

'I'm a Canadian,' the copper-bearded Gwilliams replied. 'I ain't got feelings one way or the other.'

'You got to have. You're always braggin' about these pioneer men you shaved. Sometimes you say you're an American. I don't think you know what you are, Corp, but anyway, you were down in Americy a lot. You got to have some side to you.'

'Well, it's true I was brung up there, some. But as to the South wantin' to leave the Union, I guess it's up to them. I don't see why the North should try an' force 'em to stay in. I don't hold with slavery, myself, but that ain't what the war was started about. That came in later. It was all started about the break-up of the Union. In some ways that's what these Maori wars are about too. The Maoris don't want to be governed by someone else. They want to make their own laws, and you can't blame 'em for that. But the governor needs to have control over the whole island to make things work overall, that's a fact also. So you got two facts that crash head-on into each other like chargin' bulls. The only difference between the American war and this one is the geography. You can split the North and South along a border, but you can't do that here 'cause the British is all in pockets and pieces. Now, if the British said, "We'll have South Island and the Maoris can have North Island," it might work for a while. But then there'd be a war sooner or later 'cause neighbours always end up hating each other's guts.'

Harry Wynter said, 'You talk a good argument, Yank.'

'Well, my brains ain't mushed-up like yourn, with too much bad gin, and too many kicks to the head.'

'I don't start them fights,' yelled Wynter.

'The hell you don't,' Gwilliams yelled back.

Always, two of the group's three pack-mules became restless when the soldiers argued and they kicked out at the air behind them to make manifest their displeasure. The third was a mild contented soul who was happy to simply chew on hay and mind his own damn business. King told his men to calm down and went to quieten the animals.

The mapping team were out in the bush close to the Ruahine region. Giant kauri trees, like ancient forest kings, dominated some smaller trees known as 'five-fingers', under which the men had pitched their tents. Ta Moko was teaching the pakeha about the landscape and its creatures. The Maori was a good tutor and enthusiastic concerning the nature of his birthplace. He pointed out the kea and kaka parrots, and called them 'nuisance birds'; taught the men which fungi were edible and which were poisonous; caught skinks for them to study closely; taught them how to catch tereru and tui birds with a long pole and a noose to cook in a hangi. He showed them how to make pendants out of hardened globs of kauri gum, to take home with them. Life was like a holiday for these army men, whose contemporaries were either marching around parade squares or guarding some perimeter.

However, there were minor problems that marred this walk through paradise. The stores were not lasting well, which is why Ta Moko had turned to fungi, birds and plants. All the sugar had been lost when they rafted down some rapids; the flour had got wet and turned to paste; and the bacon had developed a green fungus which, though probably harmless, put the men off eating it. They had been living on coffee and dried apples for a fortnight, plus the country fare provided by their very able guide and mentor. Jack, who had now joined his team, was particularly upset that his only pot of jam had been broken and the contents quickly devoured by the local insect life.

Sergeant King was grumbling as usual about the bush and the fact that it slowed down his work of mapping.

'This?' said Gwilliams, from the other side of the campfire. 'This ain't nothin' compared to the mapping of America.'

King snorted. 'What do you know of such things?'

'I may be just a barber, but I ain't dumb. I listen to stories, same as everyone. There was a pathfinder we had, who went over the Rockies in midwinter. Frémont was his name. This was back in 1848, when they was trying to get a railroad through the mountains to California. They went into San Juan Mountains of Colorado and got lost in snow higher than houses, wanderin' around in blindin' white tunnels. Froze, they did, in the bitter cold. There weren't no game, the pack animals all died, and they ended up eatin' each other. The weak ones was left to die while those with a bit more heart found their way out. It was wrote up by a man called Charlie Preuss. Now them's problems, Sarge. You ain't got near half them problems here.'

'He's right, Sergeant,' said Jack, warming his hands over the flames of the fire. 'You have very few obstacles here, compared with India – or the Colorado mountains. Why, there's not even a snake to sneak into your tent at night. Certainly no bears, or tigers, or any creature with malicious intent. We're lucky.'

Just at that moment a very large rat decided to dash out and make off with a large chunk of the fetid bacon. It ran over Jack's foot and he leapt in the air and drew his revolver, firing wildly at the rodent, missing with every shot. It disappeared into the darkness of the ferns that covered the ground, the meat in its fangs.

'Big bastard,' grunted Gwilliams. 'How come you missed 'im, Captain?'

Jack shuddered. 'I was aiming rashly.'

'You was, you was,' agreed his corporal. 'Nasty beggar, eh? How come you got such big rats, Moky?'

'This is not our rat, it is yours,' replied the Maori with dignity. 'You bring him in your ships.'

'But you got rats, right?'

'Not so big ones. They are nearly all gone, our old rats. Your rats have killed them all.'

Jack knew the talk was getting rather danger-

202

ous, since some Maori drew an analogy with what had happened to the rodents of New Zealand, believing the pakeha would eventually exterminate them in the same way his rat had annihilated theirs.

'Never mind whose rat it was – it stole our bacon.'

'Lousy bacon, anyway,' said Gwilliams.

'We could have boiled it,' said Jack, 'but now it's gone.'

There was the sound of a branch cracking, out in the darkness.

'That ain't no rat,' whispered Gwilliams, leaping to his feet.

The other men immediately jumped up also, reaching for their weapons. First thoughts were of a hostile Maori party. They moved away from the light of the fire and melted into the shadows. King tried to take a precious box of instruments with him, but it was too heavy and he had to drop it again. They waited with beating hearts in amongst the five-finger trees that surrounded the camp.

Shortly afterwards, two figures came into the light of the fire. One was a bent wizened old Maori man wearing only a pair of ragged trousers. The other was a small boy of about five years wearing a coat, shirt and trousers. Both were barefoot. The old man looked about him with rheumy eyes while the boy bent down and picked up a cold roasted drumstick and absently began to eat it.

'*Tena koutou!*' called the old man in a cracked

voice.

Ta Moko was the first to respond. *'E mara!'*

The soldiers now emerged from their hiding places, relieved that it was only harmless Maori, but still slightly wary. It was possible the old fellow was a decoy – but unlikely, since the Maori preferred open battle between heroes to subterfuge.

'Ah, pakeha,' muttered the old man, through a toothless mouth, his red tongue flashing. 'I see you.'

'I see them too, Grandfather,' said the boy, still munching away. 'They are afraid of us.'

'You watch your mouth, boy,' growled Harry Wynter, 'that's my chicken you're eatin'.'

The child looked at the drumstick. 'Not chicken, fool – kaka.'

'I'll lay you one...'

'Quiet, Wynter,' snapped Jack. He addressed the old man. 'What are you doing out here in the wilderness?'

'I am taking the boy to his mother – over there.' The elderly Maori pointed south. 'His family was sick and I looked after the boy for some time. But back there –' he pointed over his shoulder – 'there are bodies of soldiers. Five men.' He stamped the ground with his bare foot. 'Too hard for me to dig. But you could make them graves, sir.'

'I killed them all with my spear,' cried the boy, throwing the kaka bone into the fire. He stood akimbo. 'I am a great warrior.'

'You're a blamed pain in the neck, brat!' snarl-

204

ed Wynter.

The boy began to chant, and dance backwards and forwards in the way of a warrior preparing to attack the enemy.

'I shall break your thin arm bones in two,' cried the child, addressing Wynter, as he performed a creditable haka. 'My war club will crack your whitey head like a duck's egg.'

He stuck his tongue out fully, down to the tip of his chin.

The old man said, 'Don't listen to the boy. He has imagination.'

Jack nodded. 'Nothing can be done tonight,' he said, 'but tomorrow morning I would like you to take us to the place where you found the bodies. For now, you may eat with us, and sit by our fire. We are honoured to have your company.'

'No,' said the boy, looking at his grandfather. 'We will not sit with you. You are pakeha, our sworn enemy. My father has killed many pakeha and will kill many more. It is true I did not kill these soldiers, but it must have been my father. My father will kill you too, when he comes this way, so you had better go home, you bloody pakeha.'

'If that half-pint don't shut his mouth, I'm goin' to shut it for him,' grumbled Wynter. 'He's makin' my nerve-ends ragged with that squeaky voice of his. Brats like him should know their place. We was taught to be seen and not heard. A good beltin' is what he wants.'

No one took any notice of this speech, which

sent Harry Wynter into the sulks.

Ta Moko took care of the old man and the boy, giving them some food and water. The old man asked, 'Do you have whisky...?'

King, later talking with Jack, said, 'Do you think there was a massacre here? Maybe these soldiers were sent to find us and were ambushed?'

'I don't know, Sergeant, it's possible. Certainly I've never heard of any other pakeha straying this far from safety. I had thought that we are the only ones out here. Unless something has happened back in New Plymouth that requires our presence, though I can't think what.'

Ta Moko came over to where Jack was sitting.

'I have talked to the old man,' he reported, 'but he swears neither he nor the boy touched the bodies. He believes it to be bad luck to take anything from the dead. I believe he is telling the truth.'

'Fine. Thank you, Ta Moko.'

King said, 'Sir, they could be a scouting party. Perhaps the generals are thinking of marching this way?'

'We won't know until the morning, and I'm not going to spend the whole night guessing, Sergeant. Get some sleep.'

The following morning the old man and the boy led the party to a place on the edge of a forest. The smell of death has long arms and it reached out to them before they were anywhere near the cadavers. When they reached the place where the bodies lay, they found a bivouac made of staves and ferns. Inside this shelter lay a row of three bodies, as if sleeping, while the other two were sitting upright, blankets wrapped around them, staring at each other across a cold dead fire. One of the sitting dead had gripped his own hair at the point of leaving this earth, and his fingers had locked in that position, remained there, clutching, until there was very little flesh on the claws, only white bone.

The bodies were fetid; life having left them a good while ago. This was no recent slaughter, but something that had happened months previously. Eyes had been eaten by ants, which even now formed a trail into the recesses of the corpses. However, though the bodies lying in the bivouac had been knifed or bayoneted, no wounds could be found on the upright bodies. Some of the weapons were stacked in a wigwam-shaped sheaf not far from the ashes of the fire. They were found to be loaded, though the metal barrels were red with rust. As firearms they were now useless lumps of iron, their working parts seized by rust.

Both of the sitting bodies, glaring at each other with sightless sockets, were carrying knives and pistols on their person. These were revealed when Gwilliams and Ta Moko tried to lift one of the dead men and his clothes fell apart like worn tissue paper to expose a small arsenal. One of the corpses had no fewer than four pistols and three knives, plus his bayonet. The other had a similar number of bladed weapons, but only two pistols. There was dried blood on the blades of the bayonets carried by both men as if the steel was used at the very last moment.

King said to Jack, 'Cut down while they slept.'

'And the two at the fire?'

'There you have me, sir.'

'Gwilliams, what do you think?' asked Jack. 'Do you believe it was a Maori attack?'

Gwilliams screwed up his face and shook his head. 'What I reckon is the two at the fire killed the others – stabbed 'em in their sleep. Poor bastards didn't even have time to struggle. Two or three quick stabs of the blade. I'll wager they didn't even wake up.'

'I'll go along with that,' King said. 'The sitting men were still holding the bloody bayonets they used on the sleeping ones.'

'And the other two?'

Gwilliams shook his head. 'How they come to be sitting up, looking at each other, has got me beat. Ain't they got marks on 'em?'

'Not that I can see,' said Jack.

Ta Moko inspected the corpse on the far side of the campfire ashes, which was still in its original upright position.

'Yes,' Ta Moko said, 'this one has a hole in the back of his skull.' He bent his head and inspected the face of the dead man. 'And some front teeth missing – he was shot through his mouth.' He looked across the ashes again. 'His friend over there did not like the staring contest and in the end drew a pistol and ended it.'

'But why?' asked King, throwing up his hands. 'What was it all about? Did they just get

208

lost in the bush and go crazy?'

They found out when they lifted one of the cadavers in the bivouac. It was heavy. Very heavy. The pockets of the man's breeches were full of gold dust. When they checked the other corpses, they too had gold on them: some in dust and some in small nuggets the size of grave gravel. Only the last man to die had no gold hidden on his clothes. Instead, they found it in his stomach – or where his stomach used to be. It appeared he had swallowed gold dust and so killed himself. There was no explanation for this bizarre twist that sounded logical to Jack and his men. Each of them made up his own story, but in all the made-up tales there was something missing – reason. But where there is gold, reason often goes flying off somewhere, and madness takes over.

'Manius Aquillius, the Roman general, he swallered gold,' said the classical scholar, Corporal Gwilliams. 'He was made to. Ancient king by the name of Mithridates got a hold of him and poured melted gold down his throat. Choked on molten gold. Ain't that a dandy way to go? Better'n a length of hemp round your neck.'

'How do you know all this crap?' asked Wynter. 'Who put it in your head?'

'Read it in the preacher's books,' explained Gwilliams, 'man who took me in and raised me like his own. Anyway, Captain, what are we gonna do with all this yellow metal? Share it out?'

Wynter looked eagerly at his commanding officer.

'Yes, the corp's right, sir. Only thing to do. Share it out. Finders keepers.'

Jack sighed. 'I'm sorry, men, I can't do that. I know it's a disappointment to you, but it can't be done. Sergeant King has just reminded me there was a robbery last year, down in Central Otago. I'm certain this gold had already been purchased by the government agency from the miners and was on its way to Auckland. These soldiers were escorts on that convoy. They shot the officer and their sergeant and were never seen again. Well, we've found them.'

Wynter looked frantic. 'Yes, but, Captain, no one will know. You take the biggest share, 'cause you're the officer. You don't need to do this one by the book, sir. None of us will let on, will we? Just divide it up as you see right, and we'll all keep mum.'

Sergeant King said, 'Private Wynter, get those thoughts out of your head. Do you want to end up like these dead men? That's what gold does to you. It robs you of your honour and sensibility. Think of what your friends and relations would say; your fellow churchgoers in your village back home in England. Where's your honesty?'

Wynter was almost crying now, knowing that even if the officer wavered, which did not look like happening, the sergeant was so bloody stiff with righteousness, there was no bending him, let alone getting him to break. Sergeant King was incorruptible.

'I an't got no honour to be robbed of – an' my sensibility says take the blamed gold and God-damn any noble thoughts.'

'Blasphemin' won't help you,' Gwilliams muttered. 'My sentiments is with you, Harry, but I ain't goin' to get tried and shot for a hand-ful of dust. Come on, let's bury these poor bastards. They tried the bad way, and they failed at that too.'

The three Maori watched all these exchanges between the white men with mild interest. The boy had not seen such animation in pakeha before and wondered what it was all about. Even a child so young, with little knowledge of the world, had heard the 'word ', but he had thought little of its value. He owned no sheep or land either, but if asked he might have chosen those over this cold yellow stuff. His grandfather was aware of the importance of gold, but his life was almost over and any improvements to his last years in the world would come more from his fellow men than from a precious metal. Ta Moko was willing to accept what the captain thought right, for the captain knew the rules and knew the penalties for breaking them. If he was to become rich, all well and good, but if he was to remain poor that too was fate.

They dug a single shallow grave and put all the corpses in together, which was probably a last touch of irony for the souls who had once filled these husks. They died hating each other and now were going to spend eternity in a group embrace, bone locked with bone. Gwilliams chalked an epitaph on a rock face nearby. It read: 'They died for love – not for a woman, not for a man, but for a lump of metal.'

Sergeant King put all the gold in a set of double saddlebags, which one of the pack-mules would carry. The moon-coloured dust and grit filled two leather wallets the size of dinner plates and the mule King chose was the contented beast who took everything in its stride. He himself intended to lead the beast in the morning. He staked the beast on a patch of fresh grass and left her to graze contentedly.

Once the first sentry had been set, the rest of the men went to sleep around the fire. Their dreams were of many things but riches were paramount in most. One or two of them were heard to groan softly with the knowledge that they were so close to wealth but unable to grasp it. Even Ta Moko was tempted by the gold that lay just a few feet away. But the Maori, like Jack and King, was fully aware that such a theft would only end in misery. There were countless such stories: from the goldfields of Australia to the gold mines of Otago. Men who took part in such robberies eventually turned on one another. Death and betrayal were the usual rewards of such an enterprise.

Shortly before dawn, Jack was shaken roughly and sat up to see his sergeant looming over him.

'Sir – the pack-mule's gone – the one with the gold.'

'Wandered off?' muttered Jack, not happy at

being disturbed. 'We'll look for it when it gets light.'

'No, sir, not wandered off. Wynter's gone too.'

Jack sighed. 'Of course he has.'

Thirteen

They struck camp and Jack organized his men into two pairs thinking it was both dangerous and foolhardy to split them further. Sergeant King and Gwilliams were one pair; the captain and Ta Moko were the other. Unless he was absolutely crazy, Harry Wynter would have followed the stream from which they drew their water. This course ran north to south. King and Gwilliams took the northern route, while Jack and the Maori took the southern. The old Maori and his grandson left them to their search, shaking their heads and wondering about these pakeha, whose ways were strange and hard to fathom.

'Why did you put that man on the last sentry duty on his own? You might have guessed this would happen. This time Wynter's gone too far,' said Jack to King before they parted. 'His prior record makes this a hanging offence. They won't hesitate to give him the full penalty after all his other misdemeanours.'

King looked pained. 'He deserves punishment, sir – but death?'

The captain was scratching his stump, a certain sign that he was greatly disturbed. King

214

handed his commanding officer his chibouk pipe so that he could smoke his way through his anger. Once King had lit the pipe for him, it being a difficult action for a one-handed man, Jack puffed away and answered the NCO's question.

'The man is incorrigible, Sergeant. I can't do anything with him – never have been able to. You only know part of his history. The document listing his wrongdoings is longer and denser than a baron's genealogy chart. This is really the last straw. The men who took that gold murdered their officers. In stealing the gold from them, even after death, Wynter is collaborating. He'll swing, I'm sure of it. Ugly though it may be, I can see no way out of it for him. This time he's had it.'

'It might be better to shoot him and have done with it, sir.'

'Who's going to do that? You? Your skill with firearms is such you'll probably hit your own foot.'

'Well, I was thinking of Gwilliams – he's a sharpshooter.'

Jack shook his head and said sardonically, 'You're going to ask Gwilliams to execute his own comrade?'

King shrugged and said, 'They don't get on well together.'

'They drink together every night they're off duty. They may hate each other's guts, but they're all they've got. Even a cold-hearted man like Gwilliams would be loath to shoot his drinking companion.'

'I suppose you're right, sir. We'll have to take him in.'

Jack said, 'I'll bear in mind what you said though, should it be me who comes across him first, if I can put my scruples away. But between you and me, I would find that hard to do.'

Jack and Ta Moko set off south shortly after this conversation, following the brook, taking one of the two remaining mules. The other animal went with Gwilliams and King. It was rugged country with boulders and trees hindering a swift journey. Jack was cursing his private to high heaven, yet he had known all these years that it would at sometime come to this manhunt. Harry Wynter had been a shade away from the noose or the firing squad many a time. He was one of those unfortunate characters who seemed determined to have himself executed so that he could then blame the State or the army for his early demise. If there was life after death, the angels and archangels, or devils and demons, depending on how lenient was the great Judge, would regret the day that Harry Wynter entered their portals.

Ta Moko had looked for a trail beside the stream, of course, but Harry Wynter was not an idiot. He had been a member of a guerrilla group for many years and even someone with his low intellect had learned the skill of surviving in enemy territory by that time. The private had no doubt stuck to the gravelly stream bed for many miles and would therefore leave no prints, mule

216

or man. By midday they had made only seven miles and there was still no sign of where Wynter had left the stream. Jack reminded himself that he was chasing a man who had walked from the Crimea to India and had survived a journey that had killed all his officers and most of his comrades. Wynter was a hardened trekker, with feet of marble, and he could keep a steady pace for hours.

'We'd better stop here for a rest, Ta Moko,' Jack said, when they came across a glade. 'I need to change my socks.'

The rocks they had traversed had been serrated like steak knives and were sharp enough to penetrate the soles of Jack's boots. When he took off his footwear, he found his feet were torn and bleeding. He did his best to clean them up and put pads on the worst cuts, but he knew they would eventually slow him down a lot. His feet were definitely not made of any stone whatsoever. Any long journeys in his earlier life had been made by horse, while Wynter had always had to walk. Back home, many labourers walked ten or more miles to find work each day. Some walked twenty. Men like Jack, born into the aristocracy, had feet almost as tender as those of a baby. Of course he had done some walking since then, one or two long marches without a mount, but the damage had been done in his childhood and was not rectifiable now.

Ta Moko's feet, on the other hand, were bare. But they showed no sign of damage. He had some sort of trick of treading on the edges of sharp stones and rocks, and coming off unscathed. Forced treks like this one were meat and gravy to a Maori. He looked with sympathy at the bloody remains of the officer's toes and heel pad, and shook his head.

'We must slow down, Captain, to give you chance to heal.'

'Can't do that,' muttered Jack, whose further discomfort was a sodden blue jumper, which had been soaked in the spray of a waterfall they had passed. 'We must catch this man if we can.'

Socks changed, pads on wounds, they ate a fish which Ta Moko caught from the stream. Jack had never eaten anything so muddy-tasting in his life, but he knew that a beggar could not be a chooser. Ta Moko however seemed to consider the fish a great delicacy and kept smacking his lips long after the meal had been eaten.

'You must ride the mule,' said Ta Moko firmly, 'before your feet are cut to pieces.'

But the mule was already giving trouble. He had stopped once or twice with an obstinate air about him and Jack was afraid they would have to battle with the creature all the way. If he climbed on the mule's back and added to the weight of the equipment already there, he was sure the beast would rebel with the stubbornness for which they were renowned. Nevertheless Jack envied the hooves which clattered amongst the rocks, wondering why God in his wisdom had not thought fit to endow man with such wonderful permanent shoes.

In the afternoon they entered a narrow rocky-sided valley which was deeper than others they had come through. Kingfishers flew down this channel at great speed, diving for small shards of silver that wriggled in their beaks. A low mist hung about the ferns and tree-parasitic plants, which needed this kind of environment to flourish. The dampness of the valley floor made it soft to walk on and Jack even took off his boots so that he could feel the moss under his feet. This green carpet lasted for three miles and it saved Jack's tears for a while, though he knew it could not last. Nor could they stay there for the night, because the moisture-filled air would have soaked them. To sleep in such an atmosphere would invite respiratory problems. As well as tender feet, Jack had a weak chest and he knew they had to get out of the valley before he started coughing and gasping. He hated these weaknesses in himself but could only try to thwart them.

Night fell before they reached the end of the valley and they proceeded over the last few hundred yards by dark-lantern. Jack's idea of taking off his boots and socks had not been a good one. He had not realized that the moss had been full of mites, sometimes called sand-fleas by the pakeha, which had bitten his ankles and feet quite savagely. So as well as the flesh wounds he had swellings to contend with. It meant he could not replace his boots and had to walk barefoot over the new stony ground which met the end of the valley.

'How I hate that man,' Jack told himself, as he

inspected his extremities. 'I could cheerfully watch him hang at this moment in time.'

In the light of the fire Ta Moko lit, however, he watched the bats, darting this way and that, taking insects out of the air. It was not an unpleasant land, these islands of New Zealand. Not like India with its terrible biting insects, snakes and wild beasts. And even in the summer the heat was not appalling, as it had been in the Far East. There were diseases here, of course, but nothing compared to the Crimea or the Indian subcontinent. The only creature that gave Jack any trouble at all, and it was simply because of its size and revolting looks, was the giant weta insect, which was so fearsome and ugly it disgusted him. Jack would find these creatures in his clothes and shudder like a small girl.

The pair rigged a bivouac for the night, and Jack wrote up his official report diary, similar to a sea captain's log, which would condemn Private Harry Wynter. Had they caught the man within a couple of miles of the last camp, he might have had a chance, but Jack knew that this was the last escapade of his troublesome private. This report in his diary would put the noose around Harry Wynter's neck. It was not without some misgivings that Jack closed the cover of the black book, wrapped it in a waterproof skin, and put it in his saddlebag. Then he relaxed and smoked his chibouk for a few peaceful minutes.

'Ta Moko,' he said to the Maori, before they laid down their heads for the night, 'he must have left the stream now. Do you think he went the other way, and Gwilliams and King have him by now?'

'No, Captain – I have seen his prints, just before we made camp. They are still following the stream, but on the far bank.'

'Good, good. I wonder if he will break for open country.'

'He will die if he does. The tribes there will kill him.'

'What if he offers them gold?'

'They will kill him and *take* his gold.'

'Of course.'

Jack lay down in the darkness of the wilderness, wondering if he was going to sleep despite his physical fatigue. His mind was still buzzing and that was what kept people awake. His thoughts were swirling round in there; circular thoughts which seemed to have no end or beginning. Nathan was probably on his way to Australia by now and would not be around to help with the court martial. Nathan's influence might have saved Wynter if he had pleaded some sort of temporary insanity. But who would believe that a man who stole a fortune in gold was insane? Wasn't that the sanest thing on earth to do? To make oneself rich overnight and never have to worry about money again. No panel of officers was going to be convinced of madness in that respect. Nathan and Jack together might have argued that long years in the field had turned the man's head, but Jack could not do it alone.

They set off after Harry Wynter just after dawn. The sun came up over this green and pleasant land, glancing off the hills and honing the rivers like silver knives, so sharp the brightness hurt their eyes. Birds littered the trees and ran through the undergrowth. Insects formed smoky clouds over favourite shrubs and bushes.

Wynter's course was erratic and meandering and frustrated his pursuers with its unpredictability. Jack decided his private was either lost or had some thought of disguising his trail with loops and turns. It was, the captain decided, most likely the former. Despite being with a 'mapping group' for several years, Wynter had made no effort to learn the skills of navigation. Being the lowest member of the force he left the responsibility of pathfinding to his superiors, of whom there was always at least one with him. He had never been required to find his own way out in the field. Thus it was almost certain he did not know where he was going or what he was doing. At least, Jack believed that until late in the morning, when he discovered his spare compass was missing.

'Did I give you a compass?' he asked his Maori guide.

'Compass? What would I want a compass for? I know my way around these hills without pakeha toys.'

Ta Moko was irritated with the chase. Jack knew he had expected to catch the runaway very quickly. It hurt the Maori's pride to be outrun by a pakeha and a stupid one at that. But Jack knew they had made the usual mistake; the one all men made with Harry Wynter. They had underestimated him. Jack was fairly certain now that Wynter had stolen maps from the sergeant's folder too. The private knew exactly what he was doing and where he was going. Furthermore, his walking skills were second to none. He and his mule would keep up a pace that would be difficult to keep up with, let alone gain on.

Yet still, as Jack trudged through bogs brimming with mire, and along stream beds, and through tangled bush country, he could not imagine what was in Harry Wynter's mind. All those years when Wynter had not bothered to learn navigation, but knew the value of compasses and maps, Jack should have learned how the man thought. He should have been able to predict Wynter's moves. A good leader knows his men inside out, yet Wynter always had the ability to surprise Jack. Sometimes the surprises proved just how stupid the man was, but other times some hidden skill would come out.

It had to be remembered, while out in the wilds of New Zealand, that in civilian life Harry Wynter had been a bodger for a while. Bodgers mainly lived in the beech woods of Buckinghamshire and made rough chair legs out of greenwood, using a pole lathe made out of a springy sapling. It was a hard life, living in the open most of the time, using a bivouac for a shelter. Purchased food was not easy to come by in the forest, so bodgers lived for a greater part of the time on what they could find in the way of fungi, berries, roots and edible plants, supplementing their diet with the odd rabbit or wild bird. Harry Wynter certainly had outdoor skills or he would never have survived the bodger's life. There was no reason why he could not transfer those skills to New Zealand. Of course there would be plants unknown to him here, but he was astute enough to be able to recognize poisonous fungi and berries.

So, thought Jack, was his runaway preparing for a long haul out in the bush? Was he hoping to wear down his trackers, until they gave up and went home? It certainly seemed that way. Yet Jack had with him an expert on the landscape, on living in the wild, and on tracking down men who did not want to be tracked down. Did Harry Wynter honestly believe he could outrun and outwit a determined local Maori? Surely even Harry was not that much of an idiot? And there could have been no preconceived plan, for the gold did not appear until two days ago.

So the soldier's mind was still a closed book. Not a very fascinating book, but a mystery none the less. One thing was sure: Wynter was giving his officer the runaround, and that would please him. Because they felt they were getting close, Jack abandoned the mule, hoping they could move faster without it and so overtake the malefactor in front of them. They took the remainder of their provisions on their own backs and determined to sleep under the stars.

Mid-afternoon, on the third day of the chase, Jack and Ta Moko almost ran into a hostile Maori war party. The Maoris, their bodies gleaming with water since they had just waded through a torrential river, were standing on the bank talking. Jack was close enough to see the tattoos on their naked bodies as the Maoris had taken off their shirts and trousers and had fastened them round their heads to keep them dry. Harry Wynter's tracks went right alongside the river, but the Maoris did not seem aware they were standing on pakeha spoor. They seemed in no hurry to dry off, but remained chattering by the rushing white water, one or two of them cleaning their rifles which presumably they had held above their heads on the crossing.

Jack and Ta Moko were lying in a copse where the insects and spiders were using them as bridges. If they moved they would be seen. The copse was an isolated island in a sea of grass. Jack hoped the Maoris did not want to light a fire because the only source of wood for miles around was his hiding place. Then it began to rain, which was miserable for Jack and Ta Moko, though the Maoris by the river simply looked heavenward and laughed, carrying on with their conversations. They did, however, dress themselves which gave Jack hope. But even when the rain stopped, some twenty minutes later, the Maoris remained.

Finally, that which Jack dreaded most occurred.

A tall lean Maori left his group and walked up

the slope to the copse. If he had wanted to urinate he would have done it down by the river, so Jack knew he had come to defecate. Naturally he chose to do it by the bush behind which Jack and Ta Moko were lying. When the smell hit them Jack made a face at his Maori guide, but Ta Moko was in no mood to reciprocate. Then one of the Maoris down by the river decided, as a joke, to fire his musket over the trees to hurry his friend. This resulted in every bird and insect being stunned to silence.

'*Pöauau!*' yelled the Maori with his pants down.

The group down by the river laughed and jeered.

But a great danger had now asserted itself. Within the eerie silence the gunshot had caused, Jack could hear his pocket watch ticking. It sounded, to his ears, louder than a long-case clock. Surely the Maori on the other side of the bush could hear it? From that side came the tearing of grass and a grunt as the man finished his business. Jack willed the birds in the trees and the insects in the grasses to begin their chorus again. But they failed to respond to his prayers. The Maori stood up and seemed about to leave but then stopped. Jack knew he had heard the ticking and was listening. At that moment the group by the river called up to him, and they started ambling away to the west.

Still he listened, cocking his head to one side, clearly unable to discern where the sound was coming from. Jack hoped the man would think it was a beetle or insect of some kind. But the sound was too regular, too much like the ticking of clockwork and the Maori began to circumnavigate the bush.

Jack leapt up, but before he could do anything, the hostile Maori fell at his feet with a groan on his lips. He lay there, full stretch, now unconscious. Ta Moko was standing over him, with his stone *patu* in his right fist.

'Quickly, we must move,' said Ta Moko.

Jack and Ta Moko scrambled down the slope and ran eastwards. Luckily this was the direction taken by Wynter. Both knew the hostiles would soon miss their companion and go back and look for him. Then they would search for tracks, which would not be hard to find. The chase was now a threefold affair, with two pursuing one, and seven taking up the rear chasing all three. Jack and Ta Moko decided at that point to give up their chase and headed up into the hills, to seek somewhere to hide. They found a stony plateau, which they crossed without leaving prints, and thence to a cave. There they remained for two days, knowing the Maoris would be scouring the region for them.

On the sixth day they slipped out before dawn and retraced their tracks to the river. Once again they started out on the trail of the gold thief. When they reached a ford, they found that Wynter had crossed the river at that point, and to Jack's astonishment was heading back in the direction of New Plymouth.

'The man must want to be hanged,' he said to

Ta Moko. 'Once in India he tried to commit suicide – and failed. Surely this is no way to take one's own life? Hanging is a dreadful enough thing to watch – it must be a thousand times worse to have to participate. I wonder if he thinks he'll get the firing squad. He won't. Not for this.'

Jack and Ta Moko were hounded all the way back to the garrison at New Plymouth, but the hostiles never caught up with them. They found Sergeant King and Gwilliams had arrived a day before them. King met them coming through the main gate. King was clearly agitated, but Jack put this down to the fact that a man was soon to hang.

'Where's Wynter, in the stockade?' asked Jack, wearily trudging towards his quarters.

'No, sir – in his billet,' came the reply.

Jack almost stopped in mid-stride.

'In his billet? Surely not under open arrest?'

'Not that either.'

'Well, don't just stand there, Sergeant – tell me!'

'Private Wynter came back with the gold and reported to the orderly officer. He said he had been out with his mapping party when they had come across the victims of a robbery, probably the Otago robbery.' King's face was blotched red and Jack could see his sergeant was seething. 'However, he told the officer he – Private Wynter – had not trusted his commanding officer and NCOs to bring in the gold. He said he had heard talk of deserting with the money and sailing to Australia in a Maori skiff.'

'*What?*' cried Jack. 'That infamous...'

King continued, almost choking on his words. 'Wynter informed the authorities that he had gathered up the gold, put it on a mule, and brought it in for safe keeping. It was a very clever ruse, Captain, because he told them, "I couldn't be certain sure that they *was* goin' to take the gold – after all, it were an officer I've 'ad the honour of servin' under for many a year now – but I *thought* I heard it said. I didn't want to be part of no robbery, sir, for that's a hangin' offence, sure, so I brung it in anyway, then if I *were* wrong there's no harm done, is there, eh?"'

'He said that?' Jack expostulated. 'Why, I haven't given that man credit enough for his fiendish imagination. That is the cleverest lie I've heard in a long time. I'll strangle him. I swear I will. He has led us the sorriest dance ... I'll kill him with my bare hands. Where is he?'

Jack stormed into the billet that housed Harry Wynter and two dozen other soldiers. Wynter was lying on his cot, staring at the ceiling. Someone yelled, 'Officer present!' and all but him jumped up and stood to attention. Harry Wynter rose slowly and saluted; an insolent smile on his face.

'Sorry to beat you back, sir. Guess I've got better feet than the rest on you.'

'I'll beat your bloody back,' shouted Jack. 'What was this all about? I don't understand it, Wynter. Was it just to run us ragged? If so, you were playing a very dangerous game.'

The other soldiers in the room were round-eyed and glanced at one another, still remaining at attention.

Wynter turned an innocent face to his room comrades, then back to Jack again. 'Captain – I swear. I just wanted to see the gold get back safe. That's what I told the officers. It's the truth.'

'You lied, you insufferable toad. You insisted that you heard talk of desertion. There was no such talk. There was no such conspiracy.'

The look of innocence grew wider. 'I'm sorry, sir, I thought there was. I wasn't *sure* I heard such. I know me ears an't what they were, afore cannons did for 'em, but I did hear *somethin'* around those lines while I was fallin' off to sleep. I told the officers I *could* 'ave bin mistaken, but couldn't take the chance, see? You can understand that, sir, not takin' the chance? No harm done, after all.'

'No harm ... you nearly got us all killed, soldier.'

Wynter grinned. 'No, sir, not you. Take more'n a thing like that to get you killed, wun't it?'

Jack stared at his man for a full minute, but he knew that if he did not get out of the billet, there and then, he would strike him. King was concerned about this too, and steered his captain towards the door.

'I'll do it later,' he told Jack, 'behind the wash-rooms.'

'No, no, don't do that, Sergeant,' said Jack

wearily. 'I think he's beaten us this time. I'll see what I can do.'

Jack went back to his quarters, bathed, and changed into full dress uniform. Then he reported to General Cameron, who had already been informed of the affair. Jack stood before the general's desk, ready to give an account of himself. The general, a grave expression on his features, tapped with his pencil on the wood-work.

'What do you say to this accusation, Captain Crossman?'

'Sir, the man is an incorrigible liar. He has been under my command for several years now and has been nothing but trouble.'

'But, forgive me, Captain, for playing devil's advocate, but of course if it were true, you would say that.'

'It is true, sir. I hope you are not insinuating that *I* am a liar?'

The general rocked back in his chair and stared at Jack through narrowed eyes.

Jack continued. 'I can bring you a dozen reports and as many live testimonies to sub-stantiate my claim, sir. It is there in writing. It can be heard from the mouths of my NCOs. The man has an animal cunning. I have no doubt he intended to steal that gold – I can only think that by our dogged pursuit we forced him to return it to the garrison.'

The general's chair came upright again with a snap.

'About that gold, Captain. There is a small

amount missing. I say, *small*, but of course that is relative to the whole. In monetary terms I would put the value at over a thousand sovereigns.'

Jack was astonished by the general's vague look.

'Well, there you are, sir.'

'Well, there I am not, because this Private...?'

'Wynter.'

'Yes, this Private Wynter claims that the original thieves must have used the missing gold in some way.'

Jack laughed. 'They went on a shopping expedition in the bush?'

General Cameron frowned. 'No, Captain, they used it to bribe Maoris to let them through their territory.'

'Oh.' Jack was crestfallen. 'I suppose...'

'Or someone else could have taken it.'

Jack realized the general was again making veiled accusations regarding him and his NCOs. He was allowed no time to dispute this imputation because the general continued with, 'There's no proof, either way. Certainly I can't court-martial a man without the tiniest shred of evidence. He would claim he thought he was doing the right thing in bringing in the gold himself. It's a strange and funny do, Captain. I really don't know what to make of it.' General Cameron gave a huge sigh, then said, 'But on the plus side, most of the gold, the greater part of it, is now in our hands again. I will be mentioning your name in that regard, in my official dispatches, and no doubt there will be a commendation. With regards to this soldier, if it is as you say, I suggest you settle with him quietly. Get your sergeant to do it. Or await the next opportunity to punish him for some misdemeanour. You tell me he crosses the line often? Then throw the book at him next time. Give him the maximum. That'll be all, Captain.'

'Yes, sir. Thank you, sir.'

Jack left with the general saying after him, 'Good work on that gold – and the murderers got their reward, eh? God sees all and metes out justice. He doesn't always need us...'

Fourteen

June was a miserable month; day after day of rain, cold swirling winds blown from Antarctic regions, and the long dark nights did nothing to improve the men's spirits. Whales could be heard moaning out in the winter seas, calling to each other like night owls on the British landscape. A sort of heavy gloom settled over the hills and valleys around New Plymouth. Soldiers and settlers alike kept to their quarters and only ventured forth when it was absolutely necessary to do so. Even the Maori huddled together, wrapped in woollen blankets, like sheep on a mountainside.

In Taranaki, rebel Maoris gathered at the mouth of a river known as Katikara. They were intent on building a *pa* from which to taunt the British soldiery. However, Jack's spy network, though still a fledgling organization, was beginning to show profit. Jack received warning of the rebels' intentions and informed General Cameron – the same man who had refused to court-martial Harry Wynter – and the general's response was much as Jack expected. It was the sort of reaction Jack had been getting from generals since first becoming an intelligence agent in the Crimea. The general treated the information with disbelief.

'Balderdash! They wouldn't show their hand before they had built their *pa*,' bawled the general. 'That isn't like the Maori.'

'They haven't shown their hand, General,' said Jack, exasperated. 'This is inside information. My spies have penetrated the rebel meetings. This time we know what they're going to do *before* they do it.'

'Oh, I don't know, Captain.'

'Sir, this is my job. I have been doing it now for several years. If you do not act on my information, what use is there having a branch of intelligence at all? If you wait and do nothing, you will lose more men when you do have to act. They *will* build a *pa*, have no doubt on that score, but if we move now we can intercept them before that happens. They will be caught by surprise and for once we'll have the upper hand, instead of the other way around.'

After a long period of silence the general's eyes narrowed. He shook a finger at Jack.

'If this turns out to be a wild goose chase – why, man, these expeditions cost money, and there's precious little of that in the army coffers at the present time. The government at home thinks we can operate on dry leaves out here. The duke is threatening to take all British troops out of the islands for good and leave it to the militia. What a precious mess the settlers will make of it too. Half of them don't know one end of a rifle from the other. But...' He swallowed,

235

his Adam's apple bobbing before Jack's eyes. 'I'm going to take your word for it, Captain, and if your word turns sour on me, I'll stamp you into the ground.'

'Yes, sir,' said Jack, now fearful himself that the Maori spies he had working for him had got it wrong. It was possible, of course, that one or two of them were actually working for the other side. Now his name, rank and reputation were on the line. 'I'm certain you won't regret it.'

General Cameron himself led the column that marched to the mouth of the Katikara River. To his mild astonishment, for he had been more than convinced that Captain Fancy Jack Crossman had received false information, the Maori were there. Cameron attacked at once, using field guns to batter the enemy in half-dug rifle pits and trenches, and then sending in Colonel Warre's 57th – Middlesex men for the most part – who carried out a bayonet charge on the shattered defences. Around three dozen Maori were killed, many more wounded, with the loss of only three British soldiers. It was true that as usual several of the enemy escaped into the bush, to live to fight another day, but on the whole General Cameron was pleased.

He was not pleased enough, however, to remember that it was Captain Crossman's group who were largely responsible for his success. No mention was made of Jack, or to Jack, regarding the incident. Governor Grey congratulated the general himself on the affair, but the shadowy force who had made this happen

236

were forgotten. This was to set a precedent. After all, the general might have argued with himself, it was not as if members of an 'intelligence network' did the actual fighting. Spies were helpful but could be likened to cooks. Kitchen staff dished out essential meals that were gratefully received but once eaten all interest in them died. They were left to wash the dirty dishes in sordid silence.

Over the next few months Jack continually 'passed on the word', putting Cameron in a favourable position. You did not get huge pats on the back for simply passing on the word. You got them for acts of bravery and valour, like the one performed by Drummer Stagpoole and Ensign Down who risked their own lives to save that of a wounded comrade under heavy fire.

Up in Auckland, the settlers provoked the governor into attacking Waikato tribes just south of them by complaining that they themselves would be attacked if he did not do so. It was Grey's intention to destroy the king movement and stamp out insurrection before it was allowed to flower. A chieftain called Rewi had publicly called for the Maori to 'kill all pakeha'. Grey was not going to put all the work on to regular soldiers, however, and insisted that the settlers provided four hundred militia men to assist Her Majesty's forces. All sorts of tradesmen, farmers and artisans signed up: from butchers to cobblers to shepherds. They exchanged their cotton and leather aprons and crooks for muffin caps, blue jumpers and blue trousers with a smart red stripe down the leg. The militia were conscripting only single men. Those who wanted out simply proposed to their best girl and got married in haste. Some married men who were eager to fight denied they had ever been to the altar. In any war there are always those with zeal and those who prefer to watch from the sidelines.

Despite all his high ideals and the danger of disobeying an indirect order from Lovelace, Jack was unable to stay away from Amiri. Now that Jane was not coming, the captain slipped yet again from his pedestal. Strangely he found that now he had taken up with the Maori woman again his headaches had returned. Sometimes they were so savage he was confined to a dark room by the surgeon, who could do little for Jack's suffering. Once again he sought local remedies, which did sometimes ease the pain. However, he was beginning to believe it was God's punishment for his adultery.

'Are you unwell tonight, my man?' asked Amiri softly, as she entered Jack's quarters by the back door, tiptoeing in the gloom.

Jack's voice came to her from the desk under the window and she saw his hunched shape against the evening sky.

'Oh? Amiri? No, I'm well enough today – I just haven't lit the lamp yet...'

'What are you writing, Jack?'

'I – I'm just finishing a report.'

'Is it not a letter to your wife?'

The figure stiffened in the chair, then slumped

again.

'Yes – yes, you're right. It is. You know me too well, Amiri.'

'Please do not think I am jealous. She is your wife. You met her long before you saw me.'

'It's not that.'

'Oh – it is the guilt?'

'Yes, yes, I am a weak man.'

'It is different for soldiers – you might die tomorrow in battle.'

'There are no excuses, but thank you for trying.'

Amiri lit the lamp and saw that Jack was looking worn and haggard, probably with the pains from his head.

'Are you not sleeping, Jack?'

He gave a short laugh. 'Not much.'

'Come here.'

He went to her and she made him sit on the edge of his cot while she massaged his neck and shoulders.

'I am unhappy too, Jack, with the war.'

'Aren't we all?'

'But the governor. He is bringing many Australians to our country and is promising them land. There is no land to give. It belongs to the Maori. There is talk of five thousand men coming. My people are being turned out of their villages and told to go and live elsewhere. What justice is this?'

Jack was always careful about what he said to Amiri. Nathan Lovelace had taught his protégé well. *Trust no one, not even your own wife.*

239

Amiri was not even Jack's wife. He kept any sensitive information to himself, for Amiri was a Maori and Jack had no doubt that her people came before her pakeha lover. He would have expected no less from her. She was a woman of the highest honour. Had he been in her position he would have had the same priorities.

'Is that so? If it is, it's quite bad, but I believe the governor is clearing a buffer zone behind Auckland. There's nothing vindictive in the move. It's not part of the land confiscation scheme.'

Amiri suddenly became angry, her eyes flashing.

'We will drive the pakeha into the sea, Jack – when the tribes all meet together, we are numberless, like the ants.'

Actually, thought Jack, it is *we* who are numberless. We who are the ants. The sixty thousand Maori were already outnumbered by the Europeans on the islands, by at least ten thousand. Poor misguided Maori people. Even now, outside in the evening somewhere, troops were singing the American civil war song, 'We'll hang John Brown on a sour apple tree,' prior to marching out the following morning to find the Maori foe. Most of the action was now just south of Auckland, but there were still the odd skirmishes round and about New Plymouth.

Amiri stayed the night and left the following morning, expressing her fear that Jack would be sent to Auckland now that the fighting had switched from Taranaki to Waikato. Jack himself feared the same and had no heart or desire to go. Yet he knew he must. He was first a soldier and all else came second. His whole adult life had been spent in a uniform, of which he was sometimes immensely proud, at other times ashamed. All one could do, as a soldier, was make sure that the wearer did not besmirch his own honour. Most of the time you did as you were ordered and saw that it was a good order. When it was not, for there were fools wearing senior officers' caps as in any profession, you questioned it and did what you could to prevent a bad action. To an old soldier like Jack a court martial for disobedience was preferable to an unwarranted and terrible violation of what was lawful.

Jack watched his Maori lover slip through the murky dawn and wretchedly went back to his letter.

Unknown to both Jack and Amiri, someone saw her leave, had been *waiting* for her to leave. It was a tall Maori in a plaid shirt and grey trousers, his shotgun with a cord sling over his back, his long black hair swept back and tied at the base of his skull with a black ribbon. He let the woman cross the low bridge over the stream, then followed at a distance, tracking her more by her spoor than by keeping her in sight. Eventually he was rewarded by the destination: a cave in the hills where there were a number of other Maoris, one of whom he recognized instantly. He nodded in satisfaction. The master would pay him well for this information: very well indeed. He returned to the garrison.

Jack was indeed sent north, as expected, to assist in the fight against the Waikato tribes. On 20 November 1863, he and his men were standing on the Rangiriri Ridge looking down on the Waikato River. King-movement Maoris had built more of a redoubt this time, not quite a full *pa*, with trenches and rifle pits on the two banks of Waikata. The battlefield was some 50 miles from Auckland. General Cameron had told his officers they were to make simultaneous attacks from the front and the rear of these earthworks. First came the inevitable bombardment with Armstrong field guns – the largest of the three being the 12-pounder. The attack, as so often with long-range weapons, had little effect on the redoubt, the earth swallowing the lumps of iron with sludgy gulps. Jack could see where the battle was going and requested a place with his men in the charge that was to come, but Cameron was still peeved with him over various issues and refused permission.

'Thank Gawd for that,' said Harry Wynter. ''Bout time we did some lookin' on, instead o' gettin' our brains knocked out.'

'Your brains being where?' questioned Gwilliams.

'Never you mind,' growled Wynter, taking a silver cigarillo case out of his pocket and preparing to light one of the contents. 'You just treat me with a bit o' respect.'

Sergeant King's eyes widened. 'Put that bloody cigarillo away, you meat-headed idiot!' he roared. 'I'll give you respect with the five that make up my right fist if you don't behave.'

Jack turned to glare at his men and his eyes too went from narrow to round.

'Where did you get that silver case, Wynter?'

The private quickly slipped the case back into his pocket.

'It was give to me.'

'By whom?'

'Mate o' mine.'

'His name?'

'Can't recall.'

'Yet he gives you valuable silver cases.'

'S'right, sir. I won it. In a card game.'

'You said it was given to you.'

'Well...' Wynter grinned. 'He 'ad to give it me once I'd won it, din't he?'

Jack was certain Wynter was using the gold he had stolen from the shipment to buy such items, but he had no proof.

'We'll talk more about this later, Private. You will show me the man from whom you won that cigarillo case. Understand?'

'Sir!'

Then to Gwilliams, Wynter said, 'I never knew anybody else what said *whom* like the captain does. Is that a real word? I thought it was *who*.'

'It's called grammar.'

'Is it though?'

* * *

243

Men of the 65th, a Yorkshire regiment, had earned the nickname of the Royal Tigers in India. In New Zealand they were called the 'Hickety Pips', a mispronunciation of the Maori *hikete piwhete*. They were a hard, determined bunch and three companies were ordered to charge the Maori redoubt: a direct assault. But it took some eight attempts before they were able to storm the two outer trenches.

Down on the river, the 40th, West Country boys with long-vowelled accents, were attacking from two ships: the *Avon* and the *Pioneer*. Their objective was the central redoubt, a 20-foot-high fortification in the middle of the *pa*. Men were going down in greater numbers than General Cameron had anticipated. The smoke-laden air was full of the cries of the wounded as the rifle pits and trenches of the enemy took their toll on the attackers. Maoris were falling too, but in fewer numbers. General Cameron was one of those soldiers always of the opinion that a professional modern army is unstoppable, if pitted against a less organized enemy. But the cost was hurting him.

'Where's the 14th?' he asked a staff officer.

'They're in there too, sir,' came the reply, 'alongside the 65th.'

'Over eight hundred men,' growled the general, 'and we can't take a few Maori in a mud fort. Damnation. I *will* have them. I will. Who have we got in reserve?'

He then ordered thirty-six men of the Royal Artillery to rush the main tower with revolvers.

They went in with great bravado, firing their handguns at anything that looked like the enemy. It was a wild and extravagant gesture from the general, which might have astounded the Maoris into a panic. In truth, it was a rotten failure. The RA lost their commander, and many others, and had to retreat. Jack turned his head as he saw Captain Mercer, the officer in charge of the assault, go down under fire. He had met Mercer in the mess, two nights before. But when he looked back, there was a Maori clambering over the earthworks to reach the captain and drag him to safety, getting himself wounded in the process. It was an incredibly selfless and courageous act, which gained rare praise from General Cameron, who said he was determined to find out the name of that Maori as he was a fine and noble warrior.

Next, the order went out to the naval brigade. One hundred men in blue, armed with cutlasses and rifles, stormed the parapet of the central fortification as they might the quarterdeck of an enemy ship in an engagement at sea. Again they were caught in a hail of fire from the defenders. Naval men went down, here and there, unable to make any impression on the Maori defenders. It seemed as though the Maori citadel in the middle of the redoubt was unassailable.

'Call them back,' the general said, sighing. 'We'll hold our position here.' He looked around him. 'It's getting dark. I want the *pa* completely surrounded. None must escape. We will take it in the morning.'

Jack and his men bivouacked nearby. Ta Moko was not with them on this occasion, but Jack knew his Maori guide could have told the general that there would be escapees during the night. Indeed, when morning came, such was the case. A large number of the enemy had slipped through the cordon. Those who had been left behind wasted no time in surrendering. The toll on the Maoris was 50, but the British had suffered a similar number of casualties. It was one of those times when Jack could not help wondering if they had come to some sort of agreement, a compromise, there would be over a hundred men still walking around, breathing air, and living a life. There appeared to have been no real gain for either side. So the British had won? But was their win merely in name only? Some battle honours to go on the colours? Or was it a significant psychological victory, which was a telling blow to the Maori cause?

Over 180 prisoners were rounded up. The British troops showed these men great respect for their gallantry and General Cameron said they should be treated well. Then, with the way open south, Jack and his men were sent up to Auckland, where Sergeant King was to present some of his maps to senior officers billeted in the city. For King, it was the highlight of several years of work. He solemnly displayed the products of his endeavours before bored colonels as if they were the works of Michelangelo.

'What your man doesn't seem to understand,' a major said to Jack on the side, 'is that it's *fun* getting lost in the bush. How else are we to test our mettle if not from having to find our way out of a fix every so often? How dull it would be, chum, if we knew exactly where we were going and how long it would take to get there, *all the time*. There's no sense of achievement in treading in the footprints of a sergeant-clerk.'

In his heart of hearts, Jack was inclined to agree with the major, but of course he said nothing to King, who was like a boy presenting his handmade model to his tutors at school. This was *his* work. The fruits of his profession. Nothing could destroy King's feeling of euphoria.

Later, Jack learned that the name of the Maori who tried to save Captain Mercer was a chief named Te Oriori. Unfortunately Mercer's wound was mortal, and the chief's attempts were in vain. Nevertheless, Jack's admiration of Maoris as a warrior race had again increased with that selfless act.

Fifteen

Captain Abraham Wynter, of the Honourable Artillery Company, was in the dressing room of his grand house on Main Street, New Plymouth. There were a total of seventeen bedrooms in the huge white clapboard residence, only a half-dozen of which were ever occupied at the same time. On the occasions that Captain Wynter had held drinking and card game evenings, most guests were unable to return home afterwards (in actual fact, many were incapable of making it to the front door) and were permitted to doss in the first unoccupied bedroom they had the good fortune to stagger into, so long as it was not one of the two master bedrooms used by the host. Captain Wynter himself was a light sleeper. His troubled mind often kept him awake in the early hours of the day as he brooded on various issues which circled his brain. It took but a creak of a stair, or the wind in the eves, to have him sitting bolt upright in bed, his heart racing ahead and his fear not far behind. On such occasions Captain Wynter would take himself to his second bedroom, in an attempt to find a change of atmosphere, and blessed sleep.

Today though, in his dressing room, with his

maid and sometime bed companion assisting him, Captain Wynter was reverently unpacking and laying out the uniform which had arrived by the latest ship. Since 1830, when King William IV had taken notice of the HAC, its uniform had been based on that of the Grenadier Guards, an aspect of his newly found regiment that pleased Abe Wynter immensely. The Grenadiers were a highly respected, superior force.

'It wouldn't hurt, Sadie,' said Abe, using his pet name for his Maori maid, 'to be mistook for one o' them Grenadiers.'

He began by putting on the scarlet coat with its splendid golden epaulettes and buttons gleaming in the sunlight that speared the window. There were several uniforms in the pine wooden box, but the only one he was really interested in was the dress uniform, with its various sashes and its wonderful sword and scabbard. In a separate box was the bearskin hat, which almost stopped Abe Wynter's heart with its magnificent aspect. He put this on and was immediately over seven feet tall. Once he was fully dressed, with Sadie fussing around his shoulders with a little dusting brush, he stood in front of a full-length mirror.

'My God, Sadie,' he said, genuinely astonished at his own splendour. 'No wonder them officers look so regal-like. It an't hard to be a gentleman in togs like these. Why, I look like I was a high-born warrior from a top-class family, don't I?'

'You look like a king, master.'

He turned this way and that, admiring himself.

'Don't I just. I *feel* like a bloody king. Look at this bleedin' titfer! Like an Aussie wombat squattin' on me napper. You can't do better'n this for style, Sadie. Here...'

He suddenly drew the sword from its sheath and, whirling on her, brandished the blade underneath her chin. He flicked the steel back and forth as if fending off an enemy. Once or twice the razor-edged blade passed but a note-paper's thickness from her glistening skin. Then curiously, he suddenly held it still. Light from the blade gleamed on the upper part of Sadie's throat. She stepped back, pale with fear. She knew her master's unpredictable moods. Abe grinned, knowing he had frightened her. It was the sort of joke he enjoyed.

'You like silver, eh?' he said to her.

She looked puzzled and he explained. 'When we was kids we used to hold buttercups under a girl's chin – if it showed yeller we said she was fond o' butter. But you like silver coins, eh, Sadie?'

Sadie nodded violently. Abe then tipped the sword point down and hooked her woollen skirt with it. He lifted the hem to reveal her legs all the way up to the smooth brown thighs. He grinned again.

Sadie tilted her chin, almost in defiance. This puzzled Abe for a minute. Then he grinned and let her skirt fall. 'With legs like them, you an't got no worries about getting your gold and silver, Sadie.'

Later that morning Captain Wynter stepped from the porch of his house into the Main Street. He was wearing his full dress uniform, his hand on the hilt of his sword. He imagined he heard one or two gasps of admiration from passers-by in the street, which gratified Captain Wynter immensely.

'I am on my way to war, madam,' he told a woman who was gaping at him. 'I aim to teach them Maori rebels a lesson, if you please! Oh – Captain Wynter, at your service, ma'am.' He clicked his heels together in the manner of a Prussian officer and saluted. Then he called over his shoulder, 'Catch up, you two. Chop-chop.'

Close behind him were two of his Maoris, carrying a crate. Inside the crate was Mr Perkins' Extraordinary Steam Gun, the very one which fired one thousand shots per minute, using 900psi steam. The crate was long, since the barrel itself was six feet in length. It could even, with an attachment, fire around corners. The captain was going hunting in the bush this morning. He had been granted a column of thirty soldiers, a loan so to speak, by one of the regimental commanders, a colonel who wished at some time to purchase some land. Wynter had promised the colonel the men would be used with discretion.

Abe Wynter enjoyed the walk to the garrison in his magnificent bearskin, where his temporary loan was waiting on the parade ground. A colour sergeant called them to attention as Abe approached. The clash of arms in his honour greatly excited the ex-sailor, who recalled how proud the captains of ships had looked when marines had performed the same duty for them. He too felt proud. He was now a soldier – yet not *just* a soldier, a commissioned *officer*. And not even just a lowly lieutenant, but a full-fledged captain in a top-class regiment. That was something to be proud of, by damn, coming as he did from such humble origins. Probably half his cousins and brothers had been admitted, often under violent protest, to the sordid cells and passageways of Newgate prison in London. Some of them had never come out. One or two had been forced to leave by exiting through a small trapdoor on the floor of the gallows.

Yet here was he, Abe Wynter, inspecting a troop of Her Majesty's soldiers.

'At ease, Sergeant. That is, at ease once I've inspected 'em, and I'm satisfied as to the smartness and such.'

The colour sergeant rolled his eyes.

Captain Wynter gravely walked up and down between the ranks of the soldiers, nodding, frowning, pointing the sergeant towards a grease mark or blemish. Once the tour had finished he told the sergeant they should be on their way. 'If you follow my tracker, Kunu, he'll lead us to where these damn rebels are, Sergeant.'

'Yes, sir,' muttered the Scottish sergeant, clearly not pleased with the arrangement his colonel had made. 'Follow the tracker.'

The small column left the garrison and headed out into open country in the wake of a keen-eyed

Maori with his hair tied in a black ribbon. Captain Wynter wanted no horses or pack animals of any kind with the main party. He was of the opinion that such creatures slowed a march down. Also, they had a habit of whinnying, or braying, just as you came within earshot of the enemy, and you would arrive at their hideout to find it abandoned. It was important on this mission to catch the rebels at home. Abe wanted no mistakes. There was money attached to this venture. However, thousands of musket balls weighed heavily and could not be carried by men on foot. He needed this ammunition for the Perkins gun. This meant that pack animals would have to follow on in the expedition's wake. Abe's sixth Maori was left to haul the reserve ammunition, while the main party carried only a thousand balls.

The tracker and the soldiers went ahead, with Abe and the sergeant taking up the rear. There were four Maori taking turns to carrying the machine gun. This engine of war also followed after the rifle-bearing soldiers, as they trudged through the bush.

'So, Sergeant,' said Abe, 'what do you think of the old uniform, eh? Pretty smart, wouldn't you say?'

The grizzled sergeant, a veteran from a Burmese campaign, looked him up and down, and nodded curtly.

'Aye, it's no bad – sir.'

'Not bad? It's bloody good, Sergeant.' Abe stroked his scarlet breast with his palms. 'This is good stuff, not like that itchy blue serge you're wearin'. I don't even put on underpants made out of stuff that coarse. I'll let you into a secret – it only takes money. If you make it rich, then it's all open to you, see? I was just an ordinary seaman once. Now look at me? Captain in the Honourable Artillery Company – which, by the by, I been meanin' to ask one o' you army types. I thought artillery was big guns, but some o' the HAC, me included, an't gunners.'

The Scottish sergeant was better informed than most about such things and had the answer for the captain.

'You want to know, sir, how that comes about?'

'Yes, that's why I'm askin', man.'

'Fact is, sir, the word *artillery* was used first to mean bows and arrows – when muskets came along, they were called "great artillery". Yon HAC was probably formed early on, when it meant archers and such, ye ken?'

'Oh, so that's 'ow it worked, eh?'

'I should think so, sir.'

'Makes sense.'

The march through the bush was slow and cautious. They had at least one night in the open to look forward to, where they would not be permitted to light fires or do anything which might give warning to the rebels. When evening came round they camped by a small brook in a narrow valley. Since they were travelling light, the soldiers simply placed a blanket on the ground to sleep on. It was midwinter now and the nights were cold and damp. Captain Wynter had brought with him several sheepskins, some to lie on, some to cover him. He used his precious bearskin as a pillow. He hated sleeping in his bright new uniform, but there was nothing else for it. His Maori aides slept in a circle round him, their shotguns to hand, just in case. This helped to keep him warmer than he would otherwise have been.

Strangely – the mind is a complex machine – Abe slept more soundly out there in the mud than he ever did at home. Perhaps it was because of the exercise and fresh air, but more likely it was because his brain was freed from reminders of past misdeeds. Back at the house there were all those trappings of a rich gentleman which threw his mind back to the time when those riches came to him. Striker probably had the same dreams, the same nightmares. Abe wondered if it was one of the reasons why Striker had gambled his money away. Perhaps the load was too heavy to carry and he had jettisoned it willingly?

Abe woke as the dawn light was clawing its way up the sky. A murky mist was flowing over the damp ground. His bones ached and his temper was on the edge of nasty. Coffee. He would at that moment have given a bag full of gold for a cup of coffee. But he knew that lighting a fire would have been foolish. Why come out at all if the bird was given warning to fly the roost? He settled for a cup of clear stream water, hoping sheep had not shit in the headwaters.

Around him the soldiery was waking, exchanging greetings, while the sergeant prowled amongst them telling them softly to 'keep the noise down'.

The five Maori that Abe had brought with him were washing in the brook. They were big quiet men who asked no questions and only gave answers when asked for them. Looking at them, at their marvellous physique, Abe did not wonder they made such a ferocious enemy. They were warriors through and through. It was as if God, or Nature, had designed them for that role. They were muscled fighters in the mould of Ancient Greek heroes. Achilles himself would have changed bodies with any of these dark-skinned combatants. The British soldiers – some skinny, some fat, some heavily built, some short – paled by physical comparison and were entirely reliant on organization and discipline, and numbers of course, for their position as a great force in the world.

The march continued from early morning. When they came close to the enemy, they fanned out, approaching cautiously. The attack, thanks to the Maori guide, was a great success. They surprised the Maoris at their fire outside a cave. One of the enemy went down under fire straight away. The others, a dozen or so, had no option but to retreat into the shallow cave, which was not much more than a rock hang. A fight ensued, with those in the cave firing out at the troops in the bush, and the soldiers firing back. It was a sporadic battle, sometimes with periods of silence broken in the end by a single *crack* or a shouted jeer from one side or the other. Stalemate, in fact, though the defenders knew they were not going to escape. They had water and food in the cave, but these supplies would eventually run out. Abe Wynter's sergeant was of the opinion that it would take about a week before the spirit of those in the cave was broken.

'I can't afford a week,' grumbled Abe Wynter. 'We'll 'ave to finish them off before then. Can we smoke 'em out? Where's that damn ammunition for the Perkins? Shouldn't it be here by now?'

They tried fires, but the wind was in the wrong direction and they only succeeded in burning a huge area of bush, endangering themselves in the process. In the early evening the pack animals with the ammunition for the Perkins arrived. Abe Wynter had already carried out the erection and mounting of the steam gun, but had been reluctant to use the first thousand rounds of ammunition in case those in the cave immediately surrendered. Abe wanted no surrender. He intended to kill all the defenders before they had a chance to show a white flag.

By the time they had unpacked the ammunition, the sun was low on the horizon, a big orange ball. It was growing cold with the onset of the gloaming. Abe Wynter knew that once darkness fell it would be difficult to prevent the defenders from escaping. He and his men might catch one or two, but others would slip away for sure. He consulted his sergeant on the matter and the sergeant confirmed his fears.

'Right,' said Abe, his heartbeat quickening, 'time to use Mr Perkins.'

A charcoal fire was lit to boil the water in the generator of the engine, which would be released under pressure into the chamber of the gun. The hoppers were filled with musket balls from which the balls would drop one by one into the chamber of the gun. Finally the gun was moved on the swivel joint and aimed at the entrance to the cave.

Abe Wynter was managing the whole of this procedure himself, since no one else present had any idea what a Perkins steam gun was or how to operate it. The sergeant had not been present at the first demonstration of the weapon, there being only officers in attendance at that time. The NCO had no notion of what was to follow. All he was aware of was that the so-called captain had a newfangled weapon, which looked a rather dubious piece of equipment to the sergeant, being made up of pipes and funnels, and needing a coal fire to make it work. Indeed, it looked more like a contraption that should have been part of a steam boiler in a Chinese laundry rather than out on a battlefield.

He soon changed his mind.

Lying behind the Perkins, Abe Wynter began to fire. The soldiers around him were both astonished and horrified as the machine gun rattled a thousand shots into the mouth of the cave. Inside the cave they could hear the screams, as musket balls that did not hit any direct target, ricocheted off the inner walls of rock. *Zing, zing, zing, zing.* The noise from a thousand balls striking stone was astounding from outside the cave; it must have been terrifying within. One minute after releasing the trigger, the hoppers were empty. Abe, sweating profusely, screamed at one of the soldiers, 'Quick! Fill the hoppers again – now!'

There were cries of agony coming from the cave. A man came running out. Abe Wynter drew a revolver and shot the man before he managed to get ten yards. The soldier on the ammunition yelled that the hoppers were again full of musket balls. Abe went down behind his weapon again, his sweat soiling the collar of his precious scarlet coat. He knew what he was doing and he wanted it done.

'Sir!' cried the sergeant. 'Can't you give 'em time to surrender? Let me talk to 'em. They might—'

'Shut your mouth, Sergeant. I'm in charge here,' screeched Abe – and then he released the trigger again, pouring another thousand balls into the cave. When he had finished, there were only groans coming from the defenders' position. Still he was not satisfied, despite the sergeant's obvious agitation.

'Again!' cried Abe. 'Fill 'em again.'

Out of the corner of his eye Abe saw his own half-dozen Maoris walk off into the bush. They did not want to witness this slaughter of their own kind. They had chosen sides – for money or revenge over ancient enemies – and they knew there was no going back. But they did not need to watch this feverish butchering of men with the same ancestors as themselves. They would come back when it was all over and the screams and pleading from the cave had ceased.

Five thousand rounds went into that cave mouth. The sound of rapid fire, which had so shocked the soldiers witnessing this massacre, had left the wildlife of the evening as silent as the dead. Those in the cave had not stood a chance. Indeed, when the soldiers went to look the next morning, they were sickened by the carnage. Gory body parts lay everywhere, limbs having been ripped from sockets, heads pulped, and torsos mangled. The sergeant had seen a great deal of action, in various parts of the world, but this was one he wished he had not been part of. It had been ugly, horrifying, dishonourable, and for the most part unnecessary.

'Shall we bury the bodies now, sir?' he asked.

'Nah – leave 'em to rot,' growled the captain. 'They don't deserve a decent burial.'

The sergeant's voice was quiet but determined. 'Beggin' the captain's pardon, sir – all men deserve a decent burial. These here Maoris are Christians. They fought us fair and square. I'll no deny a Christian soul his last resting place.'

'Oh, do what you like, Sergeant. I couldn't give a tinker's damn what you do with 'em. But we've got to get going, back to New Plymouth. Who knows, there might be other war parties out here? Hey, you! Soldier! Be careful with that weapon. That's an expensive bit of metal, that is. That there gun will change the face of war.'

'I hope to God I never see the like,' muttered the sergeant. 'When that thing comes into service, I aim to take off my uniform for good and aye.'

Once the Maoris were in shallow graves with markers, the soldiers packed up and began the march back to the garrison. One of them happened to mention something about 'the woman'. Abe Wynter overheard.

'What woman?' he asked.

'One of them dead Maoris, sir,' answered the soldier. 'She weren't a man – she were a woman.'

Abe felt uncomfortable with this news. He did not know why, because women had been killed on the battlefield before. Chiefs' daughters and wives had been caught in crossfire, or had been part of a Maori defence, and had died as a result. This was an unfortunate turn of events which had not been in his reckoning. He had a good idea who the female Maori was, though he did not know her name, and decided that this need not go any further than the raiding party.

He asked the sergeant to call a halt.

'Listen up, you lot,' he cried. 'This 'as been a secret raid, as you might say, and is to stay confidential. It's me what'll put in the report to the colonel and I'll tell him what he has to know, understood? Any man caught discussin' these events, including you, Sergeant, will find himself up on a court martial for disclosin' secret information. This 'ere Perkins gun is a secret weapon, see, what we must keep from the enemy's knowledge. Any man here that jabbers in a tavern about what happened yesterday will regret his mouth, understand? I'll personally see him stripped and flogged.'

'I think we ken the message, sir,' growled the Scottish sergeant. 'Yer need have no fear of my men talking.'

'Good. I'll hold you to that, Sergeant. Any one of these men talks and you lose them stripes. That's a fact.'

'Yes, sir. I understand.'

The sergeant understood, but knew there was not a hope in hell of stopping the troops talking about this action. It would be all over the place before a day was out. Especially concerning the woman. Women had been killed in this war before now, but never in such a terrible slaughter as the one these soldiers had witnessed.

Abe, though, was satisfied he had put the fear of God, or at least fear of army discipline, into the troops. He was convinced they would not speak of this incident again. The column continued on its way back to New Plymouth. Again they spent the night out in the open and again did not make fires for fear of reprisals from other Maori tribes. The Maori were notoriously quick at discovering such deeds. Abe would not feel comfortable until he was back in New Plymouth, within the protection of several thousand British troops.

They arrived back the following evening. After bathing and stowing his precious gun, Abe Wynter dressed in civilian clothes and went out in search of Captain Jack Crossman. He was told the captain was at that moment in time in Auckland or thereabouts so he would have to wait to complete his business. He was glad to have something to offer the officer, whom he had kept dangling a long time. In the meantime he paid for the services of a clerk to write his dictated report to the colonel.

Abe Wynter made no mention of the dead Maori woman in his report. He knew who she was; the woman who had led him to the Maori rebels in the first place. The woman he had once discussed with his brother Harry; an indiscretion Abe wished he could now retract. However, the damage was done and, all in all, what did it matter? She was only a Maori and Crossman could get another if he wished.

Sixteen

Jack was still convinced that Private Harry Wynter had stolen part of the gold shipment that he and his men had recovered, the value of which he knew to be close to a thousand sovereigns. To a private soldier, whose pay after stoppages was around three or four pence a day, that was an absolute fortune. But how would Harry Wynter convert raw gold into money he could spend? The answer to that was obvious. He would do it through his brother, Abraham Wynter. Abe was shrewd enough to know he could skim a good profit from handling his brother's ill-gotten gains, even after declaring that he would take a percentage. Harry Wynter had no real idea of the price of gold on the market, would not know how to go about discovering it, and would be happy with what he got.

What was more, Abe was clever. He would know that money in Harry's hands would be spilt like water on drink, women and gambling. It was doubtful if the whole thousand sovereigns, given all at once, would last a week. Abe would therefore be careful to dole out the cash to Harry in small amounts. Harry would grumble but would be in no position to make a great fuss. After all he was a thief who faced dreadful punishment for his crime if he were found out. So Harry would reluctantly accept his brother's plan and make the best of a rather pleasant situation. Now, though, the private had slipped up a little and Jack pressed forward with his enquiry.

Coming before him, in the room Jack was using as a temporary office, Harry Wynter looked as if he had crawled out of a ditch. His uniform was filthy, his skin looked unwashed, and his boots were covered in mud. When he saluted, he swayed violently to one side. Sergeant King had to nudge him up straight with his shoulder to keep him from falling over altogether.

'Sergeant,' snapped Jack, seated behind the shipping crate he used as a desk, 'is this man drunk?'

'Tired, your honour,' murmured Wynter, his eyes half-closed. 'Not drunk. Leastways, I *was* a bit tipsy yesterday, but that were yesterday. Today I an't drunk, sir. I din't get me much sleep last night, bein' as I'm havin' certain dreams.'

Jack ignored the bait about dreams, which would have led to all the injustices Wynter felt he had undergone in the army.

'Sergeant, where has this man been to get in such a state?'

'He won't be able to tell you that,' replied Harry lazily, ''cos I an't told him. Oh, he asked all right, but I still din't tell him nothin'.'

'Sergeant, why is this man speaking to me directly?'

'Sir,' said King, 'I can't stop him, short of gagging him. Shall I gag him, Captain?'

Jack removed the prosthetic metal hand that he wore when he was in his dress uniform, laid it on the shipping crate before him, and scratched the sore stump which was his wrist. Wearily, he replied, 'No, no. No gagging, Sergeant.'

Thus Jack swiftly abandoned the procedure he had hoped to adopt; he had hoped to use Sergeant King as a buffer between him and Private Wynter. He had known in his heart beforehand that he would not be able to keep it up, but had thought it worth a try. He now spoke directly to the private.

'Suppose you tell me, Wynter? Why do you appear before your commanding officer in a state of filth?'

'Sir, I was as smart as you look when I started out this mornin', but was set upon by the navy on me way here.'

'The navy?'

Wynter's hideous milky eye rolled in his scarred face as he gave Jack a twisted smile.

'Not the *whole* navy, o' course. Just 'alf a dozen.'

Now it was Wynter's turn to scratch at something: the black furrow in his forehead left by a handgun he had used in an abortive attempt at suicide. Wynter had blamed this attempt at taking his own life on the 'abuse' he had received from Sergeant King and the then Lieutenant

266

Crossman. He claimed to have been callously abandoned in an Indian thorn bush, which blinded his eye and tore wounds in his body, only later to be thrashed by King for insulting the Asian host who had nursed him back to health.

This subtle scratching action infuriated Jack, who knew it was being done for the sole purpose of making him feel guilty. Yet if he charged Wynter with this accusation, he would be met with a look of astonished innocence.

'Leave your face alone, Wynter.'

'Oh, sorry, sir.' A contrived innocence springing immediately into place. 'I 'spect it was 'cos you was scratchin' your stump. Unconscious like, I did the same. We been through a lot together, an't we, sir? Battles here an' there. That's what I told them navy boys when they started insultin' you. I said if they'd seen half the action you and me 'ave, over the years, they'd take refuge in a woman too.'

King stepped away from Wynter's side and stared in shock at the private.

Jack, deep down inside, went very cold.

The captain was silent for a few moments, then he said in a low threatening voice, 'Be very, very careful, Wynter.'

'I'm just tellin' you, sir, what I heard. I din't believe a word of it, o' course, you bein' a married man of honour, but them navy boys wun't stop yellin' stuff. So I told 'em even if – even if you *was* goin' with a Maori bint, which I was certain you wasn't, there was good reason when you'd bin through so much action, like us. That was when they laid into me, sir, and I got this dirt on me. I fought 'em like a wild 'un, for the honour of the regiment, like, but they dusted me over good.'

Jack knew of course that these 'navy taunts' were fictitious. He strongly doubted there had been a confrontation at all. More likely Wynter had spent the night in a ditch, sleeping off his latest drinking bout. Where had Wynter got the knowledge of his liaisons with Amiri? This much Jack *had* to find out, to see how far his indiscretions had spread. God help him if it had reached the ears of a private soldier who hated him already! The silver cigarillo case was now irrelevant. More important was the source of Harry Wynter's knowledge. Jack fought his feelings for a few minutes. He would have much enjoyed planting a fist on his private's nose, an impossible scenario, but he had to control his cold anger and attempt to outmanoeuvre a man who owned more cunning than Shakespeare's Iago.

'I want to thank you, Private Wynter, for intervening on my behalf,' he said, much to the complete astonishment of his sergeant. 'These groundless insults are not to be borne, are they?'

'No, sir, they an't. It's why I waded into 'em with me fists.' He showed Jack a grimy set of fives. 'I showed 'em what soldiers is made of, that's certain. An' anyways, it's none of the navy's business.'

'Well, I think we have established the complete lack of evidence behind these insults, Wynter, don't you? After all, if there were any truth in the matter, I would be in deep trouble, wouldn't I? In such a case I would have conducted my affair with great caution and secrecy, which would have meant ... what?' Jack paused for thought. He furrowed his brow. 'Yes – it would have meant that someone had to be watching me, observing my movements all hours of the day, for weeks at a time. No one I know has that sort of time and energy, and therefore it could never happen, could it, Wynter? You can see that, can't you?'

'Yes, sir, there an't nobody I know who could do that of themselves.'

Of themselves? A revelation! Jack suddenly realized who Harry's informant might be. The knowledge hit him with a hammer blow. Now he remembered seeing a man, just once or twice, close to his quarters! Good God, it was worse than Jack could have imagined. The sweat came to his brow and he blinked. If this scandal broke, he would be ruined both in his marriage and probably in his career as an officer. It was not the act – many officers had been with local women – but the terrible consequences of being found out by a man who could use the knowledge to destroy him. What a stupid thing it all was! How weak he had been. Carnal lust had been the downfall of many a great man, let alone a small man like himself. All for a few moments of ecstasy between the sheets. Yet – yet, it had been more than that, hadn't it? He loved Amiri, did he not? The difference only had meaning to himself though.

Harry Wynter was jabbering again.

'Is this about the cigarillo case, sir? – 'cos I can explain that,' said Wynter, cutting into the silence.

Jack had been staring at the crate top and now his face came up and Wynter saw the horror in it. The private smiled. Triumph was his. At last he had the bloody captain on a hook.

'What? What can you explain?'

''Bout the cigarillo case, sir. It was give me, by my dear brother Abe Wynter, for a favour I done him.'

There it was, the confirmation of Jack's fears. Abraham Wynter had had him followed. Or his man had witnessed Amiri entering Jack's quarters surreptitiously. There was no doubt about it. Jack could read the message in Harry Wynter's face. It was there in every crease. Harry Wynter had been with him when Amiri had flirted with him the first time they met. He had obviously mentioned this incident to his brother, who then had had Jack watched by one of his Maoris.

'Quite so, Private Wynter, you are dismissed.'

Sergeant King suddenly found his voice. 'But, sir, Wynter previously said the case had been given to him by a comrade.'

'Well,' replied Harry, grinning, 'who's my best comrade? None other than my dear old brother. Best mates, we are and always 'ave been.' He came to attention and saluted Jack. 'Justice 'as bin done, sir, ain't it?' Then he swaggered

270

insolently from the room.

Jack buried his face in his hands.

Sergeant King was mortified.

'Sir – are you ill? Is it the headaches again?'

Jack lifted his head. 'No – that is, I'm not feeling altogether well, but you need have no concern, Sergeant. Just a little fatigue I think. If you wouldn't mind, I would like you to take Private Wynter and Corporal Gwilliams and give them a lesson on map-making today. That's all, Sergeant.'

King saluted. He clearly suspected that something had gone on between his captain and the private that had escaped him. Whether King would take it further, Jack had no idea. Perhaps he would try to question Wynter. Jack was sure Harry Wynter would keep his knowledge to himself, for if he gave it away to King, or anyone else, it would immediately become a weaker weapon. Harry Wynter was not one to let his strengths dissipate before he had used them to the full.

Jack sat staring bleakly at the wooden walls of the room he occupied. What was he to do? Confront Abraham Wynter? Where would that get him? What about leaving sleeping dogs to lie? In which case he would have the affair hanging over his head for ever. If only there were someone he could talk to, to get advice. He wished Nathan Lovelace, though he would have been excruciatingly embarrassed to take Nathan into his confidence. Steel-souled Nathan did not understand the failings of men.

Later in the day, Sergeant Farrier King came to see him.

'Sir, I may have got us a new Maori man – you know, for your network? I thought you'd like to see him yourself. Recruit him personally.'

Jack was lost in his own thoughts. He had been so distracted and dismayed by Harry Wynter's inferences he had hardly left his shipping-crate desk all morning. In the early afternoon he had paced up and down, trying to see a way forward. He certainly could not punish Harry Wynter in any way, though the man's insolence warranted some form of punitive action. Nor could he make any sort of rebuttal. The facts were the facts, and Wynter knew it. Now that the knowledge of his affair was out in the public domain, Jack's marriage was under serious threat. It would have been one thing to admit such a misdemeanour to Jane privately, quite another for her to discover that even the rank and file knew of her husband's indiscretions. Jack's mind had blazed with feverish thoughts and his spirit had plunged into the deepest imaginable misery. He would rather be dead.

'Sir?' said King. 'I said...'

'Sorry, Sergeant, I did hear you,' murmured Jack, 'I'm just not feeling myself at the moment.'

'I understand,' replied the sergeant, quietly.

Jack's head came up, glad to be able to change his emotions, glad to have a target for anger.

'Oh, you do, do you?' he snapped.

He had never seen eye-to-eye with his senior NCO. Sergeant King and his obsession with map-making was a constant source of irritation to him. Sergeant King was more of a civilian surveyor in army uniform. He could not shoot straight, his discipline consisted of taking soldiers behind the latrines and knocking their teeth out and he obeyed only those commands which he felt were justified. It was true that King's intelligence and dedication to his profession made him valuable to the army, but Jack would have much rather have had a sergeant with the mind of a good thoroughbred horse. One who thought less of charts and coloured inks and more of following through his captain's orders.

'That is, I know why you're down, sir.'

'I think this conversation should stop here, Sergeant.'

'Well, sir,' said King, 'I would stop it here, if I thought it was the best thing for the group. But it seems to me that this problem you have goes too deep to be left alone. It will affect us all, when we're out in the bush, where our minds need to be sharp as tacks.'

You see, thought Jack to himself, this was just what he hated about this man. King had the impertinence to intrude upon his commanding officer's very private business. It was no use Jack doing his 'how dare you, this is my personal life, I do not need a sergeant's advice' speech. It would be like water off a duck's back. Jack tried to imagine what an officer like Lord

Cardigan or Wellington would do with an audacious sergeant who had the temerity to patronize them. Why, the man would be sitting, hands tied behind his back, astride a newly sharpened wooden horse within seconds! Yet Jack was no Cardigan or Wellington; he could not explode in wrath and destroy this upstart. His nature was to writhe in cold anger and try to demolish the man with an aristocratic stare. Sergeant King's nature was to ignore haughty stares and continue intruding upon his officer's private trials and tribulations.

'You see what I mean, sir? It's not just about you. It's about all of us. It's about keeping our minds honed to the work and staying alive in dangerous situations. It's about keeping our heads clear.' The trouble with King was he had been born an intelligent man and made a great deal of sense. 'You see, sir, it's not like we're just going off into battle. If that was what it was, the fighting would take your mind off what's worrying you and I wouldn't have the sauce to say the things I'm saying. It's hard to worry about things when people next to you are getting blown to bits and heads are flying off bodies. But what we're doing takes slow and deliberate thought. Out in the bush we have to think clear. Your head's not clear, sir. It's full of dark dreams. You could kill us all by just – well, by just going in on yourself, sir.'

Jack picked up his iron hand and used it to point at King's face, hoping to intimidate him.

'And you, Sergeant King, have a solution to

my problems, do you?'

'No, you know I haven't got that, sir. Look, can I just say if it were me – caught out like you've been – I'd make a clean breast of it, sir. Write to Mrs Crossman – tell her. It's no good you look at me like that, Captain, we all know. Harry Wynter doesn't keep things like that to himself. It doesn't matter to us, does it? We're no saints. I got an Indian woman into trouble when I was younger, didn't I? But think about it, sir, getting it off your mind, I mean. If Harry Wynter has anything to do with it, she'll hear anyway. Sorry to intrude, sir.'

King stood before him, a square man with a square jaw, square fists and a square honest expression. Jack's anger melted and the feelings it had temporarily replaced returned with a vengeance. His spirit plummeted like a stone thrown into a chasm. He only wished it would hit the bottom and his heart would stop with the impact.

'I'll leave you now, sir. Sorry again.'

King saluted smartly, turned, and left the room.

Jack sat there for another half-hour, then picked up his pen and began to write a letter. Once it was finished, he sat back and read it three or four times, before putting it in an envelope and sealing it. Then he leaned back and relaxed. King had been right. He did feel a great deal better, a great deal less fraught. The letter had not been sent yet, but just getting his confession on paper was cathartic in itself. He did not exactly feel purified, but his mind was clearer and more alert. It was no good wallowing in self-pity anyway. No good telling himself he had been a stupid fool or any of that rubbish. There was no healing in that, only self-recrimination. If Jane were devastated, he would have to take her disappointment in him on the chin. Things would never be the same again between them, their union would always remain stained, but that was the price of his folly and he was going to have to live with it.

He left the building for the first time that day, taking the letter with him to the mail room. Sergeant King intercepted him on the way. He quickly stuffed the letter inside his tunic before King could see it.

'Sir, have you thought about what I said – about the Maori, I mean?'

'Ah, yes, the potential agent?'

'Yes, sir. I've got him in my quarters, if you want to talk to him. He's a Waikato man.'

'Right. Good work, Sergeant. I'll see him now.'

Jack went with King and interviewed the man in question, who turned out be a shifty-eyed creature interested in money. Jack did not mind that the man was mercenary – most of his Maori spies were not in the work out of love for the pakeha – but the captain had the feeling that this particular fellow was one of those who worked both ends. He would be taking information back to his tribe, as well as bringing information out of it. Such men were useful in other ways. It was just as important to sow false rumours amongst the Maori, as it was to discover the truth about their movements and intentions. Jack paid the man, told him he was now a servant of Queen Victoria's secret army, and began to question him on the situation amongst his people.

'You know, sir, about Orakau? This was a bad thing.'

Jack did indeed know about the battle in question. After the fight at Rangiriri Ridge, the Maori had fallen back on their old ways of retreating from *pa* to *pa*, keeping just out of reach of the soldiers who were trying to lock them down. Stronghold after stronghold was captured, but without any resolution. Then came the battle at Orakau, in the Waipu basin, where about 300 warriors including some women in the *pa* were attacked by British forces. The defenders held out for several days, despite lack of food and water, braving the storm of lead and shells that was hurled at them. Then a trench was dug by the British sappers and hand grenades lobbed from there right into the heart of the besieged *pa*. Those within the *pa* were by now exhausted by lack of sustenance, and their ammunition had almost run out. A call was made to them to surrender, saying the troops greatly admired their courage, but the day was lost to them. The Maoris replied that they would fight to the death and could never make peace with the pakeha.

Not long after this, the Maoris suddenly left the *pa* and at a measured pace trotted through the British lines, much to the astonishment and bewilderment of the attackers. At first not a shot was fired from either side, but then the soldiers began rounding up the retreating Maori, taking prisoners and shooting those who resisted. Just under a third of the defenders managed to escape, including their Chief Rewi, leaving behind prisoners and their dead. They also left, within the *pa*, many wounded Maoris, including women. For once the soldiers forgot themselves. They had been fighting a bloody battle for several days and their blood was up. They ruthlessly bayoneted several of the wounded Maoris, including the women, and only stopped when officers ran amongst them commanding them to desist. This was an unusual occurrence amongst troops, who ordinarily respected and admired their heroic Maori enemy, and they were condemned for it.

'Yes, indeed, it was a bad thing,' replied Jack, 'but in war such things are bound to happen, for men fall foul of themselves.'

'It was bad,' continued the Maori, 'but it means the Waikato no longer wish to fight. This war will now go to Tauranga.' This was on the east coast. 'The Ngataerangi there have built a road to their *pa*, so the pakeha do not get tired and turn back. The pakeha will be able to find their way easily to the fighting grounds.'

Jack had heard that certain chiefs did such things. Inwardly he smiled. It was typical Maori humour that one could not help but find endearing. 'How many Maori defend the *pa*?'

'There are two hundred and fifty. Some Koheriki are there with the Ngataerangi. There are two *pas*, one small, one big...'

Jack questioned the man closely on the details of the landscape and the force of warriors that were there. He learned that the *pa* was on a ridge, high up, near a borderline between Maori land and settlers' land, just two miles from the sea. There was a fence that ran between the two territories, with a gate in the middle. Jack decided to pass this information on to General Cameron, who would no doubt want to bring in the navy as well as his own men. The new spy was paid off, but Jack was reluctant to bring him into the live network. He let the man know that his information would be useful at any time, but gave him no indication that there were others like him. Not for the first time he felt distaste for his work, though he could not tell why. All he kept saying to himself, as he crossed a yard to reach General Cameron's office, was, 'This was not what I joined the army for. I'm a captain in the Connaught Rangers, a proud regiment – a regiment I have not had the opportunity of fighting for since I received my commission.'

Once he had unloaded his information on the general he went back to his quarters, consciously forgetting he had a letter in his pocket that had not yet been posted.

Seventeen

Captain Fancy Jack Crossman came away from the battle for the Gate Pa ragged, weary and bloodied. General Cameron had indeed attacked the *pa* from the front, while General Greer had taken up a position to the rear. Nearly 2000 men had been involved in the action, facing an enemy numbering just 250. Pakeha artillery included two 40-pounders and one 110-pounder. There were seamen, marines, 43rd Foot, 68th Foot, and various other regiments, including Jack's men from the 88th Foot. It should have been an easy victory for the government forces, but it had been a mistake to box in the Maori. The rebels could not employ their usual tactic of hit and run since Greer and the 68th had cut off their rear. And so they did what any self-respecting Maori warrior would do – they decided to fight to the death.

At twilight on the evening before the attack, over 700 men of the 68th slunk away into the murky swamps of Waimapu. Guided by a Maori by the name of Tu and one of the settlers who had a house nearby, they trudged a stretch of mud flats that went on for almost a mile. It was soggy ground and the soldiers found themselves sucked down and floundering to the tops of their calves in mire. Foul, silent curses surged through the head of the infantry soldier. More elaborate, but equally potent oaths went through the mind of his officer. It was a constant struggle to prevent the sludge from stealing the footwear of the marchers. The going was slow and tortuous. It took them two hours to cross that short piece of boot-greedy bog and they finally made it to firm ground on a spur to the rear of the Gate Pa before the moon briefly rose. A deep darkness descended and it started to rain. A miserable night lay ahead, but there was the comfort of knowing they had performed a brilliant piece of circumnavigation: to night-march a regiment through a swamp without being seen or heard by an enemy who lay watching and listening close by. Jack was all admiration.

During the battle, the fact that the Maori had no way out caused confusion, not just amongst themselves but in the ranks of their attackers. Soldiers who saw retreating Maori suddenly turn and come back at them believed there had to be more Maori reinforcements behind them and so retreated themselves. Regimental officers tried to stem the withdrawal, waving their swords in the air at the fleeing troops, and as a consequence a great number were shot dead where they stood. Jack was told that the 43rd lost more officers at the Gate Pa than soldiers of any regiment were killed in the Battle of the Alma, a fact that he appreciated, having taken part in the storming of the heights above the

Alma River in the Crimea.

After it was all over and the dust was settling Jack found Sergeant King was missing. He, Gwilliams and Wynter went into the *pa* and searched amongst the wounded.

At first they could not find him and Jack wondered whether King had been taken prisoner, or had wandered off somewhere not in his right mind. He would not have blamed the man if it had been the latter, because the hand-to-hand fighting had been fierce and terrible. Facing a Maori with an axe in his fist was a fearful thing. A Maori warrior was a fearsome creature. His physique alone was enough to strike terror in the heart of an opponent. He would twist his facial muscles into ugly expressions, and use battle cries and gestures that were both strange and frightening. It was one thing to be part of an organized attack in a line of disciplined soldiers, quite another to be thrown into a savage mêlée where men were being hacked to death by wild tattooed warriors with the strength of grizzly bears.

They turned over corpses and picked their way amongst the injured, calling King's name. After twenty minutes Jack was beginning to think they would not find him. He feared that a headless body he had seen might have been his man. The blood and gore, which had flowed from the severed neck, had covered the dead soldier's uniform, disguising any regimental markings. Jack was reluctant to go back to that cadaver and check whether it was King or not.

'Here he is!' cried Wynter, not without a trace of pleasure in his voice. 'I got him. He's wedged 'tween two dead 'uns. Might be he's dead himself...'

They took the legs of the sergeant and dragged him out from under the bodies of a soldier and a Maori. King's face was covered in blood, and there was more blood on his scalp. With his knife Gwilliams quickly shaved away a patch of matted hair from his sergeant's skull to find a deep groove beneath, probably the result of a *patu* strike. Once his face was wiped with a damp rag they found he had also been shot in the throat. The musket ball had gone right through one side, luckily missing the spine. Though unconscious King was breathing robustly and Jack had hopes his sergeant's head wound would not prove fatal. They laid him on a cart bound for a hospital in Auckland and followed behind.

As they entered Auckland, a man was waiting by the roadside and hailed Jack with a shout and a smile.

'It's me brother,' growled Wynter. 'What's 'e want to see you for, Captain?'

'You mind your own concerns, soldier,' said Corporal Gwilliams. 'That's the captain's business, not yourn.'

Jack left the column and confronted Abraham Wynter, who reached into his coat pocket and produced a folded document, which he waved under Jack's nose with a smile.

'Your deeds, Cap'n,' said Abe Wynter. 'You're the proud owner of a thousand acres of good

283

farmin' land. Sorry it couldn't be more. What do you plan to raise? Pigs, ain't it?'

Jack stared at the papers. 'I was thinking of growing pepper vines, and perhaps garlic plants.'

'Ho! Exotic, eh? Spices is it, Cap'n? Well then, you'll probably make enough money to retire afore very long. Most people likes a bit of pepper on their taters and steak. I know I do. Well, here it is then. You'll see the price at the bottom, with my commission attached. Pay me sooner than later, but until then, good luck to you, sir. Good luck to you.'

Without waiting to be offered, he took Jack's one good hand in his two, and shook it vigorously. For his part Jack felt this had come all too late. He was embroiled in an affair with another woman, his wife was nursing a sick father, and his enthusiasm for farming had waned accordingly. He wondered whether or not to reject this deal right now, by the roadside, but then thought better of it. Perhaps he ought to just look at what Abe Wynter had got for him. After all, he had pressed long and hard enough to get it. And even if he did not, in the end, want the land, there would be no difficulty in selling it on. Settlers were clamouring for farmland and sellers were making handsome profits. Jack would only have to hold on to it for a short while before putting it up for auction to make a profit.

He took the papers.

'Thank you, Mr Wynter, for your efforts on my behalf.'

'Oh, pleasure, sir – pleasure,' said the man in the tall black stovepipe hat and long black coat. 'Anything for our majesty's officers – one meself, you know. HAC. Got to stick together, us officers.'

Jack held up the papers. 'This land...'

'All legitimate. No worries there, Captain. Be assured, sir. The last owner has passed on. Squared it with the tribe chief too, so there won't be no comeback on that score. Nuthink for you to worry about whatsoever. You just enjoy your acquisition. 'Owthat rascal of a brother o' mine? Shapin' up?'

'Mr Wynter, forgive me, but we've just come from the battleground and I have a sergeant with a serious head wound. I'd like to stay and pass the time of day, but I'm sure you understand. Private Harry Wynter will no doubt give you his version of the fighting later.'

'Of course. Understand completely. Hope your sergeant's a tough 'un and comes through all right. Good day to you, Captain Crossman.' He took Jack's hand again, though it was still clutching the land deeds, and shook it hard. 'Anything else I can do for you, don't hesitate, sir, don't hesitate.'

Abe Wynter walked off, humming an unrecognizable tune.

Jack stuffed the papers into his coat and then rejoined the column, which was now trailing through the streets of the town. Despite all his previous misgivings and dark thoughts, he found there was a little hop in his step. He was a landowner. A landowner in New Zealand, one of the prettiest countries on the face of the earth. That was something to think about. It was a long way from home, to be sure – the farthest one could get unless one was interested in endless white expanses of snow and ice – but New Zealand's green hills, valleys with hot springs, lakes and mountains, appeared astonishingly fresh. New Zealand had to be the last piece of the world God fashioned, and he had done it with all the love and care that someone puts into the finishing touches of a masterpiece. It was the British Isles with thermal heating, a less harsh climate, and far fewer people. Once the fighting was over and things had settled, Jack would own a thousand acres of paradise.

Once they had ensured that Sergeant King was getting treatment for his wounds – he still had not recovered consciousness, which did not bode well – Jack dismissed his men and went to his quarters. There he bathed and dressed his own wounds, which were merely small lacerations and bruises. His head was hurting again, but he told himself that this was the result of witnessing Sergeant King's injury. A reminder. He was transferring that man's pain to his own head in some way. So he lay on his cot and, after taking a powder, attempted sleep.

A scratching at his door woke him when it was dark. He lit a lamp and lay there for a few minutes, but the scratching sound continued. Thinking it might be a rat, Jack took his metal hand from the bedside table, intending to use it as a cudgel. On throwing open the door, he found a brown kiwi rooting around by the door-post, presumably looking for worms. It scuttled away into the darkness of the shrubs. Jack stood in the doorway for a few minutes, taking in the silence of the night, and the fresh air. Looking up he was amazed by the clarity of the heavens: a mass of stars embedded in black velvet. It was relatively easy to pick out the Southern Cross, whose fifth star was visible to Australians but not visible in the more southern parts of New Zealand. There were others more familiar to a man from the northern hemisphere. Indeed, though, it was a refreshing night sky, somehow cleansing for the spirit. A whole weight lifted from Jack's previously leaden mind, not for any reason but the fact that he could see how unimportant his hour-by-hour concerns were when compared with the aeons invested in those constellations above.

He went back to bed but could not sleep. Instead, he took up a book Jane had sent him. It was a French novel in the original by an author called Victor Hugo. *Les Misérables* was not the sort of book Jack would have chosen himself; he preferred factual books on factual subjects. He soon put the worthy, and wordy, Frenchman down in favour of a pamphlet: *The Most Interesting History of Numeration, Including Irrational and Transcendental Numbers, Leading to the Complex Numbers Discovered by the Italian Mathematician, Raphael Bombelli (1526–1573)*. This was much more Jack's style and he happily lost himself in prime numbers and rational coefficients. It astonished him to learn that the 'zero' had come along in the fourth century BC, with the Babylonians.

'One would have thought,' he murmured drowsily to himself, 'that the Romans, coming so much later, would have had the sense...'

But he had fallen asleep before he could finish the sentence.

The following morning when Jack was imbibing his morning coffee at the mess, he received a visit from the overweight newspaperman, Andrew Strawn.

'Captain?' Strawn sat at the small round table without waiting for an invitation. 'I was wondering if you had anything for me on the battle for the Gate Pa. You were there, weren't you?' He let out a sort of tinkling laugh that had other officers looking across and frowning. Seven in the morning was no time to indulge in tinkling laughter. 'I understand it was quite a fight. Some are saying it's the turning point of the war, though a sort of shallow Pyrrhic victory, considering the number of casualties.'

'Why me?' asked Jack. 'There were others there – officers commanding regiments – who are in a better position to assess whether it was a great victory or not.'

Strawn leaned forward conspiratorially. 'Well, between you and me, Captain – you're one of the more articulate officers in this war. Intelligence is not a commodity which overflows amongst our aristocratic officer class. You're one of those rare ones who seem to know what they're doing.'

'You know what Lord Raglan said about officers who know what they're doing – he thought the army would be much better off without them.'

Strawn lifted a finger at a passing waiter. 'Coffee!' he said, then turning back to Jack, continued. 'You must have some opinion on the battle. I won't use your name, if that's what's worrying you.'

Jack said, 'I think the important thing is we won. Yes, there was a cost. There's always a cost, but I hope you don't expect me to criticize our senior staff, because – forgive me – I don't trust you not to use my name.'

'*A source present on the battlefield.* That's how I refer to my informants.'

'And I suppose you're invisible to all these other officers in here?'

'Ah, you mean they'll put two-and-two together. Well, I always talk to a number of them. Not just one. Believe me, Captain, I can't even remember your name. What is it? Wellington or something?' He let out another one of those horrible laughs. 'Please, let's just go over the battle with an eye to detail.'

Jack sighed and leaned back in his wicker chair.

'I don't think I'm capable of that this morning. I had a bad night and my sergeant is shot to pieces and lying on a hospital bed. I intend visiting him in a few minutes.'

Strawn scribbled something on a pad, murmuring, 'Interesting...'

'What the deuce is interesting about *that*?' asked Jack.

Strawn looked up, a frown on his broad brow. 'Why, an officer with the rank of captain bothering to visit an NCO in hospital.'

Jack realized this was probably unusual. 'You don't seem to understand. My unit is very small. Though I'm in the 88th, the Connaught Rangers, I haven't served with my regiment in years. I'm on special duties and my command is tiny – one soldier, one corporal, one sergeant. You get quite close when there's just four of you out in the bush, dependent on each other for survival.'

'Some officers wouldn't.'

'Well, I'm not some officers. The life of my sergeant is important to me.'

'You get on well together, then?'

'Not particularly. Like I say, we depend on each other. It would take me months, perhaps years, to train another sergeant to the standard of this one.'

Strawn's steaming coffee arrived and he nodded his thanks to the Maori waiter. 'What is it exactly that you do, Captain? You and your *unit*?'

'We – we're map-makers.'

'Ah – I remember now. The same sergeant of yours was lost in the bush the last time we spoke. You seemed very concerned about him then, too. Obviously, he was eventually found, but now still giving you cause for grief. He seems like a son to you...'

Jack found the thought revolting, but did not say so.

'So,' continued Strawn, 'map-making? Important stuff, map-making. My grandfather knew William Lambton, the India map-maker. And also Colonel Everest.'

'Heroes of my sergeant.'

'But not of yours?'

'My heroes are men of science.'

'And you don't consider map-making a science? No, I suppose not. It's more of an art form, isn't it? I do love the fact that when one starts to look into things like map-making a whole new language emerges. Words. I love words, don't you? Perhaps not. Now, what are those lines called, that show the steepness of heights on relief maps? Not contours, but another word...'

Jack realized he was being tested. Strawn was delving to see if he really *was* a map-maker. Perhaps the newspaperman had a whiff of Jack's prime purpose in New Zealand: the setting up of intelligence networks.

'You mean hachures?'

Strawn smiled. 'Ah, yes – that's the word, *hachures*. The thicker they're drawn, the steeper the slope, eh?'

'Would you like to join the team?'

Strawn shrieked with laughter, causing a major buried in a newspaper to look up and mutter, 'I say there, keep a lid on it, fellah.'

Strawn snorted in the direction of the major, and then turned back to Jack. 'Well, sir. What about this battle? The Gate Pa. A milestone in the Maori wars? I understand many officers were killed in the assault. General Cameron is blaming Governor Grey for that. Apparently before the battle Grey ordered the Tauranga commanding officer not to move from his redoubt, which allowed the Maori to build that formidable *pa* and hold it against a vastly superior force.'

Jack now realized that blame was being apportioned. He really wanted nothing to do with the politics of war. However, he knew he would have to give an opinion or Strawn, like all crafty reporters, would make something up. 'It was certainly a key battle. Men fought bravely on both sides. I could not say whether the building of the *pa* made any real difference – you'd have to ask an engineer for an opinion on that. There was chivalry from the Maori. I saw one Maori woman face rifle fire in order to get water for a wounded British officer. There were other such gestures. It's true that at one point our men panicked, but things like that happen in war. In the heat of the battle, with all the smoke and noise, and the screams of the dying, one becomes disorientated. It's easy to become confused in those winding trenches the Maori dig. It's like trying to find one's way through a maze.' He paused. 'Let me give you some advice, if I may. Try not to apportion blame for any perceived mistakes. Leave that to history.

We – you and I, and the rest of New Zealand – are too much on top of things at the moment. Let a bit of time pass in order to reflect.'

'I'll bear that in mind,' replied Strawn, scribbling. 'Thanks, Captain.' Strawn rose to leave. 'Hope that sergeant of yours recovers without too many problems. Oh, and, by the by, that land dealer of which we spoke last time I saw you – Wynter? Abraham Wynter. He just led a successful engagement in the south, against a pocket of rebels. Wiped out a whole lot of them. There's talk of a medal.'

Jack was surprised. Abe Wynter had said nothing when handing Jack the deeds to his land. And the Wynters were not renowned for their modesty.

'Thanks for that information.'

'You're welcome.'

Jack put Abe Wynter out of his mind. He had other matters far more important than concerning himself about medal winners. He left the mess and made his way to the military hospital. Nearing it, he could smell those smells which turned his stomach. Jack, like many people, hated hospitals. They were supposed to be places where men recovered from illnesses and wounds, but more often they were halls of pain. The surgeons did their best, of course, but they were considered butchers by the men, since most of their work consisted of hacking off limbs. Some surgeons used chemicals to render a man unconscious before cutting, but others considered this unethical and would only amputate while a patient's eyes were open and comprehending. One or two military surgeons were often more concerned with whether soldiers were malingerers or not, even as they were chopping through gristle and bone.

There was the smell of urine and faeces mixed with blood as Jack walked along a narrow passageway to the long room where the wounded from the Gate Pa had been taken. Indeed, this was one good reason to hate hospitals, if there were no others. At first he could not recognize his NCO amongst the lines of patients, since he was looking for that signature shock of wild hair. Then he remembered; King had been struck on the head and would no doubt be wearing a white turban of bandages. Indeed, it was so, though the turban was soiled. When he finally saw him, in a row of wounded and injured soldiers, Jack thought he was dead. King had his eyes closed and his mouth open. But on a quick enquiry with a nurse, Jack discovered that King was simply asleep. His mouth was open because he needed to breathe, his nose having become clogged with dried blood which the doctor saw no necessity to remove at this time. Jack went to his sergeant's bedside and it was almost as if King knew he was being observed; his eyes opened very slowly.

'Sir?' he croaked.

'I'm sorry, King. Does it hurt you to talk?'

'No – doesn't hurt. Just feels strange. Surgeon said my air pipe was holed, but it's closed up now, I think.'

'Ah. Good.'

Jack had no idea how to converse now that he was here. He had always had trouble making small talk and he considered hospital visits the worst in the world for this kind of thing. Even if it were his own brother in that cot, he would have had trouble thinking of something to say.

'You did well – in the battle.'

King shook his head, grimly.

'No, sir. I didn't kill any Maori.'

'Well, that's not always a good measure of how one has done, to count bodies. Sometimes it's the saving of lives which brings credit to a man.'

'Didn't save anyone, either.'

This was hard work. Fine, Jack thought, if he does not want praise then I will give him none. Let him stew in the belief that his wound has been for nothing. This was what he disliked about Sergeant King, the man always ran counter to what Jack required. Would it have hurt King to accept the praise gratefully and thank the man who offered it? A little bit of politeness and a few manners went a long way. But, no, King had to reject any comforting talk. The sergeant was as blunt as a Maori club. He met everything head on with the absolute truth, when truth was not necessarily what was required. Sometimes what was needed was a few white lies, just to ease the situation and make people feel better. Jack's feelings hardened and he met truth with truth.

'Well, then, you got your wounds for nothing.

How about the head? Any pain there?'

'No – no pain. Just a buzzing in the ears.'

King tapped the side of the turban.

Jack was slightly annoyed. He still suffered headaches occasionally from the blow he had received from Potaka's club. Perhaps this sergeant's skull was that much thicker than his own? For a few moments, in his irritation, he allowed himself to be mollified by the idea that this was the difference between an aristocrat's skull and the skull of a peasant. It only lasted seconds, before he became ashamed of such thoughts. As a man who believed in science, he knew that this was a myth, just as royal or noble blood was a myth. The queen's blood was no different from the blood of a scullery maid. A sergeant's skull was no thicker than that of a baronet.

'You're lucky,' he told King. 'Mine still hurts.'

'More brains,' croaked the sergeant, trying to smile. 'More brains to damage.'

'That's unlikely. I'm no academic. You're the man with the mind, Sergeant, the map-maker. I'm just a soldier.'

'Modesty, sir, you think around corners – I can't do that.'

'Well, let's not argue about it,' Jack replied, pleased by this praise. He looked around the ward at the various cots bearing inert soldiers. There were some hideous wounds. Skull clefts open, limbs missing, horrible holes in various places. Men looked back at him with vacant eyes, those who were not totally blind. Several pairs were Maori eyes. One or two were groaning quietly. Some, he did not know how many, were no doubt dying. A hospital was of course a place where a man could be nursed back to health, but it was also a place in which a man's spirit could dive straight down to hell. A soldier could come in here with a very treatable wound, but spend time looking at what might possibly happen to him in the future. It was enough to depress the most stalwart of souls. A mildly eccentric fellow thrown into Bedlam might end up completely mad in the company of the insane. A youth with a wounded hand, left amongst the legless, armless and blind, was not likely to imagine he had lost his sight or limbs, but he was likely to witness such suffering that he fell into a state of dejection from which he might not recover.

'Are you all right here, King? I mean, I can get you moved.'

'I'm fine, sir. To be honest, don't feel like being moved at the minute. There's no one with diseases here, if that's what you're thinking. Everyone's a war casualty. No body fever. It's a fact you can't catch another man's bullet wound.'

Jack had not been thinking that. But King was right. If they started mixing the sick with the wounded, then that was the time to get his man out of there.

'All right. I'm going now. If you want anything, send for me.'

King managed a creaking laugh. 'Send for the

captain? Me, a sergeant? That's likely, sir.'

'I mean it. Gwilliams will be in, no doubt. Send him if you have need of me.'

King's eyes fixed on his, full of seriousness.

'You're a good man, sir. Too good, in that way. You need to look to your old ways a bit more, now you're an officer.'

'I don't think that's true. Colonel Lovelace would do the same. It's because we're such a small unit.'

'Beggin' the captain's pardon, Colonel Lovelace might or might not come. If he did it would only be to listen, in case I had anything of import to tell him – not because he felt the slightest pity.'

Jack was inclined to agree with his sergeant, but he did not admit as much. He stayed with King for a short while longer, then felt he was able to go on his way. Once outside the hospital he breathed a little more freely, having been strongly affected by the misery within. It was not so very long ago that he had lain in such a bed with a crushed hand and other wounds and had thought he would never again feel normal.

The evening air on the way back to the billets revived his spirits somewhat. He could smell the sea, which always had an invigorating effect upon him, and also herbs and blooms amongst the greenery of the parklands close by. New Zealand had that refreshing element to it. There was a cleanness, a clearness, about this country which was what attracted him to owning a farm on its landscape.

A farm! He remembered the deeds in his pocket. Stepping into the light of a window, he took the papers out of his pocket and peered at them. His eyes travelled down the lines until he reached the name of the man who had previously owned the land. A shock went through him. He stared at the name disbelievingly. Then he recalled what he had been told about Abraham Wynter's recent military activities. A second, much greater, shock went through him, coupled with a terrible fear.

'Oh God, no!' he moaned. 'It can't be. It must not be. Oh God, what has the man done...?'

Eighteen

Naturally, considering the history between Abe and himself, Striker did not trust his old shipmate not to attempt to kill him any more than he would trust a rafter rat not to eat his cheese. The secret between the two of them was so ghastly they could hardly bare to look one another in the face. For his part, Striker was happy not to see Abe, even though this horrific bond between them had drawn him to New Zealand once he had lost his gold. Abe, however, was always coming round to 'see how his old shipmate was doing' and Striker could see in the man's eyes that he was always disappointed to find Striker in good health. The pair of them kept up this false behaviour, this pretence, of being great friends. Certainly Abe's Maoris thought they were, for the locals nodded and smiled when the two men slapped each other on the back and exchanged hearty greetings.

Yes, and the gold. Striker could not imagine how Abe had managed to keep his, and even turn it into a vast fortune. For his part he had felt a sense of relief once it was gone. It felt filthy. And when Striker had developed consumption, the ex-sailor felt it was fitting. He knew he deserved punishment and the Lord had decided to give it to him in spades. Striker took his just deserts like a man, accepted them for what they were, and tried to get on with his life.

But the sense of guilt was greater than the sense of relief he first experienced on ridding himself of his fortune. It returned to swamp him again. So now here he was, confronting his sins every time he saw his erstwhile companion. Yet Abe seemed to go from strength to strength; nothing bothering him except the living presence of an old shipmate. Striker had heard that recently Abe had been out with that rapid firing gun of his and earned himself a medal or two. Maybe that was what Abe was doing. Serving the pakeha cause in order to try to wipe clean the slate? It could not happen. There was no slate. It was a rock face engraved with their crimes and it could never be erased, not in this life.

'We go out now?'

The Maori named Tarawa, whom he and Abe called Kipper (because of his fondness for smoked fish), stood in the doorway of his hut.

'Yes, yes.'

Striker lifted himself gently from his bed, only to enter a fit of coughing that ended in quite violent spasms, causing his pale narrow chest to bend backwards and forwards like a sheet flapping slowly in the wind. The Maori viewed this display with a blank expression, waiting patiently for it to pass. Then, once Striker was able, he went forward and assisted the pakeha to his feet. He kept his face averted, not wanting Striker's

301

stinking breath in his nose or mouth, fearful that the disease could be passed on that way.

Striker gradually recovered his breath and, along with it, his composure. He pulled a nankeen shirt on over his head, then climbed laboriously into his pants and sandals. Tarawa brought him some fruit and bread for his breakfast, and coffee, which he sorely needed. Finally he spoke to the Maori again.

'What's the day like, Kipper?'

'The wind is light.'

'Enough to take us out?'

'Yes, Striker. Enough to take us out.'

'Good. Well, let's get about it then.'

They left Striker's hut and walked down the beach to a small sailing craft drawn up on the sands. Tarawa himself dragged the vessel down to the water's edge, since such heavy work was beyond Striker's strength. Then the pair of them pushed it out into the surf and jumped on board as it crested a wave. Striker tumbled into the bottom, but laughingly got to his feet and found a perch.

'Bugger! I used to get into these things like a fairy settlin' on a flower bud,' he said, wheezing. 'Don't ever get this bloody disease, Kipper. It takes every ounce of power out of you. Not that any on us gets it on purpose. Some is lucky, some ain't. I was just born unlucky.' He paused, before adding, 'Now that there *Captain* Wynter, he's one of the lucky ones, give or take a setback or two. Whatever he does he comes out smellin' of honey.'

'The captain?'

'Yes, the bloody captain. Shit, he's no more captain than you or me. Not really. Money's the only thing he's got. Forms his character, it does. His whole person is fashioned of money. When he dies you'll find a casket of coins where his heart should be. Same with his soul. It'll have the Queen's head on one side and a date on the other. He's always been Newgate material, our Abe. His neck was made to wear a noose. But that luck of his keeps findin' him silk collars 'stead of hemp.'

Striker knew Kipper only understood half of what he was saying, but he said it anyway. Kipper, having raised the sail, was now busy baiting the hooks with clams and the torsos of hermit crabs. They would manage two lines each, he and Striker. Striker much preferred line fishing to using a net. He liked the feel of a fish on the end of a line, the tug and jerk of a live creature deep below the surface of the water. It was like reaching into the unknown, testing, testing, then the quick bite and the yank. Then the zigzagging line cutting the surface about. This was much more thrilling than throwing out a net and dragging in all sorts of weird fish life. Why, only the night before Kipper had been throwing out a circle net around a rocky area and pulled in the ugliest fish you ever saw. A stonefish, he called it. It was like a lump of stale bread dough with a tail, covered in warts and bumps, sort of greeny-grey in colour. On its back was a set of spines that Kipper very carefully avoided and there were small fins coming from its sides. The eyes of the creature looked dead. Striker curled his lip in disgust on seeing the fish.

'You ain't goin' to eat that, are you?' he had asked Kipper, who had shaken the fish free of his net. It had landed in a rock pool and simply lay there, looking bloated; its miserable mouth curved downwards to its underbelly. 'It looks poison to me.'

Kipper had nodded. 'Yes, poison. The spikes.'

'The spines are poisonous? Deadly?'

'Yes. Takes one or two hours. Maybe.'

'Shit. Well, we don't want him for supper, do we? We don't want him *at all*. Best leave him and be wary of where we tread in future if that's what's under the water. Bugger. Why God made such things is beyond everything. Had a bad day, I reckon...'

Striker's attention was then taken by Tarawa pointing to a dark patch of ocean that seemed to be alive with silver knives.

'Aha!' cried Striker, the excitement rising in his corrupted breast. 'Bonito if I ain't mistook!'

Down came the sail and Tarawa rowed swiftly towards the shoal while Striker finished baiting hooks. When they got to the tunny the lines went over the side and they began pulling in large silver striped fish. Striker chortled the whole while and Tarawa grinned.

This was the life, thought Striker. Not dead gold, but live silver. This was what it was all about as far as Striker was concerned. Who needed a bank when there was the ocean's bounty to reap for nothing? A morning's work, that was all. Hell, he thought, Abe could keep his fortune. There was nothing like a fish roasted on coals to satisfy a man, then lying on his bed listening to the combers booming down the beach, curling and clawing at the shingle. Abe could keep his dishes of partridge and pheasant and his silk sheets and cushions. He could keep his power too. Striker wanted nothing more than a morning out on the shining sea, the sun on his neck, and the line in his hand taut enough to sing in the wind. The rest was all free and gratis, with no worries attached.

By the mid-afternoon Striker was feeling weary and asked Tarawa to take them in. The Maori raised the sail once again and they sped towards the shore. Striker was aware that much of the work had been done by Tarawa and so resolved to do the cooking, even though he felt exhausted by a day out on the ocean in the heat of the sun. He gathered some driftwood to use as kindling, then brought some logs from the shack, and made a fire on the beach. By the time he had stripped a green stick of its bark and skewered a bonito, the sun was falling down the face of the sky. A hazy purple glow turned the sea into a king's robe. Striker looked up and caught it at its best.

'Oh God,' he said, reverently. 'Would you look at that, Kipper? You couldn't buy a sight like that in Liverpool. Worth a ransom, eh?' He bent once more to his task. 'And smell that fish!

Does that make your mouth water, or no? Have we any bread?'

'Yes, Striker, we have bread.'

'You are a trump card, Kipper. Can we toast it a bit? Not too much – not so much so it burns, but just to warm it a little?'

'Do put it by the fire, Striker.'

Not long afterwards they were enjoying their repast in the gloaming. The heat was still in the sand and it was pleasant to sit watching the stars speckle the heavens. Striker saw a falling star and watched its silver track streak down the evening shades. For some reason it filled him with sorrow, possibly because he had seen just such a sight as a boy of six, sitting on the back of his father's tumbril. He felt tears come to his eyes, but wiped them away quickly in case Tarawa noticed them glistening in the firelight. He was not sure how Maori felt about men crying. He was inclined to think it was unmanly.

Tarawa rose just before the end of the meal.

'Where are you off to?' asked Striker, surprised.

'I must visit a bush.'

'Oh – off you go, then.'

The Maori rose and was soon swallowed by the twilight. He returned some minutes later and resumed his meal. Some roosting birds were making a racket in a nearby tree. Tarawa threw some stones up at the branches and the birds scattered into the darkness. They returned almost immediately and continued with their cacophony until they were settled for the night.

Striker suddenly felt exhausted.

'I'm off to bed, Kipper. See you in the morning.'

'Yes – in the morning, Striker.'

The sailor turned fisherman dragged his feet up the sea strand to the hut perched on the rocks above. The twilight had almost turned to darkness, but the starlight was bright enough for him to find the doorway. He knew exactly where his bed lay in relation to the door. He sat on its edge and removed his sandals, threw off the blanket, and flopped back.

An excruciating pain seared through him.

Striker's eyes went wide with hurt and fear. He screamed at the top of his ragged lungs and fell out of the bed on to the dirt floor. He was in agony. Every nerve-end in his body seemed to be burning. An unbearable deep-seated pain was growing within his torso, as if he had swallowed a cache of sulphur and someone had put a match to it. For the next few moments he crawled around on the floor, clawing at the earth, gasping for breath, trying to fight the torment within. Then, somehow, despite the terrible pain, he managed to get to his feet. He staggered to the doorway and propped himself against the post.

'Kipper! For Christ's sake, Kipper!'

The Maori came to him, carrying a flaming log.

'Help me, man,' groaned Striker. 'I'm hurt.'

'I am sorry, Striker,' said Tarawa. 'I am very sorry.'

Striker blinked away the hot tears in his eyes.

He could not comprehend what the Maori meant. Tarawa seemed so calm, so distant, so unmoved by his plight.

'Wha—? What do you mean you're sorry? Can't you see I'm in agony?'

Tarawa was looking over Striker's shoulder. Striker turned his head and in the light from the torch, saw the dying stonefish. It had been placed in his bed so the dorsal spines would pierce his flesh when he lay down. Tarawa was trying to kill him. Tarawa *had* killed him. God, it hurt. It hurt so much Striker knew he was going to swoon.

'Murder!' he moaned. 'You've murdered me, you bloody bastard. What did I ever do to you?'

'Nothing to me, Striker.'

Striker knew who had killed him of course.

'It – it was *him*, weren't it? The captain?'

'I am truly sorry, Striker. I will pray for you in church. Your soul will go to heaven.'

'Sorry? You fucking bastard. Sorry don't do it.' A wave of agony went through him and his legs went from under him, his body folding and sliding down the doorpost to the floor beneath. 'Fetch me a fucking priest, Kipper. You can do that much for me. I've been good to you. A good friend,' he managed to blurt before he passed out. 'I need a priest. Help me. Oh Christ, I'm dying. The pain...'

The Reverend Chatterton had lit his lamp and was carrying it to his kitchen when there was a rapping at the back to his house. He went to the door and opened it. A Maori stood there, his facial tattoos glistening in the lamplight. Reverend Chatterton was a great champion of the Maori cause and immediately believed one of them – a man named Tarawa – had come to him to enlist his help in some dispute over land rights or something of that nature.

'Come in,' said the priest. 'Don't be concerned.'

'No, no. You must go down to the shoreline, sir. There is a man there who asks for you. He is dying.'

The shocked reverend took a step backwards.

'The shore? Where on the shore?'

'By the Two Maidens.'

Chatterton knew the Two Maidens, a cleft stack whose shape suggested two women holding hands. Everyone knew the landmark.

'Where is he? On the beach?'

'No, sir – in a hut. You will see.'

With that the Maori drifted away, into the street beyond.

Chatterton was still in a state of shock. Dying? Why? How? Was this a trick of some kind? Perhaps he would be ambushed, not by renegade Maoris, but by settlers. He was not liked for his support of the Maori people. It would not have been difficult to find a Maori who would betray him, however. All races, all manner of men, had their traitors. What should he do? Take this at face value, or call out the troops, go down to the shore with a bodyguard?

But if the man *was* dying? It would take some

time to gather soldiers. If he were to help this man he would have to go now, this instant, and trust in the Lord. Yet he admitted to himself, he was afraid. He was, besides being a priest, a human being. He was capable of fear. Oh, yes, fear had been a companion on many occasions. What should he do? He had to make a decision. Yet the Maori had looked calm enough. Why had he not helped the person in trouble?

But of course he had to go, danger or not.

There was a woman who helped around the church, cleaning and assisting with the flowers.

'Missie? I am going out.'

A faint 'Yes, sir' came from the depths of the house.

'If – if I'm not back within an hour, call Major Nielson.'

'Yes, sir.'

Chatterton was still wearing his cassock from evening service. He swept out into the night and headed for the beach. Two Maidens rock was only about ten minutes away. He hurried along a track strewn with crushed seashells; the hem of his cassock swishing against his legs. Now that he was out in the night, he felt braver. In fact his confidence had returned and was high. It was just the shock of those first few words uttered by the Maori. *He is dying.* Hopefully that was an exaggeration. Perhaps the man was simply drunk. Some of the Maoris tended to embellish when they retold situations. A man flat on his face, arms outstretched, would not necessarily be inspected closely.

The vicar looked up as he walked. Ah, a crescent moon. How attractive. Golden horns. The horns of a dilemma. Could he work something in to his next sermon about the moon? Of course he had to beware of animism. You had to be careful when dealing with a people whose pagan gods had only just been tucked in the bottom drawer. It would not take much to get them to open that drawer again.

Now there – there was the Two Maidens. No sign of the man or his hut – wait, there it was! He had forgotten to ask whether it was a Maori or a pakeha. Did it matter? Not really. A man was a man, for all that.

'Help me!'

For the second time that night the vicar felt a great shock wave pass through him. A gaunt pale figure had staggered out of the dark and now clutched him around the neck. Chatterton reached up behind and unclasped the hands with his own. He found himself staring into a haggard visage in the moonlight. Then the man, now he was not supported, slipped down to the ground. Feeling guilty at his own reaction, Chatterton bent down and took the man's head, resting it on his knee so that the fellow's back was supported by his leg.

'Are you ill?' he asked. 'What's your name?'

'Strickland. I've been poisoned,' groaned the man. 'Great pain. Terrible pain...'

'Don't talk, sir. I know you. Yes, I know you. You're the fisherman. I remember – you bring Missie fish. Poisoned, you say? Who? How do you know?'

Strickland stared with wild eyes into Chatterton's face.

'I'm dying.'

'Well, perhaps not,' said the vicar in the most reassuring tone he could muster. 'If we can get you help...'

A hand came up and clutched at his shoulder.

'I'm dying, I tell you. Stonefish. I've been stung by a stonefish. That bloody Maori put it in my bed. There's no way back from that. I'm slipping away now. I'm not a strong man. Too much liquor. Too much work on the ships. The consumption. My body's weak. A strong man might last another hour, but...'

'A stonefish?' Chatterton, like many vicars of his time, was an amateur naturalist. He knew what this man was talking about.

'Oh dear. Oh dear. You are going, most certainly.'

'Yes, I must confess.'

Chatterton was a little distressed by the urgency of the tone.

'Oh dear. I'm not a priest of the Catholic faith. I can't give you absolution, or last rites, not the Roman kind. I can give you comfort, if you wish, and of course if you are truly repentant of your sins, let me hear them.'

'I just have to tell somebody. I don't want to go to my Maker like this. And somebody's got to pay. Abe Wynter. He was with me. He's the man who murdered me.'

'Murdered you? With – with a *stonefish*?'

'Yes, yes. It were like this, vicar.' His burning eyes were boring into Chatterton's own. 'There was three of us in Australia. We struck it rich, see – found gold. There was me, Abe and Danny. Daniel Kilpatrick. We – we felt like kings. We *was* kings for a time. Then we did somethin' stupid. We got ourselves lost, out in the desert. It's a rare desert that Aussie outback! Nothin' there at all. Just broken white trees, rocks and dust.' Strickland licked his lips as if speaking of the dust had made them dry. 'You can walk and walk, the sun blazin' down on your neck and head, and after several days everythin' still looks the same. It's as if you're standin' still, just moving your legs, the earth goin' under your feet. Crazy. It drove us all crazy, the sameness of it. Nothin' changed. Every day we woke up parched and desperate hungry, and all there was was these broken white trees.'

'But you had water? You had to have water.'

'We had water but no food. Some Abos found us the water, but then they wandered off, wouldn't come back when we called to 'em and we was too weak to give chase. They didn't have no food to give us, though they'd scratched a hole out of this dry dust bowl, which let up some dusty water. Well an' all, we stayed lost and looked to die. It weren't no good being rich as kings when we had no food. Looked like we was done for – would've bin – then Abe ups and takes a rock in his fist, and walks up behind Danny and cracks him on the head. Killed him stone dead.'

'Mr Wynter – Captain Wynter killed his comrade?' whispered Chatterton. 'Why, what good would that do? Did this Danny have food hidden away? Had he been hiding it from the pair of you?'

'No – no, he didn't have no food. Abe killed him to eat. We ate Danny's legs an' arms, and Abe had some of the soft meats. I think Abe ate Danny's heart, which is why he's always nudgin' them Maori, saying as how him and the Maori are alike. You know the Maori used to eat their enemies, so I'm told. Abe thinks that makes him and them brothers under the skin.'

'Oh my dear God,' murmured the Reverend Chatterton. 'You can't mean it? He ate another man.'

'Our shipmate, Danny. I ate him too. Had to. Starvin' to death. You'd do it too. We killed him and ate him.'

'But – but to eat human flesh when you're starving to death is bad enough – to *kill* a man in order to do so...'

Strickland tried to stand up. He started shouting. 'That's what I'm tellin' you, you silly old fool. It were a desperate enterprise. That's why I'm confessin' it. I – I gotta go now. It's gettin' cold and dark.' He held up his hand. 'Is my fingers there? I can't feel my fingers. Oh Christ, this pain. It will go, won't it, vicar? It will go when I...'

The body convulsed so hard it jerked itself out of Chatterton's arms. When he next lifted

314

Strickland's limb it was limp and lifeless. Horrified by this, and by what he had heard, Chatterton got to his feet and began walking back to his church. He needed desperately to pray for a while, to get his mind back in some order. He was far from calm. His nerves were shot and his thoughts ricocheted wildly around inside his head. *To kill and eat a friend!* How dreadful. How terrible. Someone would have to be told, of course. Major Nielson. He would tell Major Nielson then leave it to the army to deal with.

After a short session on his knees, murmuring orisons that were meant to ward off future nightmares, but would fail in their purpose, the good Reverend Chatterton went to see the major. Nielson immediately sent out a party of soldiers to recover the body, then he questioned the vicar closely. Had it seemed as if this fellow Strickland was in his right mind? Could there be some fantasy here, provoked by the poison he had supposedly ingested? In Chatterton's opinion, was there a case to answer or were they the ravings of a dying madman?

'Fetch the Maori,' said Chatterton, realizing this was the best idea he had had all evening. 'I know the man. Tarawa's his name. Bring him in and question him about the stonefish. Inspect this Strickland's bed for the deadly fish. If that part's true, then I expect the rest of it is too. Why would a man make up a story like that, when he knows he's dying?'

Nielson was not at all happy that he had to

deal with this situation, since it looked very messy.

'Aren't you people supposed to honour the secrets of a man's confession? What about confidentiality and all that, Edward?'

Edward Chatterton was indignant. 'I'm not a Catholic priest. I don't have any such constraints. I can tell deathbed confessions to whom I like. Listen, George, if you're going to be sticky about this, let me remind you I have had a traumatic evening. A man has died in my arms, complaining that he has been murdered, and confessing to murder himself. That's a shocking thing to have happen when one is settled for the evening with a nice cognac and a quiet time with a book to look forward to. I thought you army types were ready for any emergency?'

Pride came forth. 'Well, yes, we are – but all the same...'

'All the same, what?'

'Nothing. I see your point. You have done your duty, Edward, and now I must do mine, however unpleasant the task. You realize of course this man Abraham Wynter is a captain, in the Honourable Artillery Company? No? Well, he is. Makes it damn awkward, really. A commissioned officer eating people? Of course he was only a seaman then, a deckhand I expect. It sounds very much like he was a runaway and deserter too. Jumped ship no doubt to do this gold digging? Many of them do, y'know? Oh, well, he'll have to be brought to book. Daniel Kilpatrick? At least you got a full name out of

316

him, before he expired. Well, we can check on this Kilpatrick, and Strickland. Abraham Wynter, eh? Supposed to be some sort of hero at the moment. Destroyed a nest of rebels down south. Well, he's got himself a hornets' nest now, hasn't he? Go to bed, Edward. I'll see to this. Sorry I flew at you. Shocking business, eh? Nasty. Very, very nasty. Ah, here's my lieutenant back with the body.'

Nineteen

It was clear from the document in Jack Crossman's possession that the land he had acquired through Abraham Wynter had previously belonged to Potaka, the Maori who had begun by being Jack's enemy and had eventually become his friend. It was also clear that Potaka and his men were now dead, annihilated by Abraham Wynter's rapid-firing steam gun. What was not known, but was feared by Jack as he travelled back to New Plymouth, was whether Amiri had also been killed in the same ambush. On arrival Jack learned from Ta Moko that Amiri was indeed one of those shot to pieces in the rebels' cave.

'Oh God, no,' he said, almost breaking down before his Maori guide. 'This is my fault! If I had not been so greedy for land—'

Ta Moko interrupted him. 'You were not to know, Captain. And if not you, some other pakeha. This man Wynter, he is not a man to concern himself who buys what he has for sale.'

A rush of emotions flooded through Jack, including guilt and anger, and great sorrow. Potaka had chosen sides in a war and though his end was horrific, it was no worse than being blown to pieces by a shell, or cut down in a hail of rifle fire. Jack was sad that his friendship was over, but it had been a dangerous thing in any case. Had someone in authority known he was fraternizing with the enemy, he would have been in serious trouble.

But Amiri was a different matter. He had been in love with Amiri. It did not matter to him whether she was a rebel or not; her passing caused him terrible anguish and there was a rage in his heart for the man who had taken her. He knew he would have to kill Abe Wynter and fortunately the man was of the same rank. Jack knew what he had to do: force Wynter into a duel. Not so long ago Jack had fought a duel with a Captain Deighnton over nothing. Now he was ready to do the same with Captain Wynter, this time he had something to fight over.

'Where is Abraham Wynter?' he asked Ta Moko. 'Can you take me to him?'

'He is not here, Captain. He has flown.'

'Flown?' Jack wondered whether Ta Moko's English had suddenly failed him. 'What do you mean, *flown*?'

'Sir, he has run away.'

Jack was at a loss. 'I was led to understand – that is, I heard he was some kind of hero, for this action.'

'Yes, Captain, he was. But no longer. They are hunting him. No one knows what he has done, but one Major Nielson wishes him captured for a crime.'

'And you don't know what this crime is?'

319

'No one does.'

'Major Nielson must or he would not be after him.'

Jack knew that Nielson was the Provost Marshal in New Zealand, the army's policeman. He left Ta Moko and made his way to Nielson's office. He found the major bent over a pile of papers, smoking a large cigar. Nielson looked up when he entered and though Jack knew him, he did not know Jack. A frown appeared on Nielson's brow.

'Can I assist you, Captain?'

'Captain Crossman, sir, of the 88th. I am here on special duties connected with Colonel Lovelace.'

The major frowned even more fiercely, then his frown cleared and he said, 'Oh, one of those.'

'Yes, sir, one of those.'

'What is it then? Be brief. I'm due to go to dinner with the general at six.' He glanced at the clock, which told both men it was 5.44. 'I rather hoped to finish these papers, too – but...' He gave a gesture of helplessness, then, 'Anyway, go on. You have some information of import to impart? *Import to impart*,' he repeated, 'I must tell Edward that one. Sort of rolls off the tongue, eh?'

Jack fumed with impatience.

'I understand you're hunting down Abraham Wynter. May I ask why?'

The major pursed his lips before saying, 'No, Captain, you may not. At least, you may ask, but

320

you will not get an answer.'

There was a heavy lump in Jack's chest as he tried to contain his frustration. He knew he would get nowhere, however, if he revealed his feelings to this senior officer. Persuasion was what was required, not a display of wild emotions.

'Sir, as you now already know, I am a spy. I am here setting up intelligence networks throughout New Zealand. As a spy I naturally deal in secrets. Secrets by the dozen. Secrets by the hundred. I began my career in espionage as a sergeant. I am now a captain. It would follow that I am able to keep secrets, or long ago I would have been discarded by my superiors or executed by the enemy. Colonel Lovelace, and before him, Colonel Hawke, held me in esteem. I do not say that to draw praise to myself, nor am I boasting. It is simply a fact. I am good at intrigue, which is not necessarily praiseworthy in the eyes of many men.

'Sir, I have particular reasons for wishing to know Abraham Wynter's crime.' Jack bent the truth somewhat. 'I was close to turning the leader of those Maoris he slaughtered in that cave. Unfortunately my duties took me to Auckland, and I was not able to complete my work. May I ask whether his crime has to do with the action he took on that day at the rebels' hideout? If so, I should very much like to join the hunt for this man.'

Major Nielson leaned forward. His hands were now linked together, elbows on the surface of the desk, and he rested his chin on his knuckles. His eyes were fixed on Jack's own.

'Something has just occurred to me, Captain. Tell me, in the course of your duties for Colonel Lovelace I imagine you have acted as an assassin, have you not?' He leaned back in his chair again and picked up his smouldering cigar, making it glow like a torch with a single draw. 'I am familiar with the work of Colonel Lovelace. We went to school together and purchased our commissions in the same year. Come, come, you need not be coy with me, Captain. Do tell.'

A denial immediately sprang to Jack's lips. Any decent army officer would be revolted by the idea that one of his colleagues was an assassin. But something in the major's expression made Jack hold back on his refutation. Instead he said, 'There have been occasions when all other methods have failed to produce a desired result.'

The major nodded, still staring into Jack's eyes.

'There is no hunt for Captain Wynter,' he finally said.

Jack's head went up. 'No hunt? But...'

'Oh, he's wanted all right. We're – that is, *I'm* hoping he'll die out there in the bush. I don't want him back here. If there's a trial, there'll be a scandal. The army doesn't like scandals, as you well know. This wouldn't stop here. Every newspaper in Britain would make it headline news.'

Jack's mind was in a spin.

322

'But what's he done, Major?'

'Killed a friend. Two actually.'

'But that wouldn't make headline news.'

'And eaten one of them.'

Jack's head jerked up again. 'What – cannibalism? Here in New Zealand? A European?'

'Not here. In Australia. There were three men who discovered gold, then were lost in the desert. Two of them killed and ate their comrade when they were starving. One of those men was Abraham Wynter. The other was a seaman called Strickland, whom Wynter had killed in a most horrific and bizarre fashion.' The major leaned forward. 'Now, Captain Crossman, you know as much as I do. The only other parties to this information are a priest and the general, neither of whom will ever divulge the latter part of this man's crime. We are saying we want him for the murder of Strickland. You seem to want Wynter for other reasons, or you would not be in my office. My suggestion to you is to go out and find him – but don't bring him back. Am I understood?'

Jack could not believe his luck.

'Thoroughly, Major.'

'Good.' Nielson rose from his desk, pointing as he did so. 'That missing hand – it won't hinder you in this task?'

'I hardly know it's gone, sir.'

The major nodded and crushed his cigar butt in the hollow of a brick on his desk that he kept for the purpose. 'I must go to meet the general. I will tell him only that I have engaged your services in tracking down Wynter. He will know what we know without being told. When you return – supposing you do return – you will say that you attempted a capture and your quarry resisted. Is that all clear?'

'Absolutely.'

Jack turned to leave, when the major added, 'Oh – and no witnesses.'

As Jack walked back to his quarters he pondered on that last remark. He would need Ta Moko to track for him. How would that work, when he came upon Abe Wynter? Was he to send his Maori off somewhere to do shopping while he destroyed his man? These senior officers wanted everything wrapped up neatly in a nice parcel that would not come apart. Well, they could not have it all ways. Jack would do his best. In any case, what the army wanted kept quiet was the cannibalism. Ta Moko was not privy to that information and it was doubtful whether Abe Wynter would have told anyone. A man was being hunted for murder. That is all anyone needed to know.

'Wha—' Jack's heart skipped a beat as he came up against someone in the gloom, almost bumping into the fellow who was standing stock-still in his path.

'Sir?' said Harry Wynter. 'You left us up there in Auckland. We follered you back.'

Private Wynter sounded pained, like a wife or child who had been abandoned on the road.

'Oh, Wynter. I thought you were your brother for a moment.' Jack breathed more easily. 'Is

Gwilliams with you?'

'Yessir. In the billet.'

'You'd better join him. I have something to do over the next few days. You will make yourselves useful around camp.'

'We an't comin' with you?'

A feral dog slunk between them, passing through these two human pillars as if they were stone.

'No, this is something I have to do alone.'

In the gloaming Jack saw Harry Wynter's blind milky eye turn in its socket. It was a disconcerting sight. Harry's breathing had quickened and Jack knew something of importance was coming.

'You're goin' out after *him*, an't you?'

There was no real gain in lying to this man.

'I have been ordered to bring your brother in – dead or alive.'

The reply was belligerent. 'Why can't we come with you?'

'I would think it was obvious, Private Wynter. This is your *brother* we're talking about. You would be too personally involved. How do I know what your feelings would be? No, it's best you stay here and await the outcome. If – if things go well and we capture him and bring him back for trial, you may stand as a character witness if you so wish.'

'*Character* witness,' snorted the private. 'He an't got no character, that bugger. He's a murderin' bastard, an't he? Killed his best friend over what? A drunk argument, or somethin'? I just thought, well, we're your men, me and the corp. You don't do nothin' without us, normally.'

Jack saw it then. Harry Wynter felt he was being sidelined. Nothing angered the private more than being ignored.

For once Jack Crossman decided to justify himself to this soldier who gave him so much trouble.

'Private Wynter, this has nothing to do with your worth or enterprise. I value both. In truth I have been ordered to do this mission alone. I need Ta Moko of course, but not for his fighting skills – I need him to track for me. Gwilliams and yourself are soldiers I would not normally be without, as you say, but on this occasion I have no choice. A major has ordered it so.'

'Oh, well, if a major said so,' mumbled Harry, 'then it's gotta be, an't it? Good luck, sir. Bring the bugger in.' Amazingly he came to attention and saluted Jack. 'He's my brother, but he's done a bad thing this time. No one wants to see his brother hung and I'm askin' in advance if I can be excused the execution.'

Once again this strange excuse for a soldier had the ability to surprise his commanding officer.

'Of course, Wynter. I would not expect you to witness the execution of a member of your family.'

'Thank you, sir.'

They parted and Jack continued on back to his quarters in a bemused state. He slept badly that night and rose before dawn. Ta Moko came to him as soon as it was light and Jack told the Maori what they had to do.

'We must travel fast, so there'll be no sneaking through enemy territory.'

'They will let us through. I will make them,' said Ta Moko.

Jack was not sure how the Maori was going to do that, since not all Maoris were best friends with each other, but he left it at that. Jack dressed in his uniform, including his sword. He was not going out to kill a man in the camouflaged oddments he normally wore out in the bush. Gentlemen were quite particular about dressing for the occasion – they even had the 'right clothes' for fossicking or for collecting seashells on the beach – and Jack was only an exception in common times. Today was uncommon. Ta Moko was dressed in his usual canvas seaman's trousers cut short at the knee and a thick woollen plaid shirt. He normally carried an ancient musket but Jack now gave him a new Enfield rifle, which Ta Moko accepted as though it were the crown jewels. They took with them just the minimum rations. Ta Moko was expert at trapping birds and other creatures. They would neither thirst nor starve.

The manhunters, for that was what they were, travelled on foot, swiftly through the bush. Ta Moko had made many enquiries the night before and knew the general direction in which their prey had travelled. Ta Moko also learned that Abe Wynter had taken three of his six Maoris with him. The other three had refused to go, even with the promise of a great deal of gold. It seemed that Wynter's plan was to find a hideout where he could hole up until the army – and the government – forgot about him. Then he would make his way to the coast, hire a native boat, and escape across the ocean, probably heading for Australia.

His reasoning was fairly sound. If he went now for a boat, the navy would be on high alert for him. They would be checking all the native craft that took to the high seas. There was only one direction to go and that was north. Abe Wynter was not a man to spend the rest of his life on a Pacific island amongst savages. And if he went south he would end up in the freezing waters of the Antarctic. So hiding out until the furore died down was the best of his options. Also, he knew that the army would not be anxious to find him and grandstand his crime. They would be horrified if his story reached the newspapers. The navy would not be so fussy. The army's embarrassment was their smugness.

Jack and Ta Moko made good progress over two days. Sure enough, any hostile Maori they encountered proved an initial problem but these were quickly solved by Ta Moko.

'This officer is seeking another for *mano-o-mano*,' he told the rebels. 'There is to be a fight to the death. The other killed the woman of this man by foul and underhand means.'

Magically, they were given free passage. No Maori would stand in the way of single combat between two rivals fighting over such a terrible transgression. It was a miracle they did not all trail behind the manhunters in order to watch the spectacle. They slapped Jack's shoulder as he passed and wished him luck.

'God be with you. May you cleave his head!'

For more than two weeks they scoured the hinterland seeking the runaway captain. At night they lit no fires so had to eat their meat fresh off the bone; a difficult task for Jack's inexperienced teeth. Ta Moko found them wild root vegetables to eat and water in plenty to drink. Jack's beard grew shaggy and uncomfortable, but he took no time to shave. One thing was good: he slept well out in the open, dropping off exhausted with the end of each old day and waking fresh with the following new dawn. His spirit began to flag however, when there was nothing to show after the passing of two whole weeks. Then they came across a lone elderly Maori, an eremite who tried to go by them without a word. Although the old man would not stop, Ta Moko would have none of it and questioned him by walking backwards and talking into the old man's face. Jack's guide learned that a white man and three or four Maoris – the old man was not good at counting, he told them – had settled at an abandoned hut not one day's travelling from where he stood.

With the elderly Maori's description of the area in his head, Ta Moko set out with Jack to find their quarry. They took fifteen hours to reach the place and arrived at dusk. Voices could be heard from a clearing amongst a grove of flame trees. Creeping on their bellies, Jack and Ta Moko observed the hideout from the forest pale. A fire had been lit in front of the hut. The roof of which had collapsed in one corner. Abe Wynter was sitting in a makeshift chair staring moodily into the flames of the fire, while his three Maori were squatting nearby, talking to each other in low voices.

Jack and Ta Moko retired and found a place to sleep.

At the first light of dawn Jack scraped the fuzz off his face, using a hunting knife and cold water. It was not the best of shaves, but it would have to do. Then he tidied himself as well as he could, brushing the mud from his uniform and boots with a clutch of twigs. Finally he nodded to Ta Moko, and they made their way back to the hut in the clearing.

The one thing Jack did not want was to step out and get shot to death before even opening his mouth. So he and Ta Moko positioned themselves in the trees and Ta Moko yelled at the Maoris sleeping around the fire. Abe Wynter was nowhere to be seen, but Jack assumed he was in the hut still asleep.

At the first yell, the Maori were on their feet, guns pointing at the forest, yelling back. Ta Moko told them in their own language not to fire. He said he and his pakeha could have killed them while they slept, but were only after their boss. 'This has nothing to do with you,' he said. 'This is a fight between two pakeha. Whatever gold you have been paid, you will be allowed to keep. You will be permitted to go free after the fight is over, whoever wins the battle. This is single combat between two white men and we are here simply to watch the outcome...'

Jack observed the Maori men nodding.

During the exchange, Jack was watching the doorway of the hut, waiting for the tall pale figure of Abe Wynter to emerge. No one came out of the dwelling, even after a lot of conversation between Ta Moko and Wynter's Maoris. Jack was beginning to wonder if there was a rear exit and his quarry had slipped away, when he saw Wynter ambling up a path from a stream far below dressed in shirt, boots and breeches.

Abe Wynter had heard the Maori shouting and was returning from his ablutions, wondering what the noise was all about. As far as he knew it was an argument only between his Maoris, which was not an infrequent occurrence.

'What the bloody hell's goin' on?' he grumbled, peering at his men. Then he appeared to notice for the first time that they had armed themselves. 'What's this then, eh?'

Jack stepped out of the woods and faced Abraham Wynter.

'Arm yourself,' said Jack, coldly. 'We are to fight, you and I.'

Wynter had a pistol stuck in his waistband and he snarled and whipped it out, pointing it at his adversary.

'All right, officer – I'm armed. Now what?'

'Have you a sword?'

331

Wynter waved the muzzle of the pistol.

'I don't need no sword, I've got this!'

Ta Moko stepped from the trees and stood behind Abraham Wynter, his Enfield aimed at Wynter's back.

'Put down the pistol,' said the Maori, 'or I will kill you.'

Wynter's face screwed into a mass of wrinkles. He glanced towards his own Maori. They were leaning on their own weapons, making no attempt to cover Ta Moko. The expression on their faces told the tale. They were not going to interfere.

'Oh – that's how it's goin' to be, is it?' shouted Wynter. He lowered his firearm and stalked towards the hut. 'Yes, I got me a sword all right, Captain Fancy Jack Crossman. If it's a fight you want, I'll give it you. You sure you can duel with a lowlife like me, out of the gutter? I thought you lot only blazed with gentlemen of rank? I might wear a captain's uniform, but I'm still what you lot call trash, mister.'

'I'm prepared to make an exception.'

Jack drew his sword with a ring, the blade flashing in the early morning sun as it slid metallically from its scabbard.

Abe Wynter vanished into the darkness of the hut. Ta Moko kept the doorway covered in case the malefactor came rushing out firing. He did come flying out, but with a different weapon in his fist. He had a broad-bladed cutlass in his hand and instantly hacked at Jack with several savage strokes, battering at the defensive blocks

Jack was forced to adopt. Jack was immediately put on his back foot, off-balance and caught out by the wildness, the suddenness of the attack. Wynter's face was twisted into a grimace of fierce determination. He yelled as his heavy cutlass smashed down on the lighter sword of his opponent, while Jack desperately sought to ward off the blows which chopped down at him.

'Thought I'd be an easy mark, eh?' cried Wynter, triumphantly. 'Don't you underrate a sailor, toff. I've boarded more vessels than you've got shiny buttons on your coat. Think you could take *me*, what's bin in a score of frays from here to the shores of Barbary? Ha, you make me sick, you fucking toffs. I been killin' xebec pirates my whole life.'

All the while he spoke Wynter was crashing heavy blows down on Jack's guard. The broad blade bit hard. Under this onslaught Jack continually failed to regain his balance. Finally Wynter's attack forced Jack over. He fell backwards with an outstretched left arm. There was no hand to prevent him falling flat. Only the stump of his wrist. Pain shot up Jack's arm and caused him to wince. Abe Wynter called out in elation, thinking he had now got the army officer in an unrecoverable position.

Still Jack's skilful defensive overhead blocks saved him from a cloven skull. This way, that way, Wynter could not break his guard. First, Jack managed to get to his knees. Then he got to his feet again. Wynter's fury began to abate. Jack continued to parry, parry, parry, but with no chance to thrust. Wynter's aggravation started to show as he grew tired. He could not find a way past Jack's guard no matter what. And they both knew the reason. Ferocious his attack might be, it was of limited scope. Nearly all the blows were downward strikes at the head. Once or twice Wynter tried a swipe at Jack's left side, but the murderer knew this was dangerous since it left him wide open too long.

Exasperated, Wynter now took his cutlass in both hands. He hacked with all his strength at the sword edge which was frustrating his efforts.

'You will not break this blade,' said Jack, 'it was forged in Toledo by a brilliant craftsman.'

'I – will – break – you,' gasped Wynter, the lightning scar on his face livid now. 'I – will...'

This time he took his cutlass right back over his head, hoping to deliver a tremendously powerful blow and thus break the guard.

Too far.

Wide open.

At last!

Jack swiftly thrust his own blade deep into Wynter's chest, twisting it, searching for the heart.

Wynter had had the upper edge for so long he had forgotten his opponent was able to attack as well as defend. His cutlass remained over his head. He glanced down in surprise at the glinting steel that was buried in his breast. Then he looked up into Jack's grim face.

'You bloody bastard!' Wynter croaked. 'You've...'

He slid from the sword blade and fell flat on his back without another word. For a few moments he stared up at the sky, his puzzled eyes seemingly watching the clouds drift overhead. There was no terror there. Only, at the last, annoyance, though with himself or others it was impossible to know. Abraham Wynter's throat rattled for a minute or more, and then gave a horrible gargle before he passed into another world.

Jack stood there, swaying, gasping for breath. He was spent. That last, that only thrust, was all he had left in him. Had it failed he must surely have died in Wynter's place. Ta Moko came to him and put his forehead against that of Jack's. For a while the Maori just stared into Jack's eyes from less than an inch away, fiercely triumphant. Then he took his head away and gripped Jack's shoulders with firm hands.

'You win,' he murmured to Jack, then, nudging the body with his toe, 'you lose.'

Twenty

Major Nielson did not look at Captain Crossman, as the latter placed his report on that man's desk.

'Thank you, Captain. That will be all.'

'You don't want me to tell you what happened?'

'I'm sure it's all in your report, Captain. I think the less spoken about this business the better. Good morning.'

'I think it has to be said, sir, that it was not an assassination. I intended to kill him, but not dishonourably, not in any underhand way. No shot in the back, no stabbing in the dark. It was all open and witnessed. He made the first move – his Maoris will attest to that – and we fought with swords. I'm lucky to be standing here. Wynter was no slouch with a cutlass. I'm sure I wouldn't have been the first man he dispatched with it had he succeeded in his wishes.'

Nielson now looked up. There was a cold embarrassment in his eyes.

'Still, a killing is a killing, Captain. No doubt it was not cold-blooded, but it was not on the battlefield. We do not take pride in such things. They are not battle honours, after all.'

'My report says that Wynter refused to be captured. I'm not sure that's wholly correct. I did not give him the chance to surrender himself. True, he did not offer, but no such request was made. He knew I had come for his life.'

'Captain Crossman, did you have personal reasons for wanting this man dead?'

Jack was taken aback. Someone had been talking.

'That's neither here nor there, sir. I was following your orders.'

Nielson put his elbows on his desk, knitted his fingers, and said very clearly and precisely, 'What orders, Captain?'

Jack nodded. 'Ah, yes – like that, is it?'

'On the other hand, I accept whatever you have to say in this.' The major patted the report. 'There will be no enquiry. No recriminations. Your word is accepted without question. The matter is closed. There will be no more discussions. Am I understood?'

'Perfectly, sir.'

Jack left the office with an anger lingering in him. They had wanted Abraham Wynter dead, but once the deed was done, it became unsavoury. Well, that was the army for you. You did your job, you carried out your mission, but there would be no praise for work well done. Had Lovelace been here, he would have approved. Lovelace had no scruples about such matters. His assessment of the operation would be that it was an action carried out capably. Colonel Lovelace was more interested in an efficient means of carrying out the army's aims and goals than legality or protocol.

The first person he ran into was Private Harry Wynter.

Wynter stared hard at Jack. The private was dishevelled; his forage cap was out of shape and askew. His coat was unbuttoned and his breeches hung low at the belt. The boots were unlaced and filthy with mud and horse manure. One good eye in his face looked red-veined bleary. Stinking breath issued from his slack mouth. Harry Wynter had obviously been drinking and there was a belligerent look about him. He placed his legs apart in a fighting stance.

'So you did for my brother,' he said. 'Ran 'im through, I 'ear? Ran 'im through without so much as a by-your-leave. This an't no officer-cum-private talk we're 'aving now. This is just you an' me, mister, man to man. Why'd'ya kill 'im, eh?'

At first Jack was not going to reply, but then decided this man, with whom he had spent the last few years, deserved at least an explanation for his brother's death.

'He murdered a man, Wynter. Your brother killed his own shipmate.'

'Then 'e deserved a trial. 'Ow was he guilty, without no trial, eh? Tell me that, officer.'

Jack sighed. 'You don't know the whole, Harry. I understand your filial indignation. He was your brother. But the man was evil.'

Private Wynter blinked. It was the use of his first name that took him by surprise. Captain

338

Crossman had *never* called him 'Harry' before. He had called him a lot of other things, some of them quite ugly and obscene, but never by his given name. It took the wind out of his sails and put him in the doldrums for a few moments.

'What whole? What did he do otherwise, then?'

'You really don't want to know, believe me. As he was a relation of yours, it would upset you.'

Jack was astonished to see that tears came to the eyes of the private. This too was a first. He had never seen the man weep before. There were white tracks down his dirty face, running down from his bad as well as his good eye. He blubbed for a few minutes, streaking the grime on his cheeks. Then he found his voice again. A high squeaky voice.

'So what do I tell me sisters, eh? That I just stood by and let it happen? What kind of brother does that make me look?'

'They would understand if they knew what I know, Harry. You would too. But – well, it's not pretty.'

'I have to know, sir. You know I have to know. I could never show meself in England again, if I didn't. I didn't like the bastard, he always done me down, even as a kid. But blood is blood. If it was you, you'd be the same. I know you got a brother, 'cause he was at the Crimea with us. How would it be if I'd've killed your brother and said nothin' about the whys and wherefores? You'd hate me rotten, wouldn't you, eh? There's the truth of it. An' nobody goes out to kill a man who an't had a trial. Not unless there's somethin' sneaky goin' on. I 'ave to know, sir. I just 'ave to.'

Jack thought about his brother James and realized Harry Wynter was right: he deserved an explanation.

'This must go no further than us, you understand?'

'Why?'

'You'll know why, when I tell you. Your brother did not kill only one man. He murdered another poor fellow in Australia. A shipmate named Daniel Kilpatrick.'

Harry Wynter frowned.

'Still an' all, a trial—'

'He killed him to eat.'

Jack had at last managed to get it out.

Wynter looked puzzled. 'To eat what?'

'Your brother was a cannibal, Harry. He murdered Daniel Kilpatrick to eat his flesh. The other man, Strickland, joined him in devouring their friend, though we understand Strickland had nothing to do with the murder itself. They cooked the Irishman on an open fire out there in the Australian desert, and then they ate him.'

There was at last a shocked look on Harry's face.

'No? Honest truth?'

'As I stand here. Strickland told the whole story as he lay dying. Men rarely lie when they are about to face their Creator. In any case, the army could not take the chance. Abraham was a

340

murderer anyway. There is no doubt what with the evidence we had – two witnesses, including the Maori who actually did the deed – your brother would have hung. Kilpatrick never came out of the desert with the other two men. Therefore the story is very likely true. There can be a fragment of doubt of course. Strickland might have been lying to revenge himself on your brother, but for what reason? He knew Abraham would hang for his murder anyway, so why would Strickland embellish it with the cannibalism? There is no greater punishment than the gallows.'

'Abe – a cannibal? It's hard to believe.' Harry Wynter stood there, swaying, contemplating this heinous sin. 'He'll go to hell for that, certain sure.' Another pause, then a typical Harry Wynter observation. 'Mind you, 'e always did like his meat. If there was Sunday pork scratchings on the plate and Abe was there, you didn't get a look in. Proper pig, 'e was. My sisters would tell you that.'

'Do you see then that we couldn't let this reach the newspapers, for your family's sake as well as that of the army?'

Harry knew damn well the army could not care less about his family, but he tightened his mouth and nodded.

'This won't go no further then, sir? Just you an' me, and the bleedin' staff officers?'

'There are only three others who know of the cannibalism. The general, a major, and a padre. None of them are inclined to talk, or I wouldn't have been ordered to kill your brother.'

'You was ordered to, was you?'

'Yes.'

'Well, then, you 'ad to do it, didn't you? No question. You'd bin court-martialled otherwise, eh?'

'Yes.'

Private Wynter came to attention and saluted his commanding officer.

'Permission to go off an' bury the sod, sir?'

Jack was a little perturbed. 'The Maoris brought the body back then?'

'Yessir.' Harry's face suddenly became thoughtful. 'Happen the padre won't want to put him in holy turf if he's a murderer though.'

'My advice is to get a Methodist minister to do it – they're often less fussy about consecrated ground.'

'Good idea, sir.'

With that, the private shuffled away, his boot-laces trailing around his feet and threatening to trip him at any moment.

Jack had the weary task of travelling north again to bring Sergeant King back. He took Gwilliams with him, leaving Private Wynter to arrange his brother's funeral. The sergeant was in much better health and spirits when they found him. He was sitting on a lawn in front of the hospital, sketching a hillside.

'How are you, Sergeant King?' asked Jack. 'Ready to join us yet?'

'Oh, yes, sir. Fit and well. I don't suppose I

could march the length of the Great Trunk Road, from Calcutta to the Khyber Pass, which if you remember was some one thousand five hundred miles. Having done that once as a young man, I have no desire to do it again. But I could manage a few of them. Miles, that is.'

'Excellent. We'll take the leisurely way back to New Plymouth and go by ship. That will give you a greater convalescence period. The sea air will do us all good and give us some breathing space from these interminable wars.'

'That's the best idea I've heard yet, sir,' said Corporal Gwilliams, his bronze beard quivering. 'Can we do that? I mean, what about the general?'

'The general will have to do without us for a week or two.'

It took a week to get Sergeant King out of the hospital and ready for the voyage. The three soldiers went down to the docks on a blustery Thursday morning, their spirits higher than they had been for a long time. There they walked the wharfs and jetties, looking for the ship that would take them round the island to New Plymouth. As they ambled along the quayside, they watched as a large ship entered Auckland harbour. No doubt, Jack thought, it is bringing more settlers from England and from Australia, which does not bode well for the natives of the islands.

'Well *damn* me,' cried an indignant Sergeant King, pointing. 'Look at that, if you like!'

Jack and Gwilliams followed the line of

the finger.

There stood Harry Wynter, on the quay, sur-rounded by trunks and chests. He was dressed in a tall black stovepipe hat, still shining with newness. A black frock coat was on his back, covering what appeared to be a frill-fronted white silk shirt. He was wearing black leather gloves, carrying a gold-topped cane, and his shoes gleamed below the pinstriped trousers. Harry Wynter looked every inch a gentleman.

'Wynter!' roared Sergeant King. 'I hope you have got a good explanation for this!'

The gentleman turned and grinned with an ugly visage.

'Oh, Sarge? 'Ow's it swinging? And sir? An' not forgettin' the bloody Yankee corporal. Whaddya think, eh?' He opened his coat and did a twirl for them on the edge of the dock. 'Not bad for a private.'

Jack suddenly saw the light. He grinned. 'You inherited your brother's fortune, Wynter?'

'S'right, Captain. Lock, stock and barrel. Rich man, me brother. Now it's all mine. I'm off back to good old England, on this 'ere ship. No more army for me. I'm packin' it in while I still got one good eye and some hair on me head, even though both of are white. Good luck, Corp. Fuck you, Sergeant. And, Fancy Jack, if I don't never see you again, it won't be too soon, which I'm sure you'll understand.'

'There's a lot of trunks and chests here, Wyn-ter – have you been shopping?'

'Nah, not so much. It's stuff me brother

344

owned. See that big one over there? Guess what? It's a Joseph Bramah pan closet toilet, that's what. Sat on it only this mornin' afore it was packed. Marked me territory, so to speak. All gleamin' brass an' steel an' a lovely warm beechwood seat so's you don't get a cold arse while you're crappin'. Not bad, eh, for a fellah 'oo only the other day had to go behind a bush and use a fistful o' rye grass for the wipin' away?' Something else seemed to occur to the rich man. 'Oh, an' by the by, Captain. That little bit o' gold what was lost when I brought in the loot from that robbery? It was found in a barn. An't that somethin'? It must 'ave still bin in the donkey's saddlebags and 'ave dropped out into the straw when I weren't noticing.'

'You returned the gold you stole from that cache.'

Wynter winked and smirked. 'No point in gettin' hung for a miserable bit o' yellow when I got all I need, now is there?'

With that Private Wynter began pushing his way up the gangplank to board the vessel, despite the annoyance of the disembarking passengers who were trying to come down. He barged past one lady, but on seeing that she was a little distressed, he turned and apologized. Her beauty was obviously not lost on the ex-private, for he lifted his tall black hat and bowed as low as he could, given the circumstances.

'S'cuse me, ma'am,' he said. 'Don't mean to be a roughneck. It's what the army does to you, but I'm recently out of all that. Nowadays I'm tryin' to be a gentleman.'

'I'm glad to hear it,' replied the woman, smiling at the delivery of this speech. 'I forgive you.'

Down on the quayside, Jack looked up, startled, on hearing the lady's voice, having been lost in his contemplations of Wynter's – and his – good fortune, for they had both got rid of each other in one fell swoop.

'Jane?' he said, his brow clearing. 'Jane, darling. You're here.'